Amish
Mystery
COLLECTION

Samantha Bayarr

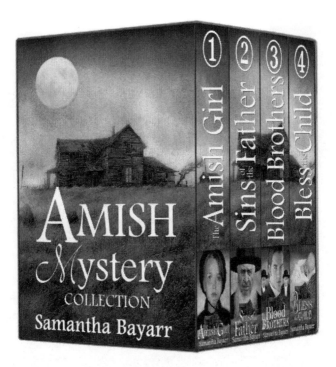

1 The Amish Girl

2 Sins of the Father

3 Blood Brothers

4 Bless the Child

AMISH
Mystery
COLLECTION

Samantha Bayarr

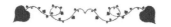

Table of Contents

The Amish Girl

BOOK ONE
Pigeon Hollow Mysteries

Samantha Bayarr

A note from the Author:

While this novel is set against the backdrop of an Amish community, the characters and the names of the community are fictional. There is no intended resemblance between the characters in this book or the setting, and any real members of any Amish or Mennonite community. As with any work of fiction, I've taken license in some areas of research as a means of creating the necessary circumstances for my characters and setting. It is completely impossible to be accurate in details and descriptions, since every community differs, and such a setting would destroy the fictional quality of entertainment this book serves to present. Any inaccuracies in the Amish and Mennonite lifestyles portrayed in this book are completely due to fictional license. Please keep in mind that this book is meant for fictional, entertainment purposes only, and is not written as a text book on the Amish.

Happy Reading

Chapter 1

Ten-year-old Amelia bolted upright in her bed, her heart racing from the crack of lightning that split the air on such a quiet, summer night. The crickets' song had suddenly stopped, and all she could hear was the muffled sound of her own heart beating.

Tilting her head to listen, her eyes bulged in the dark room as she tried to focus. The pale moonlight filtered in through the thin curtains beside her bed, a gentle breeze fluttering the sheers against the sill. Outside her window, the cornstalks in the field swayed, flapping their leaves with a familiar rhythm.

It smelled like rain was on the way.

She sucked in a ragged breath, her exhale catching as if she was out of air. Her heart beat faster still, fear flowing through her veins like ice water. A bead of sweat ran down her back between her shoulder blades, causing her to shiver.

Had she been dreaming?

Scooting to the edge of the bed, her legs felt a little wobbly as she let her feet down easy against the cool, wood floor. It was a comfort on such a warm night, though it increased her risk of wetting her pants.

She reached for the door handle, but pulled her hand away, the hair on the back of her neck prickling a warning. Tip-toeing back to her bed, she climbed in under the quilt, crossing her legs and leaning on her haunches to keep from wetting herself.

An unfamiliar voice carried from the other room, causing her heart to race and her limbs to tremble. It was an angry voice.

Another shot rent the air. It was the same noise that had woken her.

Her mother cried out, calling her father's name.

"*Mamm,*" Amelia whispered into the night air.

Once again, she pushed back the light quilt, her need to see her mother forcing her wobbly legs to support her tiny frame. Moving slowly, she made sure to be quiet, cringing every time the floor planks creaked.

It was unlike her parents to be so loud in the middle of the night, but something was terribly wrong.

Wondering who belonged to the mysterious voice, she listened to him arguing with her mother. Her voice was shaky, like she was crying, and it frightened Amelia.

"We don't have any money," her mother cried. "Please don't do this!"

Where was her father, and where had the other man come from? Who was this man, and why was he upsetting her mother? She peeked around the corner from the hallway, spotting a man dressed in black, with a gun raised and pointed at her mother.

Amelia shook, and her teeth chattered uncontrollably.

A single lantern flickered from the table, her eyes darted around the dimly-lit room, trying to place her father. She pulled in another ragged breath when she spotted him lying on the floor, blood pooling around his head. The noise that had woken her hadn't been in her dreams, it was the gunshot that had killed her father.

Every instinct in her warned her to hide, but her feet seemed unwilling to take her back to her room.

"This is your last chance," the gunman warned. "If you won't give me my money, you lose your life!"

"No!" she screamed. "Please, I don't have it."

"I had to spend the last ten years in jail for nothing," the man said through gritted teeth. "While the two of you spent *my* money on this nice farmhouse, and all those acres you have out there? You've been enjoying your life all these years with your horses and chickens and such, while I've been locked away with nothing!"

He aimed the gun at her, and she dropped to the floor, crying and pleading with him to spare her life.

He ignored her pleas.

Amelia shook violently, her gasp masked by a second gunshot, killing her mother right before her eyes.

She let out a strangled cry, and the man holding the gun turned toward her, his eyes locking with hers for a moment.

"Well, now, isn't this a nice surprise!" he said, tilting his head back and laughing madly.

His laugh sent chills through her, causing her bladder to empty uncontrollably.

For a moment, Amelia was paralyzed with fear, her feet unmovable in the puddle of urine. Lightning lit up the room, a crash of thunder bringing her back to her senses.

She forced her feet to propel her forward, heaving them as if they were chained to the floor. Swinging open the back door, she ran toward the cornfield that separated them from the Yoder farm. Glancing over her shoulder, she looked back to see the man was behind her, hobbling as if he had a lame leg.

"Don't run, little Amish girl," he called after her. "I'm not going to hurt you!"

She entered the cornfield, visualizing the path she took on a daily basis when she visited with Caleb, her neighbor and friend. She'd never come through it in the dark, and her mind was too cluttered with fear that ripped at her gut to follow the path. Bile rose in her throat, but she swallowed it down as she ran. Cornstalks whipped at her face and arms, her mind barely aware of the stings that meant they'd drawn blood.

She stumbled, her breath heaving, as she scrambled on her hands and knees long enough to right herself. Her bare feet painfully dug into the rocks and dirt in the field, but her instinct was to stay alive.

The small barn at the back edge of the Yoder property had been a meeting place for her and Caleb. A place where they'd played with the barn cats and their kittens, and washed their horses after a long ride. But most of all, it was a place she knew there was a gun. Caleb had taught her how to shoot it, using tin cans for practice, but she'd never thought to turn it on a human—until now.

The main house was still too far away. Amelia knew her only chance of surviving this man's fury was to surprise him with the unexpected. All she wanted was for him to leave her alone, and she didn't have the physical strength to run any further. Pointing a gun at him the way he'd pointed it at her mother was the only thing on her mind. It drove her to reach the barn before the man who intended to kill her.

All she could think about, as she ran faster than she'd ever run before, was getting her hands on the gun she knew was in the Yoder's barn. The gun would give her power—the power to stop this man from killing her. Neither her *mamm* nor her *daed* had a gun, and now they were dead—both of them. Amelia didn't want to die. It was one of her biggest fears in her short life, and right now, that fear drove her to stay alive at all cost.

She entered the barn out of breath, her eyes struggling to focus. If not for the large window near the tack room filtering in the flashes of lightning, she would not be able to find her way. Crawling under the workbench, Amelia grabbed for the strongbox that housed the gun. The lock on it had long-since been broken, but she shook so much, she struggled to pry open the rusted lid. A flicker of lightning revealed the Derringer inside the metal box, and she snatched it quickly, and cracked the barrel forward. She'd done it a hundred times before when she and Caleb practiced, not knowing she'd ever have to use it to defend herself.

Shoving her shaky hand inside the box of ammunition, she grabbed haphazardly, and then loaded two bullets. Gripping the small handgun, she aimed it toward the door, waiting for her stalker.

"Come out, come out, little Amish girl. I'm not going to hurt you," the man called out to her.

Amelia sucked in a breath and drew the loaded gun out in front of her, darting it back and forth until her eyes focused on her assailant. Lightning blinked him in and out of her sight.

She flinched when he struck a match and lit the lantern hanging up just inside the doorway, turning up the flame until it lit up the room.

Amelia stayed crouched down under the work bench in the tack room, gun extended in front of her. She held her breath when she saw the look in his eyes, and knew he meant to do her harm.

The man spotted Amelia's feet underneath the work bench and smiled widely, but it wasn't a kind smile. "Why are you pointing a gun at me?" he asked. "I'm not going to hurt you!"

Her entire body tensed up, fear making her grip on the gun grow tighter. She stared at him, breathing hard through clenched teeth, her hands shaky.

He laughed at her. "We both know you aren't going to shoot me."

She pulled back the hammer of the gun fast and sure, without taking her eyes off of him.

His hands went up in mock defense, but he laughed nervously. "This isn't funny, Amish girl. I put my gun away, but you better put that gun down before I have to hurt you!"

She raised the gun as he moved slowly toward her, keeping it trained on his heart. Though she only meant to intimidate him the way he was doing to her, she had no intention of pulling the trigger. Her aim was too accurate.

"Put the gun down, little Amish girl," he said through gritted teeth.

Thunder rumbled, making her jump as he lurched toward her.

She let out a scream as she accidentally squeezed the trigger, a single shot discharging with a puff of smoke from the end of the barrel. Her eyes closed against the explosion that rang in her ears like the crack of thunder from the oncoming storm. When the smoke cleared, she could see that the bullet had gone straight through the man's chest, and he'd collapsed to the ground in front of her.

She kept the gun trained on him, staring into his unblinking eyes; her hands shaking and her breath catching, as she strangled the whimpering that intermittently escaped her lips.

She hadn't meant to shoot him; hadn't meant to kill him, but now he was dead—just like her parents.

Chapter 2

Amelia woke up gasping.

She'd had the dream again.

Beads of sweat rolled down her back between her shoulder blades, her breath heaving as she shook off the bad memory.

She stretched her weary arms and yawned, remembering that today was different.

Today was the day she was going home.

She wiped away bittersweet tears from her eyes, looking at the alarm clock she'd punched the snooze button on more than once. She sprang from the bed, knowing if she was late for her last session with Sister Agnes, she would not be leaving today. The nun had warned her that her final evaluation was required by the state in order for them to release her, and if they thought in any way she wasn't ready, she would remain at Fenwick Hall for another six months, until she would be eligible for another evaluation.

Everything was dependent on the answers she would give the psychiatric nun today, and those answers, carefully calculated, stood between her and freedom from the cold halls of the institution.

She swiped at the snarls in her long, brown hair with a brush, and then twisted it to a perfect bun at the nape of her neck. Picking up the prayer *kapp* she hadn't worn since she'd first arrived at the state-run facility, she pinned it to her head as a symbol that connected her to her past. It had yellowed with age, and was a bit too small, but she suddenly felt lost without it. Almost as if today had transported her back to the life she'd left behind when she'd become a part of the *English* world.

She readied herself in the light brown dress she'd recently sewn, removing the old prayer *kapp,* and replacing it with the new *kapp* she'd also made in preparation for her return to the Amish community. She would return to her home, whether she was shunned or not. It was the only home she had.

She studied her reflection in the mirror as she contemplated the day she'd almost been dreading for the past eight years. Her intention was not to deceive the nuns with conniving answers today, but to gain passage to the long-awaited freedom she'd dreamed of.

She knew she wasn't ready to trade the safety of the orphanage for the home she prayed she'd never have to return to, but she feared if she didn't leave now, she might never go. Not because she didn't miss her home; she simply wasn't ready to face the ghosts that would likely haunt her for the rest of her days. She would never forget the sound of the gunshots that had brought death that night, nor the smell of gunpowder she could still sense if she closed her eyes even for a moment. It had made for many a sleepless night, lending itself to the sort of insomnia that brought night-terrors at the slightest drift of her eyes.

Amelia straightened her smock apron, and hurried down the hall toward Sister Agnes's office. Holding up a hand to knock, she paused, took a deep breath to calm her nerves, and then whispered a quick prayer for courage.

She'd rehearsed what she'd say, and the casual way she would carry herself during the evaluation, but nothing could have prepared her for this meeting. Not really.

If her *Mamm* was here, she'd tell her to stiffen up her bottom lip and do chores to work through her troubles, reminding her that there wasn't anything that couldn't be worked out while busying herself with some *gut,* hard work. But *mamm* wasn't here to tell her, and it just wasn't the same as being able to hide her smile when her *mamm* would look at her firmly and warn her about what the Bible said regarding idle hands.

Her hands had been nothing but idle for the last eight years, and *Mamm* had been right. It had given her too much time to think. Too much time to worry—about what today meant.

"Come in," Sister Agnes welcomed her with a smile. "I've been expecting you."

She pointed to a chair in front of her desk, and Amelia reluctantly sat. She crossed her ankles, tucking her feet under the chair. She knew it would help to keep her restless legs from her usual bouncing when she'd come for her usual sessions. She was determined to appear calm, and remain still throughout the meeting, even if it meant she had to run up and down the fire escape afterward in order to expel the nervous energy she already felt creeping up on her.

Sister Agnes put a hand to her chin and tilted her head. "How long have we been meeting, Amelia?"

Is this a trick question?

She'd been a ward of the state for the eight years since her parents were killed. For eight years since she'd accidentally taken the life of Bruce Albee after witnessing him heartlessly shoot her parents.

"Eight years," she answered quietly, trying her best to hide her annoyance.

Sister Agnes nodded politely. "Do you believe you're ready to put what happened behind you, and start your new life?"

What kind of question is that?

She'd relived that night every day for the last eight years, and no amount of therapy had removed the memory the way she'd hoped. She'd volunteered to help with the younger children at the orphanage to keep her mind busy, but it hurt her so much when they'd get adopted and she would have to tell them goodbye. After the first few times, she'd hardened her heart, not allowing herself to become attached to her young charges. The work helped to keep her mind occupied, and if not for that, she worried she might have gone mad from all the worrying.

Amelia nodded. "I believe I am."

"How do you feel about leaving here and being on your own without your family?"

"I'm ready," she said, trying to convince herself more than Sister Agnes.

The nightmares about that night had recently returned, and no matter how many times Sister Agnes tried to comfort her, nothing could remove the fear she still felt in the very pit of her soul. The nuns had tried their best to encourage her to feel at ease about returning home, but only dread filled her. Granted, she was happy to be leaving the orphanage, but with nowhere else to go but back to the very place that caused her gut to sour, she couldn't help but feel scared and alone.

"Do you know why we couldn't place you with another family?" the nun asked.

She shrugged, truly having no idea why.

When she'd first arrived at the orphanage, she'd wondered if being placed with a nice family might ease the pain of losing her parents, until she'd seen the notes in her chart that read *not eligible for adoption.*

She hadn't meant to see the notes, but Sister Agnes had been called out of her office shortly after her initial intake, and had left the file open on her desk when she'd left Amelia alone in there for nearly half an hour. There were times over the years when she wished she hadn't been so curious that day as to read her file, because before then, she'd had some sort of hope for adoption, even if it was only false hope.

"Our intention is always to place our young ones with families that best match them, and we had gotten a letter from the Bishop in your community that went into great detail of regret as to why no family there would be permitted to adopt you."

Amelia sat up straight, giving Sister Agnes her full attention. "What did it say?"

The nun lowered her gaze. "It said you'd been shunned."

"I'm not surprised."

"What will you do without the support of your community once you leave here?"

Another shrug.

The community had turned their backs on her—shunned her for taking the life of the murderer. It hadn't mattered to them that it had been self-defense. She'd been raised to live at peace with her fellow man, and violence was looked upon as unacceptable, no matter what the circumstance. Having a gun, in their eyes, was a mortal sin, and to use it in violence—even self-defense, was unforgivable.

To the community, Amelia's sin now caused her to fit into the world, and she was shunned to take her place among the rest of the sinners. There would be no tolerance for her, and no acceptance for what she'd done. After the news circulated about the murders, the fear spread even faster, and they'd put her under the ban.

No one from the community had even attended her parents' funerals.

She would never forget the cold way that Bishop Graber had treated her during the brief, and obligatory service for her parents. It was the last thing he would do for them, and she knew, even at that young age, that he hadn't wanted to. *Frau* Graber had tried to offer her comforting words when they'd approached the state-owned vehicle she was locked in, but Bishop Graber had given her a look of disapproval. Amelia hadn't even been permitted to leave the car that had driven her to the institution. Afterward, the Bishop and his wife had left her parents' graveside, and the car had taken her away. They hadn't even given her a chance to say goodbye, let alone to mourn the loss. She'd cried quietly in the back seat of the vehicle, alone and afraid of her future.

No, they would not likely be welcoming her back into their midst. Bishop Graber was a strict man, and would not tolerate Amelia's return to the community. He'd strictly forbidden the members to take her in after her parents were killed. Because of the shunning, she'd been placed in the hands of legal authorities, who, in turn, handed her over to the orphanage.

As the years passed, she'd come to realize that it was fear that had made them turn her away, but Bruce Albee was gone, and there was no reason for them to fear her, though they might beg to differ.

In the eyes of the community, she was no different than the man she'd shot.

Surely, not even a public confession would spare her from remaining under the ban.

She was determined not to let that get in the way of her returning home.

"I suppose I'll manage the same way anyone else does when they leave home to go out into the world on their own. Mrs. Winters at the bakery, gave me a *gut*—good recommendation to her cousin, Mrs. Miles, who runs the bakery back in Pigeon Hollow. She gave me a week to get myself settled, and then to go see her for a job there. With the new job, I believe I will get along alright."

Sister Agnes smiled.

"It sounds as if you have a sound plan for your future, but how do you feel about what you did—the shooting? And how do you think it will make you feel to return to a place that brought you such sorrow? Are you ready to face all of that?"

Truth be told, Amelia wasn't sorry for defending herself, because to do so, would mean she was meant to die along with her parents. She did, however, feel a very deep remorse for taking the life of the man, regardless of his murderous acts. He'd intended to kill her that night, and for that reason alone, she could not regret what she'd done. She'd struggled with the guilt and the remorse, but only for taking his life. For eight long years, she'd lived with what had happened. The fact that it was an accident had not made it any easier on her conscience.

"I wish I could take it back, but it's something I'll have to live with for the rest of my life. I know what I did was wrong—in the moral sense, even if it seemed right at the time. I believe there are reasons it can be right—self-defense, for example, and I know the difference between right and wrong. I didn't shoot that man on purpose. It was an accident, but I accept full responsibility. As for returning to my home, I do have some apprehension, but I think that's unavoidable. I suppose I won't know how I *really* feel until I get there."

They'd had many a long talk about responsibility and acceptance, and Amelia knew it was the answer the nun was looking for.

Her nod would confirm it.

"Since your home was paid in full at the time of your parents' death, I don't worry about you keeping a roof over your head," she began. "You've proven you're capable of supporting yourself by holding down a job for the past two years. The only thing that concerns me is the condition of the home. It may not be livable in its current condition. What will you do to remedy that?"

She sighed, wondering what had become of her home since she'd been gone.

"With the money I've saved from my job at the bakery, I should be able to get some supplies if I need them. I attended a few barn-raisings when I was younger, and I'm certain I can still remember how to swing a hammer the way my *daed* taught me. He used to say I was the boy he never had!"

"It sounds as if you've got everything figured out," Sister Agnes said. "You know we'll help you until you turn twenty-one, so if you find you're unable to adjust out there, you're always welcome to come back."

"I'll be fine," she said nervously.

Truth was, she was unsure of how she would manage anything about being in the house she grew up in and all the memories—good and bad, that came along with it. She had dreamt of returning home all these years, and had not been back there since the night Bruce Albee had chased her out. She wasn't sure how it would feel to return to the home where the man took her parents' lives, but she longed to be able to call anywhere *home*.

Amelia stood up and looked out of the office window, noting how befitting it was that the grey sky matched her mood. Shaking off the stress that consumed her at the moment, she tucked away the bad memories in the back of her mind, praying they'd stay there. She was determined not to suffer an anxiety attack today.

This was the day she would go from being a scared little girl, to a brave grownup for the first time since the night that turned her life upside down.

Every detail of that night was etched in her mind, and though she missed her home, she hoped her return would not interfere with her ability to heal from the grief of losing her parents. That grief had weighed her down, and kept her from living her life. And although she would never stop missing her parents, she was ready to let go of the sadness and try to live a happy life; if for no other reason than it was too exhausting to hold onto the sadness any longer.

With so many changes coming her way, she hoped she would not fail at it and have to return to Fenwick Hall.

Her family home was rumored to have been boarded up and neglected after the removal of her parents' bodies, and the evidence had been collected by authorities to close the case. She had no idea the true condition she'd find the home in, but it was all she had left of her childhood—before that dreaded night that had changed everything.

Now, she was determined to face every bit of it, despite her fear that nothing would ever be the same again.

Chapter 3

Amelia stood in front of her childhood home, unable to move. The taxi that had brought her had long-since gone, the driver leaving her few belongings at her feet before taking off. He'd talked her ear off about the history of the house as if she didn't know, and tried to pry details about that night out of her before they reached the home. She'd kept quiet the entire time, not answering him, and though she hadn't wanted to be rude, she just couldn't talk about it with the stranger. She figured he probably thought she was a little bit looney, but she often felt that her silence about that night was the only thing she had left of her sanity.

She stood in the yard, barely able to see over the tall grass and weeds that swayed in the wind as if sending whispers from the dead. Storm clouds pushed their way overhead, threatening to release their fury on the dilapidated home. The oak tree where her tire swing hung had overgrown, draping angry branches over the width of the house, the rope frayed, and the old tire cracked and misshapen.

Lightning flickered across the dark sky, causing Amelia to flinch. The rumble of thunder rolled across the thick air, rattling the broken glass in the weathered and sun-bleached window panes. Cracked and peeling paint lent to the unkempt facade of the neglected home.

She perceived from the exterior, that the house was not inhabitable, just as Sister Agnes had warned, but Amelia had nowhere else to go. She looked at the set of keys in her hand and scoffed at the door that was half-open and falling away from its hinges. Leaves and muck piled up at the entrance, and she wondered just how long the door had been left open. Several boards still remained across the doorway, blocking her view of the inside of the home, and she imagined someone had kicked the door open—a thief, maybe, and crawled under the boards that were meant to keep such a person out. A stray board or two hung haphazardly from the windows, but had also been torn away.

Lightning cracked, and thunder roared, announcing the coming storm. She raised her gaze toward the house, shaking off the hazy memory of that night. She'd worked hard to hide the details of it in the back of her mind and close them away, but they had suddenly rushed back as if it was yesterday.

Shuddering against gusts of wind, large raindrops pelted her with an angry force, but she remained unmoved. Uncontrollable sobs consumed her as she collapsed on her haunches, crying louder with every crack of thunder.

Lord, how can I stay here after what happened? I've begged you for courage, but I don't feel it. Bless me with the courage I need to overcome my fears about this place. Send your comforting arms to help me feel safe.

Warm arms wrapped around her, picking her up with a strength only a man could have. He cradled her against the contours of his chest and brought her to the shelter of the covered porch. She continued to sob, barely aware that she'd been moved, as he set her safely onto the weathered porch swing.

I remember this swing.

Many a warm night, she and her childhood friend, Caleb, would catch fireflies in the yard, while her parents watched from the solace of the swing, swaying lazily in the summer heat.

She was faintly aware of the man rushing back out into the rain and grabbing her bags, and setting them down at her feet. He removed his black, felt hat—an Amish hat, and poured the water from the large brim.

Amelia lifted her gaze to meet the man who'd pulled her out of the rain. "Who are you?" she asked soberly.

Kneeling in front of her, he pushed back wet strands of hair from her face and smiled. "It's me, Caleb."

Her breath hitched as she put a hand to his chest as if needing to touch him to make him real. "You can't be," she said, searching his blue eyes. "Caleb is just a *boy!*"

She held out her hand at the measure of his height as if he was a young boy, and Caleb clenched it, bringing it back to his cheek. His eyes drifted closed for a moment before looking at her again.

"I *was* just a boy the last time you saw me," he said gently. "But now I'm a man. I've grown up—just like you, Amelia."

He was right. His lanky arms and legs had grown longer and filled in with muscle, and his broad shoulders were strong, like a man who'd seen many days of hard work on a farm. His jawline boasted a day's growth of light whiskers that matched his thick, blonde hair.

Her lower lip quivered as she peered into his familiar blue eyes. "You did grow up, didn't you?"

She collapsed against his sturdy frame and sobbed, but these tears were happy ones. He pulled her into his arms, kissing her forehead and shushing her.

"I've waited so long for you!" he whispered to her. "I was so afraid I'd never see you again after..." he let his voice trail off, not willing to finish the sentence, but they both knew what he couldn't say.

"I've missed you too," she said with a hiccup. "I can't believe you're here!"

"When I heard you were coming back, I couldn't wait to see you."

"How did you know I was coming back?" she asked.

"The community talks a lot," he said. "And even though I'm no longer part of it, my cousins still talk to me."

"But how do they know?"

"Bishop Graber wrote to the home where you were and asked to be notified when you'd be returning. They sent a letter a few days ago."

"Why aren't you part of the community?"

"Because of what happened," he started to say.

"Because of what I did," she interrupted him. "I'm so sorry."

"It isn't all your fault," he admitted. "I'm the one who taught you how to shoot the gun. The Bishop wouldn't listen to me when I told them my *daed* had nothing to do with it—that you and I had found the old gun in the barn, but they told him he should have had more control over me, so we were shunned."

"I'm sorry," she said, looking at him. "But why do you still dress as Amish if you're not part of the community?"

He flipped the strings on her prayer *kapp* and smiled. "I could ask you the same thing.

She forced a weak smile. "I suppose I don't know any other way."

He leaned back and pulled her tiny frame back against him. "I suppose I don't either."

The rain had calmed a little, the storm moving away from them, but with Caleb here holding her, she felt the safest she'd felt in a long time.

After a few minutes, he moved to the swing beside her, tucking his arm around her. She rested her head on his shoulder and pushed gently with her foot, setting the swing into motion. The chains squeaked more than they had when she was young, but it was a soothing sound. She missed her parents, and the feeling of home.

Looking up toward the door, she wondered if she'd be able to walk through it with Caleb here.

She shivered, and he pulled her close, but it didn't help; they were both soaking wet.

"Let's get you inside and I'll build a fire so we can get warmed up."

She took in a deep breath and blew it out slowly. "I suppose I have to go in sometime, don't I?"

He grabbed her hand. "I'll be right there with you, and I'll stay as long as you want me to."

She squeezed his hand, thinking he shouldn't have offered such a thing, because she might never want him to leave. He'd certainly grown up very handsome. She imagined they'd likely be ready to marry this season if they'd not been apart all these years. The thought made her blush unexpectedly, and she was glad it was getting too dark for him to notice.

Caleb stood up, his eyes scanning the overgrown landscape. "I'm sorry about the condition the place is in. Every time I thought about coming over and taking care of the grass or the house, I just couldn't bring myself to come here—until now."

"I don't expect you to do this—it's my house, and I've got a lot of work ahead of me, but I think I can make it work. That is, if I can work up the nerve to go inside."

He smiled. "Don't worry. I'll help you get this place looking brand new again."

With her hand tucked safely in Caleb's, she braved her way toward the front door, and then stopped, the boards across the doorway a welcome hindrance.

He let her hand drop. "Stand back and I'll see if I can't get rid of these boards."

Ducking under the slats of wood, he stood inside the doorway and kicked the boards. Each one fell with a crack that made Amelia jump, despite the fact she expected the noise. It seemed lately, every little noise seemed to magnify and put her teeth on edge.

He stepped back out to the porch and smiled nervously, trying to make light of the situation before she saw the terrible condition of the interior of the house.

"This kind of reminds me of the tree house we tried to build in that dead tree in the field, and the branch fell after I hoisted the bundle of wood to build the base. I sprained both my wrists bracing myself for that fall, and had both my arms in a sling. Remember?" He chuckled. "I remember feeling pretty special that you had to feed me lunch every day at school and help me with my school-work. I left those slings on for three extra days after the doc told me I could take them off—just so you'd keep helping me."

Amelia struggled to put the memories together, but didn't remember things the same way he'd described. She had blocked out a lot of her childhood, thanks to the years of therapy she had been through that forced her to consistently remember all the bad things. She'd spent the last eight years reliving the tragic events, and she'd not had time to remember the good things in her life, and so they'd slowly left her.

"I'm sorry, but my memory isn't so *gut* these days."

Caleb's shoulders fell and he became a little confused. He and Amelia were such good friends as children, until the tragedy happened, and she was forced into a state-run facility with no family or friends to see her through any of it. He had been waiting for the day she'd return and he could be reunited with his friend. How could she not remember such an important thing about him?

Caleb smiled weakly and shrugged; he didn't want to overwhelm her by saying too much, but he was determined to help her remember the good things she had forgotten from her childhood, even if it would take some time.

Her gaze fell. "I'm afraid of a lot of things now, and I don't know why. I don't remember enough of the *gut* things, but please—tell me as many of the *gut* stories as you can, so I'll have them to hang onto. Perhaps then, I'll be able to get rid of the ghosts of the past, and maybe, just maybe, my nightmares will go away too."

"I'm ready anytime you are," he said.

"I'm afraid," she said soberly, holding back on his hand. "I can't seem to bring myself to go inside just yet."

Caleb couldn't blame her for that; he'd begged his *daed* to burn down their barn after seeing the deceased gunman in there. Having to clean up the blood had almost convinced his father to go ahead and burn it down, but since he'd been shunned for having the gun that had killed Bruce Albee, there would be no one to help him rebuild—no barn-raising would be offered to them.

"I'll help you in any way I can."

Amelia smiled. Somehow, hearing Caleb offer to be there, even if he did seem to be a stranger to her, made her feel more at home. "I'd like that."

Amelia looked up at the home where her family was once together and happy, feeling a little less sad, and maybe even a little hopeful. She felt a little unsure about the repairs needed to make this place livable again, but with Caleb's help and friendship, she felt a sense of peace about being home.

Chapter 4

Amelia stood frozen in the doorway of her childhood home, clenching Caleb's hand as if she was falling, and he was the only thing that stood between her and sudden death.

"You're going to be fine," he assured her. "I'm going to stay right here with you."

She finally worked up the courage to take a step forward through the door. The last bit of daylight filtering in from the back windows highlighted the dust in the air. The paint on the walls had faded to a color that made Amelia's stomach turn. Except for the sound of the rain hitting the tin roof, the house was eerily quiet—like a tomb.

All the furniture was gone except her *mamm's* rocking chair near the fireplace. In her mind's eye, she could see her *mamm* rocking gently by the warm fire while mending—she was always sewing something. A new dress for Amelia, or quilt squares—anything to keep her hands from being idle.

She stumbled over the rubble that used to be her life, as she made her way to the dirty chair. She'd never been allowed to sit in it, but she lowered herself into it now. It felt foreign, and not at all comforting the way she thought it might. It hadn't brought her close to her *mamm,* and in fact, gave her a chill. She rose to her feet and looked at the chair. It was just a chair, but it represented her deep loss. Her *mamm* was gone, but the chair remained as if to be a place-holder to fill in the gap where her *mamm* used to be.

She looked around at the disheveled room that had been ransacked. Thieves had most likely broken in and taken it all, and she was thankful they hadn't set the home ablaze. She hoped that perhaps they had left something behind; anything, that Amelia could hold onto. Perhaps beneath the rubble, she could find some semblance of her childhood, but right now, all she could see was filth and chaos.

She walked across the room, the wood floors creaking beneath her feet. Her breath hitched, and tears pooled in her eyes at the site of the bloodstain that still discolored the rug—the place where her parents had been killed.

She slowly walked around the bloodstain to the kitchen, where she and her mother had spent so much time baking and preparing meals. A few broken dishes cluttered the counters, food staples had been torn open, most likely from critters foraging for a morsel.

She stood at the kitchen window above the dirty sink, the view of the outside making her heart ache just as much as the inside did. It made her sad that so many years had gone by, and no one had given her childhood home the attention she felt it deserved. It was in a total state of disrepair. It wasn't just the cracked windows, or peeling and chipped paint; it was dirty, and no one had cleaned the rug.

Why hadn't anyone cleaned the rug?

Amelia could hear the crackle of fire from the other room, the strong aroma of black locust logs mixed with the slightest hint of hickory and oak filled the stale air. With that mixture of woods, it would burn longer and hotter, removing the chill from the damp, autumn air.

Noises from the other room made her shiver. She knew exactly what was going on, without even turning around to look.

Caleb had rolled up the rug and was dragging it out of the house.

Relief washed over her, while a lump formed in her throat, making it difficult to breathe. It wasn't that she wanted to keep the rug, but removing it meant removing all trace of her parents. It needed to be done, and logic told her to remain in the kitchen until the deed was done.

When she heard movement in the front room again, she turned around to be certain it was Caleb.

It was.

She let out the breath she'd held in, folding her arms across her torso and rubbing her arms to get them warm. Her teeth chattered, and she wondered if it was safe to go back into the front room so she could stand near the fireplace and warm herself. She worried that Caleb may still be trying to spare her the evidence of death that still remained in the home. Her memories alone could not be erased of that night, and no amount of cleaning or removal of rugs would strike it from her thoughts.

Though Caleb helped calm her anxieties, she still worried that coming back to her childhood home may not have been the best thing for her mental health. She was determined to begin her life anew, but the ghosts of the past had a way of creeping into her thoughts constantly. For the past eight years, she had been labeled the little Amish girl who'd shot and killed a man, and now was the time to break free from that. She was neither Amish nor *English;* neither a daughter, nor a friend. But perhaps some of that could be changed. She had longed to be home for eight long years, but this was not how she'd envisioned it.

She stood at the kitchen window watching for a moment as Caleb tightened the hinges on the front door and tested the lock.

He turned to her as she entered the room. "It closes and locks, and even though the windows are cracked, none are broken. I can tape them, or board them up, but if I board them up, you won't get any sunlight in through them."

She took in a deep breath and exhaled slowly, not ready to make any decisions, no matter how trivial. "Do what you think is best."

"If it were me, I'd tape them until we can replace the glass."

She nodded, and lowered herself to the brick hearth, extending her hands toward the warmth of the crackling fire. She stared into the flames, her vision blurring and her mind drifting backward.

"This is your last chance," he said. "Give me the money, or you lose your life!"

"No!" she screamed. "Please, I don't have it."

Caleb brought in a fresh bundle of firewood and dropped one of the logs.

Amelia jumped up and screamed, her breath heaving, a hand to her chest as if she was suffering a heart attack. She paused for a moment as she realized that the noise had come from the log hitting the floor, and not a gunshot. She began to cry, and Caleb set the remaining logs on the hearth and pulled her into his arms, allowing her to sob.

"I'm so sorry," he said, stroking her hair. "I didn't mean to startle you. I'll be more careful not to make any loud or sudden noises. I should have known you would still be in shock just being here."

"I know it was an accident," she said with a sniffle. "But maybe it was a bad idea to come here. I'm as scared as a jack-rabbit. I can't stay here by myself. I'll end up scaring myself to death before the light of dawn."

"I doubt that," he tried comforting her. "You're a lot braver than you think. I'm not sure I could stay here alone either after what happened, and I'm a grown man now."

"I have a few dollars saved aside for making repairs, but I suppose I'll have to find a place to stay in town until I've gotten used to being on my own. Maybe then I can return."

"Or," he said excitedly. "You can stay in my room, and I'll stay in the *dawdi haus*. I'll help you fix this place up, and you can stay with me in the meantime."

"What about your *daed?* Shouldn't you ask him if he minds?"

Caleb didn't answer right away.

"I don't have to stay with you if it's going to cause trouble."

Caleb cleared his throat. "That's not the problem. He hasn't been the same because of all this, it's been really tough on him."

"I'm so sorry, Caleb," she said with a sniffle.

"With the death of my *mamm* the year before, he didn't have time to recover before being shunned. It was just too much for my *daed,* and he's not been the same since."

"I feel responsible; I'm so sorry," she sobbed.

"It isn't your fault. I'm two years older than you are; I should have known better than to teach you to shoot that gun. I only did it because I had a crush on you."

Amelia gently pulled away from him to look him in the eye. "You did?"

"*Jah,* " he said. "I loved you because you were the best friend I've ever had, but I had a crush on you, too."

"You were the best friend I've ever had too," she said in response.

He looked at her, searching for more.

She smiled. "I had a crush on you too!"

He pushed her still-wet hair off her cheek. "I'll always love you, and you're still my best friend. So, I won't take no for an answer; you're staying with me until we can get this place in shape."

She loved him still, too, but she just couldn't bring herself to say it. Those feelings scared her. She'd loved her parents, and they were gone. She couldn't take another loss if something were to happen to Caleb.

"What about your *daed?"*

"I've been taking care of him since I was twelve years old. He isn't going to know you're there."

She looked around at the puddles of water from the leaking roof, the dirt and leaves that had blown inside and covered the floor, and had to admit she didn't want to stay here. There was no furniture, no dishes, and she hadn't brought any cleaners with her. Even if she had, it would take her at least a few days of cleaning to make this place partially livable.

Not to mention, she hadn't dared to look in her room to see if her bed was still there, and even if it was, she was certain it would be unusable, and likely need to be thrown out to the road for the refuse truck. Between not having a place to sleep, and the ghosts not quite cleared from her home, she'd be foolish not to accept his hospitality.

She smiled. "You talked me into it."

Chapter 5

Caleb showed Amelia to his room, snatching up a few dirty things from the floor out of embarrassment.

"Sorry about the mess," he said shyly. "I got dressed in a hurry this morning."

She tried to hide her snicker, not wanting to embarrass him, but she thought it was cute the way he scrambled to get his personal things so she wouldn't see them. She'd already noticed that the rest of the house was not as tidy as it would be if there was a woman in the house. She thought, perhaps, she could clean a little in the morning when she woke to surprise Caleb and his father with some breakfast.

They'd had a small meal that Caleb had already prepared. They'd warmed it up when they'd gotten back from her house, and Amelia had found it awkward sitting across from Mr. Yoder at the dinner table. He hadn't even spoken to either of them. He'd looked up at Amelia a couple of times, but he hadn't said a word. His eyes were sad and aged, not at all like she remembered him. He and Caleb had always been so close, and they'd done everything together. Amelia vaguely remembered his mother, and didn't want to mention her, knowing it was probably still just as painful for him as her own loss had been for her.

His dad mostly stared off into space, and Caleb had not exaggerated when he'd told her that he completely cared for him. She'd offered to wash the dishes after dinner, but Caleb had urged her to leave them until morning. They were both exhausted, and would have a long few days ahead of them to get her house in order before she had to start her new job at the bakery with her new boss, Mrs. Miles. She was grateful she'd already had an opportunity to meet with her briefly about the position when she'd gone for a visit with her cousin at the bakery near the orphanage, but she was most grateful the woman understood her need to remain employed, as there would be no help for her from the community.

It was still storming, and Amelia was grateful she would not have to sleep in her home all alone. Thunderstorms still frightened her, because of the terrible storm the night her parents were killed.

She flinched each time lightning flickered throughout the dark room, and shuddered at even the most subtle rumbling of thunder, jumping whenever it would shake the house with a deafening force. She pulled the quilt around her tightly, wondering if she would ever be able to get through a storm without being scared. Aside from the heavy drumming of rain against the tin roof, and the steady wind scraping tree branches against the siding, the house was quiet.

She was used to hearing babies crying and children whispering throughout the night, and the soft footfalls of the nuns as they walked the corridors of Fenwick Hall. To be without those familiar noises that she'd grown used to over the past eight years, she feared she would not get any sleep. Tucking the quilt in around her shoulders, and resting her head on Caleb's pillow, she turned her face toward the soft fabric that smelled just like him; a musky mixture of his natural scent, mixed with horses and hay. She stuffed her face deep into his pillow, and breathed in fully with her eyes closed, thinking she could get used to that manly aroma. If not for circumstances that had torn them apart, she imagined she and Caleb might be well on their way to being married. Being away for so many years, had left a gap in her heart, but being with him now in his home, and in his bed, only brought a desire for him she didn't know was there—until now.

Before long, Amelia drifted off into a deep sleep, her heart feeling light, and bordering in-love.

A crack of thunder startled her, but she couldn't move. She tried to wake herself, but she just couldn't move her limbs. It was as if she was paralyzed. Her lashes fluttered as lightning flickered, lighting up the room in little snippets. The figure of a man stood in the doorway of the room, but she still could not move.

She tried to scream, but no sound escaped her lips.

Another crack of thunder brought the man to life. Chills ran cold down her spine, her limbs helpless to save her from certain danger.

Again, she tried to scream, but could not find her voice.

The man took a step into the room, lightning flickering behind his large figure, preventing her from seeing his face. She groaned, trying to flee from the threat of peril.

"I'm not going to hurt you," the man's voice said.

A shrill cry let loose from her throat as she bolted upright in the bed.

Sucking in air, she lifted her eyes toward the door where the man was, but he was not there. The door was closed, and the storm had passed.

She'd only been dreaming.

Wiping the sweat from her cheeks, she jumped when a hasty knock sounded against the door.

"Amelia!" Caleb shouted from the other side of the door. "Are you alright?"

Bone-weary, she climbed out from beneath the warm quilts and went to the door.

He opened the door before waiting for her to answer. "I'm sorry to intrude, but I heard you screaming from downstairs. I came in to put more wood on the fire, and I was worried you might be hurt."

She pushed her way into his arms, her limbs shaky. "I'm sorry, I was dreaming—about the night I shot *him.*"

Footfalls from the hall padded angrily across the wood floor. Mr. Yoder tightened a plain, brown robe around his waist, and glared at Amelia.

"What are you doing in my house?" he barked. "You've brought nothing but trouble to the community—you, and your folks, when they helped rob that bank when they were on their *rumspringa.*"

Amelia's breath hitched, tears pooling in her eyes.

"*Daed,* you don't know what you're saying," Caleb said. "We don't know that they had anything to do with the robbery."

"How else did they know the man?" he questioned Amelia. "I'll tell you how; they're just as guilty of robbing that bank as the man that went to prison for it. That's why he came after them and shot them; for spending all that money on that broken-down farm they left you with!"

She started sobbing, Caleb holding onto her with the arm he'd kept around her waist.

"You shot that man with a gun you found in my barn," Mr. Yoder continued. "Bishop Graber didn't believe me when I told him I had no idea about the gun. I blame *you* for the Bishop putting me under the ban, and I don't want you in my house."

"She was just a child when that happened," Caleb defended her. "That was eight years ago, and you should have forgiven her a long time ago instead of holding onto all the bitterness that's eaten you up all these years."

"I have forgiven you," he said, turning to Amelia. "But that doesn't mean I want you in my house. Get out!"

Amelia ran back into Caleb's room and scrambled to get her things, uncontrollable sobs clogging her throat. She stuffed her clothes in her bags, not wanting to give the man any more chance to sling insults at her.

"Go back to bed, *Daed,*" Caleb said firmly to his father. "I'll handle this."

"Get her out of my house!" he shouted as he stomped back to his room.

Caleb entered his room, and rushed to Amelia's side. He stopped her hasty packing and pulled her into his arms, stroking her hair and whispering calming words to quiet her sobs.

"He doesn't know what he's saying, Amelia," he said. "Don't pay any attention to him."

"Is that what everyone thinks? That my parents were guilty of robbery? No wonder I was shunned!"

"It doesn't matter what other people think," he reassured her. "All that matters is what *you* think."

She sniffled, leaning against his sturdy frame, burying her face in his robe. She breathed in deeply, remembering his scent from his pillow. It was a comforting smell—like *home.*

"If I was to be honest with myself," she said. "I'd have to admit I've had my doubts about the whole thing. When Sister Agnes told me I was inheriting the house and the land, and that it was all paid for, it made me wonder, but no one wants to believe their parents are capable of committing a crime. The only thing that gives me confidence is that my *mamm* died because she told the man she didn't know where the money was. She wouldn't have said that if she could have told him where it was. He might have spared her life if she'd been able to hand him over the money. My parents were not thieves, and they didn't buy my house and land with stolen money. The property isn't worth much. The amount that was stolen was more than five times what the house and acres are worth. Surely, they would have lived more extravagant lives if they had all that money. Instead, they struggled, and my *mamm* made quilts and sold them to help keep up our bills. They just weren't bank robbers. It's too horrible to even think about."

"I believe you," he said gently. "And I believe in your parents' innocence."

"*Danki,* that means a lot to me. I don't know what I'd do without your friendship right now."

"You're never going to have to find out," he said, kissing her forehead.

Tipping her head upward, she searched his eyes, finding what she was looking for as he pressed his lips softly against hers.

Chapter 6

The sun was beginning to make its way across the horizon, the joyful song of chirpy birds waking her. She opened her eyes to greet the morning, but struggled for a moment to remember where she was.

The *dawdi haus* at the Yoder farm.

Caleb had switched places with her, moving back into the main house, and back to his room, while letting her have the small house in back. After his father's reaction to her being in the house, she figured it was best to steer clear of him. Instead of going into the main house to do last night's dishes as she'd planned, she figured it was best to stay in the *dawdi haus,* and perhaps get a little bit of breakfast there, and then move on to her own house. She wouldn't burden Caleb anymore by staying here if she didn't have to. She intended to work hard to get the place cleaned enough that it would be livable.

Slipping into her work dress, Amelia headed to the small kitchen to put together some sort of breakfast. She was terribly hungry, and figured it might be the end of the day before she'd get another meal.

She was grateful to find some fresh buttermilk biscuits and honey. Caleb's honey was the finest in the county. He'd always kept his hives in a clover field, which gave it a very mild and sweet taste compared to wildflower honey.

Amelia walked over to her house from the road, avoiding the path through the cornfield. She felt she'd rather walk all the way down the long drive, and all the way around the property in order to get over to her house, rather than taking the shortcut through the cornfield that still scared her just to look at it. She walked briskly past the field of corn, trying hard to block out the screams from her parents that seemed to drift over the rippling cornstalks as they fluttered in the breeze. Stepping on a twig, the snap from it startled her as if it was a gunshot. Would she ever be able to get past the fear from that night? That cornfield was the reason she'd become an insomniac. Just hearing the leaves rustling sent shivers down the back of her neck, raising the hairs at her nape.

Perhaps selling the house and the land would relieve her of all the ghosts from the past. As she came upon her house, she thought it looked different in the light of day. Though the day was overcast, it had been almost too dark yesterday to see the house fully when she'd been dropped off, and she hadn't realized just how bad the house was, until now.

Caleb was already there, working on the outside of the house. She was so grateful that he was as dedicated as she was about getting her home back to the same *homey* state she remembered it being. Growing up in this home always felt safe for Amelia, it may not have been much, but her parents had made it the best they could. She was especially looking forward to getting the kitchen in order, where she and her mother spent so much time together.

She could already see that Caleb was busy in the back, cutting the tall grass with a sickle. It was going to take a lot more work than trimming down the overgrown landscaping to get this place an order. She looked at the sagging roof, wondering how it hadn't collapsed by now with the weight of the tree branches leaning on it, and a small section of the tin roof had blown off over time.

The shutters hung on only by a hinge, the windows all cracked, and the paint peeled and chipped over most of the wood siding. It all disappointed her. When she was a young girl, her *daed* had kept the home up quite nicely. Her *mamm* had flowers around the front, and a potted plant on each end of the porch. Her mother had loved flowers.

Caleb spotted her, and leaned the sickle against the side of the house. Swiping his black hat from his head, he wiped his brow with the back of his shirtsleeve.

"It's a little warmer out here than it was yesterday," he said. "I could've sworn winter was on its way with the rain we had yesterday, but it looks like it's going to rain again today. We should get to work on the roof if you're ready, we can go into town and get some supplies to fix the holes."

She was eager to get inside and get to work cleaning, but she also relished the idea of going into town with Caleb. At this point, any type of distraction to get her mind off of having to go into the house and face the ghosts of her past, she was up for. The way the house looked now in its condition, was nothing short of a haunted house. But only it was haunted by her past and tragedies she herself had witnessed.

Caleb helped Amelia into his buggy, enjoying the warmth of her hand as he assisted her. He placed his other hand at the small of her back as he helped her up, without thinking anything of it, as if it was the most natural thing in the world.

He settled in beside her, wondering if he should be so forward with her. He'd known her all his life, and loved her just as long, but the gap in time since he'd last seen her had made them strangers, hadn't it? He didn't think it had, but he thought, perhaps, she might, and scooted slightly away from her, leaving an inch or so between them—for propriety's sake.

Amelia tucked her arm in Caleb's, moving in closer to him, and leaned her head on his shoulder. She knew he'd put a measure of distance between them with an uncertainty of her feelings. She knew him all too well. She also knew that even though they were no longer part of the community, those who saw them together would draw a conclusion about them keeping company, and would surely gossip about it.

He smiled and leaned his head against hers for a moment, and then set the horse in motion down the road. His heart felt light, as if the weight of the past eight years had lifted from him. The years of anticipation and wonder about her.

As they drove through the sleepy town of Pigeon Hollow, Amelia noted how many things she recognized. Things had not changed as much as she'd feared they would have, but the atmosphere was certainly not the same. No longer did neighbors send up a hand to wave to them, as they had when she'd gone for drives with her parents. There had always been a sense of support from the community, and she had no idea that being shunned would feel like this.

Caleb felt Amelia become rigid next to him, and knew she was feeling the tense stares from neighbors. "Don't pay them any mind," he said, trying to comfort her. "They're only wondering if it's really you! They'll get over it in a few days and stop staring so much. In the meantime, don't let them rattle you. They're only curious. They don't mean you any ill-will."

"It feels like it from where I'm sitting," she said. "I'm sure they don't want me here because of what happened."

"When they remember you were only a child when that happened, and you've grown up, things will be different. They're just afraid, that's all."

Amelia looked him in the eye. "Afraid of *me?*"

"Nee—no! They're afraid you'll bring back the dead with you—and trouble. They're afraid of history repeating itself."

"How do you know this?" she demanded. "And how can history repeat itself, when the man who killed my parents is also dead and buried?"

He turned the horse down Main Street, toward the lumber yard. "It can't, and it won't. But that doesn't stop their wild imaginations from running away from them. It's human nature. My cousins tell me things, but sometimes they exaggerate, so who knows what's true and what's not?"

She sighed heavily. "Being back here isn't exactly a picnic for me either!"

"Don't worry about it," he said. "It's all in the past. The talk will die down eventually."

He pulled the buggy into the parking lot of the lumber yard, and hopped down to tie up the horse. Then, he helped Amelia out of the buggy, trying his best to be a gentleman. He knew this *buggy ride* didn't count as courting—they were merely going into town for supplies, but prayed it would count for something more than friendship. He'd wanted to marry her since he was ten years old, and now that they were old enough, it almost felt that too much time had passed and it was too late. He prayed it wasn't so, but that would depend on her.

She looped her arm in his, leading him toward the garden area. "Look at all the pretty flowers! I wish I had the money to plant some. Remember all the flowers my *mamm* used to have out front of the *haus?* I miss that."

"I remember your *mamm* getting after me because our goat got loose and trampled most of her flower patch, and ate the rest of it. That goat ate everything in sight, so *daed* unloaded him on his cousin, and they unloaded him on an *Englisher* who tried to bring him back!"

"I barely remember that. Seems I've blocked out a lot of the good because of the bad."

"I'll help you remember only the *gut* things."

She forced a smile, feeling uneasy about his promise. Funny thing about memories—they just weren't the same for everyone.

Chapter 7

Caleb climbed into the buggy next to Amelia, warmth radiating from her. He couldn't believe how exciting it was to be near her, and he had barely slept all night from thinking of her. Now, he'd spent almost the entire day with her, picking out supplies to fix her house up. He'd missed her so much, and hadn't realized just how much until he'd seen her yesterday. Was it possible for the two of them to pick up where they'd left off so many years ago? He realized they were only kids then, but his love for her was just as real then as it was now.

"When we get back, I'll have just enough time to clear a path before the sun sets. I'm eager to get that roof fixed before more damage is done to the inside of the house."

Amelia looked up at the sky, the storm clouds rolling in made her shiver. "Since they won't be dropping off the supplies until the morning, what are we going to do about the roof now?" she asked. "Do you have any more buckets at your house to catch the leaks coming inside?"

"I'm certain I can find a few in the barn," he said, looking up at the sky.

Amelia pulled her shawl around her, shivering and praying the weather would hold out until they got back to her house. As they passed the cornfield, wind picked up and rustled the leaves.

I won't hurt you, little Amish girl, a voice echoed over the tops of the cornstalks.

Amelia's breath hitched. "Did you hear that?" She cried.

Caleb patted her hand. "What am I listening for?" He asked.

"You didn't hear that voice—that eerie voice when the wind blew?"

He shook his head, and it brought tears to her eyes.

He hated to see her cry. He always did.

When they were young, he was there to comfort her when her parakeet had flown away. She'd cried then too, but it was nothing compared to when her parents had died. She'd been there for him when his *mamm* had passed, but his *daed* had not let him cry then. He'd cried later, and she'd held his hand, just as he'd done for her then, and now was no different. If she claimed she heard something, he would believe her. He knew even if it wasn't real, it was real to her, and for that, he would comfort through whatever troubles she encountered. It was tough enough for her to be here under normal circumstances, but to live in fear, things were going to be harder on her than he suspected.

"Don't let your imagination run away with you," he said, giving her hand a little squeeze. "I'm right here with you, and no one is going to hurt you."

Amelia felt embarrassed, thinking to herself that she was hearing things that weren't there. She hoped Caleb would not think her to be a little crazy. But she was beginning to wonder herself.

As they pulled into the yard, Amelia let out a shrill scream.

Caleb steered the horse away from the house, and away from the red splatters and splotches that covered the front door and a portion of the porch.

He hopped out of the buggy to examine just exactly what it was. When he came upon it, he realized it was blood, just as he'd suspected. He couldn't help but wonder who would do such a thing. That much blood could only come from something large. He prayed it had come from an animal that had been slaughtered, and not from a human. His heart sped up and he shook at the site of it. Amelia started to get out of the buggy, but Caleb waved a hand at her, urging her back in.

"Let me check things out here first," he whispered loudly. "Then, if it's safe, you can come in."

"I want to leave," Amelia cried.

Caleb went back toward the porch and listened, but the wind howled, thunder cracked, and lightning flickered across the gray sky. He crept up onto the porch and tried the front door, but it was locked. He walked around the perimeter of the house, checking the back door and all the windows. They appeared to be secure.

When he returned to the front of the house, Amelia was sobbing so hard her shoulders were shaking. He hopped up into the buggy and pulled her into his arms.

"We can leave if you want to," he said. "But it doesn't appear as though anyone was in the house. It looks to me like blood from an animal, and I didn't find anything other than the blood. I can hose it off in no time, so we can get back to work on the house."

"I don't think I want to stay here," she said, shaking. "I'm scared."

Caleb smoothed her hair, cradling her head against his shoulder. "I'm sure it was just a harmless prank from some of the *English* kids around here. They can be a little cruel."

"You call this a harmless prank?" She cried.

He hadn't meant to belittle her worries, but he wasn't about to fall apart with her. One of them had to keep their head, and he was determined to be strong for her.

"I only meant that there are a lot of farms in this county, and a lot of them slaughter their own livestock. I have no reason to believe that it's human blood. If you're that worried, we can always call the sheriff. But I honestly think it's a one-time prank, and there isn't any cause to get the sheriff involved."

"You don't think we should call the sheriff's department now?" She cried. "This isn't a normal prank. Eggs smashed against the house, and toilet paper in the trees are pranks, and this is definitely more serious than that. I think this was meant to scare me away."

"That's possible," Caleb admitted. "But you have to be strong and let them know that you're standing your ground. I think it was done because they are afraid of *you!*"

"I don't want people to be afraid of me," she cried. "I only want to live in peace; to be left alone, so I can move on with my life. I've been so stuck in the past, I'd like to move past it all, and I can't do that if I'm going to be persecuted."

"Let me get this mess cleaned up, and we'll forget it ever happened."

"Until the next time!" she cried. "What if the next thing they do gets someone hurt?"

"I already told you, I'm not going to let that happen."

He hopped back down from the buggy, leaving her there crying and shaking, while he unraveled the hose and sprayed off the porch and the door. Whoever had done the deed had obviously done it shortly after they'd left, because it was mostly dried, and it did not come up easily.

Amelia sniffled, watching the bloody water drain down the porch steps and onto the grass. It sickened her to see it, in the same way the blood stain on the living room rug had sickened her. But just as the rug, Caleb was removing it from her sight.

When he finished, she climbed down from the buggy, her legs wobbly, and her teeth chattering—not from the cold, but from fear.

Chapter 8

Taking in a deep breath to steady her nerves, Amelia boldly tucked her arm in the crook of Caleb's elbow, and allowed him to assist her up the steps of the porch.

"I'm a grown up now," she said, giving herself a pep-talk. "No matter how bad this is, I can own up to it and stand my ground."

"*Das gut,*" he encouraged her. "Keep telling yourself that."

She didn't imagine she'd ever be able to sleep here alone—unless Caleb proposed, and since she didn't expect him to any time soon, if ever, it looked as though she'd be spending a lot of sleepless nights here. There were too many things she couldn't push from her mind, too many ghosts that continued to haunt her. And now, it seemed, that someone was determined to make things worse for her. She wanted to believe Caleb; that it was only a harmless prank, but the sight of blood made her ill down to the very pit of her stomach. If someone was indeed trying to scare her away, they were doing a fine job of it by throwing blood on her house.

Now, standing on the porch, she stopped, unintentionally digging her fingernails into Caleb's bicep. "I can't do this!" she cried. "I can't go in there. I won't!"

Caleb's heart clenched behind his chest wall, fearing he may break down. He could not force her to go in. He would not. It was cruel, to say the least. "I'll be right here with you whatever you decide. But if you can't even go inside, you might want to consider putting the place up for sale."

"But then I won't have anywhere to live and I'll *really* have to start over again," she complained.

Caleb smiled. "I can think of somewhere for you to live. A place you've already made yourself comfortable in."

Amelia became rigid next to him. "Oh, no! That's only temporary, and *only* as long as your *daed* doesn't find out I'm there. Staying in your *dawdi haus* is almost as bad as staying here—no offense!"

He chuckled lightly. "I don't take offense to that. It hasn't been easy for *me* to live with my *daed* since all this happened. I can only imagine how much worse it might make you feel."

"If I had a *dawdi haus* I'd let you stay there— so you could get away from all that tension, I mean," she said to him.

"*Jah,* I do," he said, putting his arm around her waist. "What's it going to be? Are we going in, or are you coming back with me and staying in the *dawdi haus?* Either way I look at it, you're hiding from something—my *daed,* or the past."

She took another deep breath, hoping it would calm her nerves, but she still shook just as much. "I've already been in there, and maybe it wasn't as bad as I thought. I just got shaken up from the blood, but I think if I don't face this, I'll always be running from something, and that's no way to live."

"You're right. Let's get in there and clean the place up. I'm sure that will make you feel better about being here."

She nodded and allowed Caleb to lead her up to the house. He turned the key and opened the door, the creaking setting her nerves on edge.

Noticing her jumpiness at every little noise, he tightened his grip on her. "I'll oil the hinges so it's quiet."

She nodded, walking robotically beside him. Once inside, her gaze traveled over the dim room, feeling panic rising up from her gut. Her breaths quickened, her nails digging into

Caleb's arm again. She cringed, unable to quiet the voices from that night.

Constant cracks of thunder and flickering lightning did not help ease her fears about this place. Her breaths came quicker and the walls seemed to be closing in on her; tunnel vision made it hard for her to see, and she feared she may pass out.

"Take me back," she cried. "Take me back to your house. I'd rather face your father and all his judgment than the ghosts of this house."

"You're right Amelia," he said, calming her. "Perhaps tomorrow if it's not storming, maybe then we'll be able to get through this. I think the storm is bringing back too many bad memories, and maybe you're just not ready for all of that yet."

He cradled her in his arms, as he led her out the door and into his buggy. He would take her back to his home where she could feel safer, and he would not let any harm come to her no matter what.

Caleb clicked to Chestnut, urging the horse to do his bidding. The gelding knew the way home, but Caleb could see that the weather had even put him on edge. Amelia leaned her head against his shoulder the entire way back to his house, and he felt bad for pushing her too soon.

"We'll get an early start tomorrow; you'll see when they drop off the supplies in the morning. It'll be a fresh, new day, and we'll get that place in order so there won't be any trace of the past left in your home. Unless it's something you want to be there."

"That sounds good to me," she sobbed.

They drove up to the yard, and he pulled around quietly to the back and let her off at the *dawdi haus,* and then drove the buggy a few feet to the barn so he could pull the buggy in for the night. He was trying to be discreet so that his father would not know that she was there. It wasn't that he was trying to be sneaky, he just didn't want any trouble for her.

As he began to unharness Chestnut from the buggy, he heard Amelia screaming from the *dawdi haus* without a pause. He ran to her as fast as he could, frightened that someone was hurting her. Out of breath, he shouldered his way through the door, finding Amelia screaming at a blood stain covering the rug in the front room of the tiny home. The stain was almost identical to the one he'd found on the rug he'd rolled up and disposed of from her own home.

The only difference was, the blood was fresh.

Who would've done such a thing?

"Go into the bedroom," he ordered her. "I'll roll up this carpet and get it out of here."

She shook her head. "No! What if he's in there?"

"What if *who* is in there?" Caleb asked.

"The murderer!" she said in between sobbing.

"There is no murderer, Amelia," he said calmly. "He's been gone for eight years! This is just a prank, I'm telling you."

"Don't you think we should get the sheriff's department to tell us what they think?" she begged.

"Let me think about this for a minute," he said as he walked into the bedroom to check to make sure that everything was secure. When he was certain she was safe, he went out to the living room and made quick work of moving the sofa aside, and the two chairs and coffee table. Then he bent down to roll up the rug.

"I told you to get that girl out of my *haus*," his dad's voice thundered from the front door.

Caleb looked up at his angry father, who was dressed in rubber boots, his rubber apron, and he was covered in blood. It was what he wore when slaughtering one of the livestock, and it was apparent he'd just been to slaughter.

Caleb leered at his father. "Did you do this?"

"Do what? I've been busy most of the day getting two pigs ready for the smokehouse."

Caleb sniffed the air and realized his father was telling the truth about that much of it, but he'd avoided answering him. "Someone soiled this rug with blood. It's still wet, and this stain is too large for it to be a simple explanation!"

The man scowled, his gaze traveling to the rug beneath his son's feet. "What happened here?" he asked. "Did the Amish girl do this?"

"No!" Caleb said, befuddled at his father's statement. "I was just asking you the same thing. Someone splattered fresh blood all over her front door and her porch today, and now we come back here, and there's blood on this rug, and we have no idea who did it. And for the record; she's no more Amish than you and I are!"

"I warned you not to let her stay here," he said. "I told you she would bring nothing but trouble and *death* to this house. Get her out of here; I won't tell you again!"

The man turned on his heels without answering his son, leaving Caleb filled with fear and panic. Was his father capable of such a thing? Would he go to such lengths just to scare Amelia away? One thing was certain; he would have to discourage Amelia from calling the Sheriff's Department because he wasn't about to call the law on his own father—that is, if he did this.

He prayed it wasn't so.

Chapter 9

"I can't stay here alone!" Amelia said. "I need someone to stand guard. I'm already such a wreck, I don't think I'll be able to sleep otherwise."

She was still shaking, and he hated seeing her like that.

Caleb let out a heavy sigh. He didn't blame her for not wanting to be alone. Admittedly, he didn't like the idea of her being alone any more than she did. "I can stay on the sofa, but only until you fall asleep, and then I'll have to go," he offered. "I really shouldn't stay in the same house without an escort, but I think this situation could be considered an emergency of sorts. If my *daed* found out, he'd take me out back of the barn for a *talk* for sure and for certain!"

"I'm sorry to put you in such a spot," she said. "I wish I felt safe enough to be here alone, but whoever put blood all over my front door knows that I'm staying here, and decided to extend the warning to me here as well."

"Don't worry about it. Tomorrow, things will be better. We'll get the supplies delivered, and we should have a good portion of the cleaning and repairs done by sundown, wouldn't you think?"

The wind blew and the rain drummed against the tin roof like a brass band.

"If you'll make us some *kaffi,* I'll build a fire to take the chill out of the air. I think the temperature dropped about ten degrees since the sun went down."

She went to the kitchen to busy her hands with making a pot of coffee, while she anticipated the warmth of a nice fire. She was a little hungry, but she feared her stomach would retaliate having even a small amount of food in it until after she calmed down. The constant loud cracks of thunder didn't help any. She jumped every time, even though she anticipated it after the lightning strike.

She'd not felt safe most of her life, but now, she felt a total state of unrest. Though she missed her parents, they'd been like strangers, almost as if not related to her. An only child of Amish parents, they were always at odds, and even more-so with the community. Her *mamm* and *daed* had even seemed mismatched, but she struggled to remember why. They were quiet—except when they'd argued, thinking she couldn't hear them.

What was it they would argue about?

If only she could remember the things she hadn't wanted to, or even intended to block out. All she really knew was that her childhood home had never felt like *home* because of the tension there. There had always been an unknown source of strife between her parents, and perhaps the deaths of her parents and the man who'd hunted them had been the reason, but what was it that nagged at her so? Was she remembering things wrong?

She stood at the sink, staring blankly out at the swaying cornstalks, a shiver running through her as the lightning illuminated the cornfield. Thunder rolled, shaking the house, and then another flicker illuminated a dark figure—a man.

She slowly turned, glancing over her shoulder, but Caleb was not at the hearth.

She opened her mouth to scream, as her eyes fixed forward, searching for the figure, but he was gone.

A low groan escaped her quivering lips as she searched the darkness.

Paralyzed with fear, she was unable to move from the window as lightning illuminated the large, dark figure, as he drew closer to the window.

Her world went silent; even the thunder was muffled from the sound of her ragged breaths, which she drew into her lungs as if running a marathon.

Making another attempt to scream, she still could not find her voice.

Her eyes bulged, as she struggled to focus in the dark room, her mind searching for a way to flee the threat of harm from her stalker.

A noise from the other room startled her, and she turned in time to see Caleb entering the *dawdi haus* with an armful of firewood.

She let out the last breath she'd been holding in with a whoosh, as she peered back out the kitchen window at the swaying cornstalks.

The figure was gone.

Her thoughts switched gears as she ran past Caleb, slammed the door, and turned the lock. Whipping around to face him, she planted herself in front of the door as though to guard it from the intruder.

He dropped the bundle of wood onto the brick hearth and rushed to her side.

"What's wrong?" he asked, searching the pale figure before him as if she was a ghost.

"There w-was a man—outside the k-kitchen w-window," she stuttered.

If not for her heaving breaths and inability to reason with him, he'd probably not believe her, but one thought nagged at him.

He'd been outside just now gathering wood from the woodpile on the other side of the barn, and had not gone near the kitchen window. If he'd been approached in any way, he'd wonder if the man was a stranger, but he'd managed to escape harm.

That left only one person: his father.

Caleb shook as he pulled Amelia into his arms and smoothed her hair. "It's nothing," he tried to assure her. "You probably saw me out there when I went to get the firewood. There isn't anyone out there, or I would have seen them. I'm certain you're over-stressed from everything that's happened today. Try to get some rest, and I'll finish building the fire."

"Don't leave," she cried. "Promise you won't leave!"

"I won't leave," he said kissing her hair. He loved her, and couldn't bear to see her so distressed, especially when he was helpless to prevent it.

He promised with a heavy heart, wondering why his own flesh and blood would go to such lengths to scare Amelia.

Chapter 10

"Are you certain this is what you want to do?" he asked as he steered Chestnut toward her farm.

Caleb couldn't help but think they were making a big mistake. She'd kept him awake most of the night with nightmares, and when she wasn't screaming in her sleep, she was pacing the floors nervously, checking all the curtains to be sure they were completely closed. He was certain his father knew he hadn't spent the night in the main house, and he knew a lecture behind the barn was on the man's mind, even though he'd been too old for his *daed's* lectures for some years.

Amelia forced herself to watch the cornfield as they rode past it, trying hard to convince herself it was only a cornfield, and the stalks would be gone soon with winter approaching.

"I need to have a place to live. Your *daed* has made it clear that I'm not welcome at your *haus,* and I'm an overtired wreck. I don't think I'll be able to sleep ever again if I don't face this."

She was shaking again, and he hated seeing her like that.

Caleb sighed heavily. He didn't want to do anything that would hurt her, and he feared this move was just too much for her to handle mentally. If he had his way, he'd protect her from all of this and take her away from it all. Point was, she owned the house, and until she either gave up on it and decided to sell the dilapidated property, or walked cleanly away, they were on a course for more nightmares and sleepless nights. The only real solution, in

Caleb's opinion, was to fix the home and make it look nothing like it had when she remembered it as a child.

He clicked to Chestnut once more, urging the horse forward before he changed his mind. When they pulled into the property, a truck waited for them.

"The delivery is here," he said, trying to sound enthusiastic.

He could see by the bewildered look on her face she wasn't buying into his feigned enthusiasm, but he would keep trying to make the chore as light on the nerves as he possibly could.

A young man jumped out of the truck and greeted them. "I'm Kyle, were you expecting a delivery today?"

"Jah—yes," Caleb said.

He looked at Caleb, and then over at Amelia. "I need a signature from the home-owner."

"That would be me," Amelia said.

Kyle raised an eyebrow at her as he held up his clipboard. "My paperwork says Silas Graber."

Amelia's throat constricted. "That's my *daed,*" she whispered. "How do you have his name on there? He's been dead eight years!"

His green eyes bore into her with a frightening familiarity that sent a shiver through her. "I'm sorry, Miss. His name was probably in our system, and when you ordered the supplies and gave this address, it probably generated an automated ticket for the delivery."

She didn't ever remember her father ordering materials from the lumber yard when she was a child, but she supposed he'd had to have ordered something at least once for them to have his name in their system. She let the matter drop, and signed for the materials with a shaky hand that did not go unnoticed by Kyle.

Surprisingly, he found her to be quite pretty— for an Amish girl. He wasn't here for pleasure; he had business to take care of, and there would be no personal mingling between him and the attractive young woman.

After checking her signature, he tossed the clipboard onto the front seat and went around back of the truck to begin unloading.

Caleb approached him. "Would you like some help?"

Kyle held up a hand. "I'd be okay with that, but the company tells me I have to unload on my own, and whatever the homeowner does with it after that is his—or *her* business," he said, as his gaze traveled over to Amelia.

Caleb didn't like the way Kyle was looking at Amelia; it sent a warning straight to the pit of his gut. "I'll leave you to your work, then."

He walked back to the buggy and urged Amelia to go inside the house with him. They stepped up to the porch with the cleaning supplies they'd brought with them, and she stood at the door, not wanting to go in.

"Are you going to be able to go in?" he asked when he saw her hesitation.

Kyle brought the panels of tin roof to the porch, pausing to look at Amelia. "Do you have a key?"

She looked up at him and nodded. "I'm having a tough time going into the house," she said, quietly. "Too many ghosts of the past."

She hadn't meant to share with the stranger; it just sort of spilled from her tongue like a bad taste she needed to spit out.

"I don't blame you. I heard the people who lived here were bank robbers!"

"My parents did not rob that bank!" Amelia shot back. "So you heard wrong!"

She'd heard the rumors about her parents, but she knew better. That man who shot them had mistaken them for someone else, and that mistake had cost her everything.

"Sorry," Kyle mumbled. "I didn't mean to get your feathers in a ruffle!"

His misuse of the expression set her nerves on edge almost as much as his ignorance about her parents' innocence. She was, in fact, so annoyed by him that she turned the lock on the door and walked inside just to spite him. His comments were not going to get the better of her. If she was to survive in the limbo state that was her life, she was going to have to get thicker skin. With one foot in the Amish community, and one foot in the *English* world, she would likely suffer ridicule from every angle, and she would have to prepare herself for what would surely come her way if she decided to reside here.

She set her things down on the living room floor and looked around. The room seemed somehow different at this moment. Perhaps it was the quietness of the place, or maybe that the floor was devoid of the blood-stained rug. Whatever it was that had suddenly changed for her, she was finally eager to get the place cleaned and painted so she could move in. She hoped a new coat of paint on the walls would brighten up the rooms, and rid the home of the musty smell.

"I suppose I'll get to work on the roof so it'll stop leaking onto the floor, but I'll have to fix this hole in the ceiling too," he said, pointing up to where water still dripped into the bucket at his feet.

"You aren't going to tackle that roof on your own, are you?" Kyle asked.

Caleb thought about it for a moment, realizing he would have to. Without the help of the community, he was on his own. His cousins still spoke to him occasionally, but they would surely be shunned too if the Bishop were to see them helping him with Amelia's roof.

"I don't have anyone else to help me besides Amelia, and I don't want her on the roof."

"I'd be more than happy to help," he offered. "This was the only delivery I had today. I do it as a favor for my uncle, who owns the lumber yard. My regular job is roofing."

"That's a kind offer, but I'm afraid we don't have money to pay you," Caleb said.

"I'm trying to establish my own business," Kyle said. "So if you'll allow me to put my sign in the yard as advertisement, I'd be willing to help you out. If you were to throw in a few meals; that would be payment enough for me."

Caleb shot Amelia a pleading look. He could tell by her expression she wasn't wild about the idea, but gave him a relenting nod just the same.

She knew Caleb could use the help, but she didn't like the way Kyle spoke to her, and the way he looked at her set her teeth on edge.

"So your uncle owns the lumber yard?" Amelia asked.

"Yeah, he's my mom's brother. He took me in when she died."

"So he raised you?" she asked curiously.

Caleb flashed her a look to mind her own business, but there was something about Kyle she didn't trust, and she was smart enough to know that if a person was trying to hide something, they wouldn't divulge personal information to a stranger.

"Only for four years, until I turned eighteen. My mother took an overdose of sleeping pills when my father died. It was too much for her."

This piqued her curiosity.

"You lost both your parents at once?" she asked.

"No, my dad left me when I was four years old—not of his own free will. He went to jail for a crime he didn't commit, and when he got out, he was killed."

Amelia felt her throat constrict. There was something too familiar about his story.

"What did you say your last name was?"

"Sinclair," he answered.

Unable to put her finger on just what it was that she didn't trust about Kyle, she pushed her inquiry a little further.

"How did your dad die?"

She knew it was rude to ask, but his story was too close to hers. She had to know.

"I didn't hear details, since he wasn't part of my life. I only know what my mom said before she died."

"And what was that?" She asked.

She knew she was pushing the issue too far, but she wasn't about to stop now. She was on to something, she knew it. She could feel it right down to the marrow in her bones. She knew the burden of proof would be on her, but she was determined to prove there was a connection, somehow. It wasn't a coincidence that he was here now, offering his help, but what was it that he sought?

"My mother told me that he was innocent of the charges against him," Kyle said.

"What was it he was charged with?" she asked, pushing him even further.

"Armed robbery," he answered.

"How can you be so sure of his innocence?" she asked.

"How can you be so sure of *your* parents' innocence?" he shot back at her.

"Because the man who really did it shot both of them right in front of me!"

"That's enough, Amelia," Caleb scolded her.

She flashed him a dirty look. "I'm just getting started," she said, her voice raised. "It seems to me that our parents have something in common, and I'm going to find out just what that is."

"I think it's only a coincidence," Kyle offered. "Why don't we drop the subject and get to work on the house. We won't get to the entire roof today, especially since it's supposed to rain later this afternoon. I think we should work on getting as much of that roof covered as possible before the rain comes."

Amelia leered at him. He was indeed hiding something. Was it possible he was the son of the man she shot? Was it possible he was behind all the mischief? Somehow, facing her terrorizer made it a little easier for her to accept. If he was up to something, she would be ready for him.

"I agree," Caleb said. "Let's get that roof done."

Kyle excused himself to get the last load of materials from his truck.

"What was that all about?" Caleb asked her once Kyle was out of earshot.

"Whose side are you on?" she accused.

"I'm on your side, always," he said. "But don't you think you were unnecessarily rude to him? I need his help, and now I'll be lucky if he stays and helps me with the roof."

"You don't think this story matches mine almost exactly?" She asked him.

"No, I don't! I think you're losing control of your emotions," he said. "You're becoming paranoid."

"Who wouldn't be under these circumstances? But I'm not paranoid," she shot back. "You heard him. He's hiding something."

"You can't be sure of that," Caleb defended Kyle. "Besides, even if he is related to the man who killed your parents, that doesn't make him a murderer too. And how do you explain the fact he doesn't even have the same last name as the man who killed your parents?"

"He could have easily lied. It makes me suspicious of him. You don't think it's awfully fishy that he's here? Or the fact that he knew my father owned this house?"

"I'll admit that is a strange coincidence, but don't you worry; I'll be keeping my eye on him. In the meantime, keep your mouth shut. You don't want to make him think you suspect him."

"I will do no such thing, Caleb Yoder, and you can't make me. I think he's behind the blood on my door and the blood in your *dawdi haus*.

I suspect him of everything, and I want you to make him leave."

Caleb reflected on his suspicions of his father. "Somehow," he said. "I don't think Kyle is responsible for that."

"How do you figure?" she asked.

Caleb looked at his feet, feeling shame rising up in his cheeks, heating them. "Because I just don't. When you went back to the bedroom when I removed the rug. My dad came to the door, and he had on his leather apron and rubber boots. He'd just slaughtered two pigs."

Amelia's breath hitched, and tears pooled in her eyes. "That doesn't *prove* anything, does it?"

"Not by itself, except it came with a warning. He warned me again to get you off of the property," Caleb continued quietly. "I have to wonder if he did it just to scare you. I'm sorry, and I'm ashamed to think my *daed* could have done such a thing, but I don't think Kyle is the one you need to worry about. I think we need to get your place finished so we can get you settled in here before my father goes off the deep end."

Amelia studied Caleb's dark blue eyes. The sparkle had gone from them, and his ashen face held a sorrow she could not bear. She closed the space between them and he wrapped his arms around her, kissing her hair. He would protect her, even if it meant defending her against his own father.

Chapter 11

Amelia took a step back to look at her clean kitchen. She'd spent the entire day disinfecting everything from floor to ceiling, and she was proud of her progress. She was now ready to paint since the living room would have to wait until after they finished the roof. The leaks in there had caused damage that would involve repairing the ceiling and possibly the floorboards in some areas. Though she knew it would be close to a week before she would be able to move in, she knew each day would bring her closer to the freedom she'd wanted for the past eight years.

"Where do you want me to put the paint, Amish girl?" Kyle asked, startling her from her reverie.

Amelia felt her heart pounding all the way down to her toes. She sucked in a breath, heaving it in as if she couldn't get any air.

"You alright, little Amish girl?" Kyle asked.

"Why—are you calling me that?" she pleaded, through ragged breaths.

It was the way he'd said it that reminded her of that night when Bruce was chasing her through the cornfield.

He held up his hands defensively. "I didn't mean any disrespect," he said. "I just forgot your name, that's all. Don't shoot me or anything!"

"Why would you think I'd shoot you?" she asked through gritted teeth.

"I didn't mean anything by it," he said. "Like I said little Amish girl, I just forgot your name, that's all."

"Don't ever call me little Amish girl again!"

He chuckled. "Sorry!"

"I don't find any of this funny. Maybe you should leave. I'm sure Caleb can finish the roof on his own. We don't need your help."

Just then Caleb burst through the door holding up a bloodied hand.

Amelia screamed. "What happened?" she asked, rushing to his side.

"I was trying to move the panels of roof from the pallet to put them on the porch," he said hastily. "The wind caught them and they tore into my hands. There's an awful storm headed our way, and I was trying to put everything away. It startled me so much that I dropped the pallet, and I think I broke two of my fingers."

Kyle rushed to his side with a clean shop-cloth he picked up from the top of the stack, and wrapped it around Caleb's hand. "Let me take a look," he said, as he mopped up some of the blood. "Wiggle your fingers."

Caleb tried, but he couldn't move the last two.

"I think you're right about breaking the last two fingers," Kyle said. "But I don't think the cuts are deep enough to need stitches. When's the last time you had a tetanus shot?"

"I had to get one last year when I sliced open my leg on the plow, so I'm covered."

"That'll save us a trip to the emergency room," Kyle said. "Unfortunately, you're not gonna be able to do that roof now, I'll have to finish it myself."

Amelia narrowed her eyes at him. She had just ordered him to leave her home, and now it seemed she would need him to stay. The thought of it aggravated her.

Caleb winced as he applied pressure to the cuts.

"Let's go outside to my truck," Kyle said. "I think I have a first-aid kit out there."

When they went out the front door, Amelia could see the black sky from the doorway, and the wind had picked up. Caleb was right about the impending storm. She was ready to quit for the day anyway, but she wasn't looking forward to riding back with Kyle. They'd left the horse and buggy for Caleb's *daed* so he could go into town when they'd gone back for lunch, leaving them stranded in the storm if they didn't ride back with Kyle.

A sudden darkness fell over the house, adding a deep chill to the air. Lightning flashed, and thunder rolled in the distance, and it made her shiver. Rain began to pelt down onto the tin roof, and within minutes, it was dripping onto the living room floor again. She dashed across the wood floor toward the galvanized bucket to put it under the spot that was dripping the heaviest, her foot falling through the boards with a snap.

She cried out in pain, as she collapsed onto the wet floor. Pulling her twisted ankle loose from the floorboard, the plank of wood popped up. Although she was crying from the pain, she noticed something between the floorboards, and leaned in for a closer look. There was no mistaking the large canvas bag wedged in the dirty cocoon, water stains marring it from the leaky roof and years of lying in wait of being discovered.

Panic seized her as she leaned over the decayed floorboard to move the bag. She knew it was filled with money from the worn lettering on the front. It boasted the name of the bank downtown; the one that was robbed more than eighteen years ago.

What was it doing under the floorboards of her house?

"Are you okay?" Kyle asked from the doorway.

Amelia instinctively grabbed the piece of flooring and replaced it before he came any closer. "My foot found a loose board and I think I sprained my ankle," she answered, trying to act casual.

He crouched down on his haunches next to her and picked up her foot, touching the ankle gently. "I think you're right. It's beginning to swell, but it's probably only a sprain. The bone doesn't seem to be broken."

She pulled her foot away, feeling uncomfortable at his lingering touch.

He remained on his haunches and peered at the loose board that now covered the hidden money. She backed away nervously, wondering if she could get up and leave.

Remaining where he was, Kyle looked at her curiously, and cocked his head to one side. "I sprained my ankle once when I was younger," he began. "It was when I was four years old. My dad had taken me fishing—he used to take me fishing all the time, but this time I accidentally stepped in the bucket of bait when I backed into it trying to reel in a big fish. I tipped it over and my ankle twisted. I'll never forget that day; it was the last day I saw my dad alive."

His story made Amelia nervous, and she backed away even further, checking behind her to remember where the door was, should she need to escape.

"When my father went to prison," he continued. "My mother became addicted to pills of all kinds. Pain pills, sleeping pills, you name it. Things might've been easier for us if we'd had the money my father was accused of stealing. As it was, he claimed all along that it was four Amish kids that took the money. They never did catch those kids."

Amelia knew better than to interrupt him, and so she remained quiet, all the while, trying to think of how she would escape with her sprained ankle.

"My dad went to prison for ten long years, while those Amish kids spent that money."

"Where's Caleb?" she interrupted nervously.

He chuckled. "I sent him home to get bandages. There weren't any in my truck after all!"

Amelia's spine went cold, and her brain numb, as if someone had filled her veins with ice water. She could feel her heart racing, and she tried to scoot away from him with her left foot, her right foot unable to maneuver because of the pain. His story had gone from making her nervous, to terrifying her, for she feared that Kyle was Bruce's son. Was he telling her his sad story so he could justify it when he killed her?

She wanted to tell him where the money was, but it was not hers to give to him. He was wrong about her parents spending the money; it was still down between the floorboards only a few inches from where he stood.

There was only one thing that still nagged at her; if her parents were two of the Amish kids that took the money, who were the other two?

Caleb tiptoed through the house, not wanting to alert his dad to his presence there. He was in a hurry, not wanting to leave Amelia alone with Kyle for too long. He didn't have any reason not to trust him, but Amelia was leery of him, and if she found out he was gone, she would surely be upset with him. As he wandered through the house to the upstairs bathroom where he knew there were bandages, he could faintly hear his father mumbling from down the hall. He stepped closer to his father's room, listening to the man's ramblings.

"We should never have spent that money we stole," his father mumbled. "We should have turned it in before anyone was hurt."

Was there someone in there with him?

"That money has cursed us, Lord, and I regret not turning it in when I had the chance."

Had he heard his father correctly? It seemed that his father was praying—no—confessing to a robbery. How was that possible? He strained to listen some more.

"My gun took a man's life, Lord, and the guilt has never left me. I put that gun in my own hands and held it against innocent people and stole money that didn't belong to me. Please forgive me and lift this burden from me."

Caleb felt his heart pounding against his ribcage. His father had told the authorities he had no idea where the gun had come from. He'd lied to them—and to his own son about that night. Rumors had circulated around the community about the involvement of four Amish kids that had committed the crime during their *rumspringa,* and how they'd helped an *Englisher* rob a bank. He never thought his own parents could be involved.

Was it really possible his parents were part of that foursome?

"We were just kids," his father continued to ramble on. "But I've lived with the guilt all these years. Forgive me, Lord. Forgive me for having a gun that took a man's life, and forgive me for helping to steal that money. Forgive me for spending it."

Caleb felt fear rise up like bile from his stomach. He could taste the stickiness of adrenaline on his tongue. He had to get out of the house. Had to get away from the reality that was hitting him full-force. How was he going to break the news to Amelia that his own father was involved in the same robbery from which her parents had lost their lives?

How would he tell her that it was his father that had splattered the blood all over to scare her away? Had it all been to save him from the shame of the past? He prayed for the words to say to her as he hitched up Chestnut to his father's buggy.

Amelia rose from the floor. "I think I can walk on my ankle if I don't put too much pressure on it," she said nervously, trying to change the subject away from Kyle's rendition of the robbery and shootings.

His offended expression let her know he wouldn't be distracted from finishing what he had to say. "We would have had the money and a good life if *you* hadn't shot my father!"

Amelia could feel the blood draining from her limbs. She blinked rapidly against the flashes of lightning that illuminated Kyle, his silhouette mirroring his father's on the night she'd shot him.

"I'm sorry. I didn't mean to kill him," she pleaded with trembling lips. "I was only a little girl. I didn't mean to shoot him. The gun went off by accident."

She took a step back, stumbling against the pain in her ankle.

Kyle reached out to her, but she flinched away.

"I won't hurt you, little Amish girl," he said, holding a hand out to her.

She turned on her heels, pain stabbing her ankle, but she pushed it down; her fight-or-flight response choosing to flee.

Taking the same labored steps she'd traveled on that terrible night eight years ago, she limped and hobbled, her only goal to put distance between herself and Kyle. She mentally traveled the same trail through the cornfield to Caleb's house where she would be safe, but fear blocked the memory. Hobbling through the unfamiliar rows, her gate reminded her of her stalker's that night. He'd hobbled, and it had cost him valuable time in catching her.

This time, she was the one losing valuable time.

Whimpering uncontrollably with ragged breaths, she maneuvered through the narrow rows, struggling to remember the path that would lead to safety. She could hear her *mamm's* voice floating over the tops of the tassels, calling to her, but her mother's ghost was guiding her back toward danger.

Ignoring her *mamm's* voice and the voices of the past that haunted her, she continued to stumble through the dips and rises in the soil, while the autumn-dried stalks whipped the flesh of her cheeks and arms. She ignored the stinging pain; her goal to reach the edge of the cornfield that connected her property with Caleb's farm. She still had a ways to go after she exited the cornfield before she would reach his farmhouse, but she continued to run, her instincts the only thing guiding her through the maze that encompassed her.

Sudden pain assaulted her, stinging her flesh as she became entangled in the barbed-wire fence that separated her from Caleb and his property. Lightning flashed, and she scanned the cornrows behind her for signs of the one who hunted her like a wild animal.

Desperately tugging at the wires that held her arms, the spikes ripped open her flesh and sunk deeper, holding her hostage.

She choked down the screams she knew would be a beacon to her location, as she made another painful attempt at freeing herself from the shackles that imprisoned her.

It was all in vain…she was trapped!

Chapter 12

Kyle didn't waste any time unearthing what had been resting beneath the floorboards. He could tell by Amelia's nervous reaction she'd found something very deep beneath them. After he pulled up several planks, he couldn't believe his eyes. There was the money all along. If only he'd found it any of the times he'd ransacked the home over the years while it had laid vacant.

He chuckled and talked aloud to the bag as if it understood him. "I suppose I should be glad I didn't find you before, or I would still be tempted to keep you."

He paused. "This money isn't any more mine than it is Amelia's, or anyone else's. It needs to go back to where it was stolen from; the bank."

He pulled the dampened bag from betwixt the floorboards and let it drop to the floor with a thud.

"I don't know how my father managed to get ahold of all this money, but I hope that wherever he is now, he's realized it wasn't worth losing his life over. I hope he knows it wasn't worth the lives of two other innocent people."

"Correction!" A female voice said from behind him. "That would be *three* innocent lives."

Kyle whipped his head around to the female figure standing in the dark doorway, lightning illuminating her angry silhouette.

"I take it you're Bruce's kid?" she asked him casually.

Kyle nodded.

"I hate to break it to you, but your father was just as guilty as we were. We all stole that money equally, and we were supposed to divide it equally, but your father stole something from me that was far more precious to me than that money," she said bitterly. "Something I can never get back; my husband and my daughter!"

"Are you Amelia's mom?" Kyle asked as he stood, the bag of money at his feet.

She walked in through the door, a pistol trained on him, while scanning between him and the bag of money.

"I'm the woman that your father made a childless widow over this money, and I should think that I'm entitled to that money to make up for my losses. He killed my only child."

"Are you Amelia's mother?" He asked again, taking note of her modern attire. Wearing a pair of jeans and a T-shirt, her clothing was nothing like the conservative *Amish* garb her daughter and Caleb had worn. Her gray and brown-streaked hair was down and rested on her shoulders, unlike Amelia's, which she wore tightly bound at the nape of her neck, and covered by a white *kapp*.

"I *was* her mother," she said bitterly.

But she's not dea..., he tried to say, but she cocked the gun, causing him to raise his hands defensively.

He didn't dare say another word, although he felt it necessary to tell her that her daughter was still alive. Didn't she know?

Before Kyle could think about giving her the good news, she tossed a thick rope at him, and ordered him to sit in her old rocking chair— the only chair in the room.

"Tie your feet to the chair, and make sure the rope is real tight," she said, pointing the gun at him.

"Don't do this," he begged, as he obeyed her demand. "Take the money, but please let me go!"

"I already intend to take the money! It's mine! I'll have to give you kudos for finding *my* money. I've wondered where it was for more than eighteen long years, but I never thought my husband would hide the money under the floorboards. He kept that money from me all those years, making us scrimp and save to pay back every penny of it. I worked my fingers to the bone sewing quilts until my fingers bled, and crocheting blankets and mittens and hats and scarves, and everything in-between, while he made harnesses and furniture for local shops. We slaved all those years to pay back all that money—the money we spent on our humble little farm. Now look at it." She turned her nose up as she looked around her home with disgust. "Before my husband had a chance to turn it in, your father found us and, well, you know the rest—no sense in repeating it!"

When she was satisfied his legs were securely tied to the chair legs, she ordered him to put his arms behind him. Then she wrapped the loop of a slip-knot around his wrists and pulled it tight.

Kyle winced against the pain, the ropes cutting off his circulation. The older woman was certainly strong, he'd have to give her that.

"That's tight enough so you can't get loose," she said, laughing.

"Don't do this," he begged again.

Ignoring his pleas, she grabbed the bottles of kerosene for the lanterns and began to splash it against the walls, and all the while, Kyle was pleading for his life.

"I'll be happy to see this place go up in flames," she said, continuing to ignore his non-stop begging and alternate whimpering. "For a lot of years, I've wanted to rid myself of the prison this house became for me and my family as we slaved to pay back the money. All it did was make me angry. After I woke up in the hospital, they told me Amelia and my husband had both been killed, and after the funerals, they put me in witness protection. I've been stuck there all this time, and they suddenly let me out for some strange reason."

"You don't have to be angry," Kyle said. "Amelia is alive! She just left here. She went through the cornfield out back. She went to Caleb's house!"

"You're a liar, just like your father! She's dead and buried. I saw the casket myself."

"Let me go and I'll prove it to you! She's alive. I just spoke to her!"

"Liar, liar, pants on fire!" she sang.

Then, picking up the money, she stood at the doorway and flashed Kyle a pleased look, and then struck a match.

"NO! Wait!" he half-cried. "Please! Why are you doing this?"

"An eye for an eye!" she said, flicking the match behind her.

Chapter 13

Caleb coughed and choked, his eyes tearing up from the autumn air that filled his nostrils with the stench of smoke. Burning leaves was something he disliked the most about the season, but this smell was somehow different. It didn't smell like burning leaves; it smelled much stronger. The smoke filled his lungs, and would surely make his asthma worse.

He climbed inside the buggy and clicked to Chestnut, steering him down the road toward Amelia's house.

As he headed down the long lane toward the main road, he could see smoke rising over the top of the thick tree-line. It seemed to be coming from the direction of Amelia's house.

"Oh, *Gott,* please--*nooooo!*"

Caleb's cry rent the air, splitting the dead of night, but it wasn't enough to stop the inevitable. There was no one to call for help, no one to hear his pleas that echoed against the acres of farmland that separated him from the nearest farmhouse.

Panic filled him at the thought of something happening to Amelia, and he slapped the reins against his horse's hind flank, urging him into a fast trot. If Amelia was in danger, he'd never be able to forgive himself for leaving her alone with Kyle. She'd begged him to let him go from his employ, but he hadn't listened. She'd warned him that there was something fishy going on, and he'd put her concerns off, thinking only of himself and the help he needed with the roof.

He prayed haphazardly as he urged the horse to go faster still, being careless and unaware of the possibility of cars being on the dark, country road with him. Lightning flashed, illuminating the dark silhouette of her house, and what was left of the roof. Flames licked the blackened sky, Caleb fearing he'd never make it in time to save her. His breath came out in short spurts as he prayed for her safety.

Kyle teetered and rocked the chair back-and-forth until he tipped it over, crashing down hard against his shoulder. The impact dislocated his shoulder, sending a surge of pain through his entire body. But he knew if he didn't risk the injury, he would soon not be able to breathe. His only hope of possible survival was to get low to the floor below the smoke-line.

Mere seconds after the fall, he rolled onto his back, and then over to his good shoulder; the one he hadn't fallen on. He began to scissor kick his torso to scoot closer to the door. He had no idea how he would get out of the house when he got there, but perhaps he would have to break one of the low windows with his feet.

Knowing it was better to get a few cuts and scrapes than to lose his life, he worked quickly to get free from the burning house. He coughed and choked and sputtered, heaving in smoky breaths that burned his lungs. He knew he needed to work quickly, or the chances of him getting out of the house alive were slimmer with each second that passed.

He could already hear the creak from the floor that would give way under him. The walls and the ceiling were in flames, and he could hear the creaking of the roof collapsing.

Caleb pushed his gelding as far as the animal would go, his ears twitching, and his steps sporadic as he tried to avoid going any further. Chestnut whinnied and nickered, his hooves pawing at the pavement. The animal's instincts warned his owner of the danger of getting too close to the flaming house.

Caleb turned the buggy around and jumped out, knowing the horse would go back home.

"Go on, boy," he said, as he slapped the horse on the flank. "Go home."

Caleb ran the rest of the way, his lungs filling with smoke, his heart-rate so rapid he felt nauseated.

When the house came into view, he was shocked to see the roof engulfed in flames. He feared the worst, concerned that Amelia might already be dead inside the home, consumed with smoke inhalation.

Still, he ran fast to reach the house, hearing a faint call for help, but it wasn't a feminine voice. It was Kyle's voice and not Amelia's. Confusion plagued him over the desperate, and ragged call for help from Kyle.

Working his way through the tall grass up to the porch, he could see there would be no saving the house, but he prayed he could save Amelia and Kyle.

Even at the edge of the property, he could feel the heat from the fire like the burn of the afternoon sun on his face. The smoke was so thick it burned his lungs, forcing him into a fit of coughing.

He approached the burning building with caution, putting an arm up to shield his eyes from the almost blinding arc of fire. The crackling of the flames, and the roaring heat were overbearing. His heart heavy, he already mourned for Amelia, his fears unable to rest until he knew where she was.

He yelled out hoping he would hear the faint cries that he'd heard as he approached.

"I'm here," Kyle called him. "By the door."

Caleb stepped up onto the front porch, completely aware that the house could collapse at any moment. He put his hand up on the door feeling the warmth, but it wasn't too hot to the touch. The front window had been cracked and black smoke billowed out, blinding his view of the inside of the home.

He pushed open the door slowly and there was Kyle, wriggling on the floor, tied to a chair. He was coughing and choking, and his eyes were swollen and weeping.

He looked up at Caleb with relief in his tear-filled eyes. "Help me! Hurry! Get me out of here!

"Where's Amelia?" Caleb hollered over the roar of the fire.

"She ran over to your place almost half an hour ago. You didn't see her?" Kyle said, choking.

"No!"

Caleb grabbed a hold of the rocking chair and dragged him out of the house as fast as he could, unconcerned when he bumped him down each step of the porch. He dragged him fast into the yard, aware that Kyle was howling from the pain.

"I'm sorry Kyle," he said, loosening the ropes that bound him to the chair. "Where's Amelia? Are you sure she's not in the house?"

"Yes, I'm sure. She ran across the field almost half an hour ago."

"Did she do this to you? Did she tie you to this chair?" he asked.

"No! It was Amelia's mother!" he said, coughing.

"What do you mean, Amelia's mother? She's dead!"

"No she isn't! She was trying to barbeque me!"

"Why did she set the house on fire?"

Kyle coughed really hard, pushing the last of the smoke from his lungs. "She said it was to get back at my dad for killing her husband and daughter. She thinks Amelia is dead!"

"So you really are Bruce Albee's son?"

Kyle nodded. "I used my mother's maiden name—the same name as my uncle because Albee isn't such a respected name in these parts."

"Did Amelia take off running when she saw her mother?"

Kyle hung his head in shame. "No! I'm afraid I might have scared her, but I was just a little freaked out. I would never harm her, but I don't think she knows that."

"What happened?"

"Amelia's mother took the money!"

"What money?" Caleb asked, feeling a little confused.

"Amelia found the money from the robbery in the floorboards. I freaked out when I saw the bag of money, and it made me mad seeing it, just thinking of everything we've all lost. I believed in my dad's innocence all my life, but now I know it wasn't true. He was guilty, and we need to get the money from Amelia's mom and turn it in."

Caleb stood back and looked at his beloved Amelia's home. Smoke billowed up against the full moon, the flames illuminating the air against the expanse of farmland where it seemed to pause just before melting into the horizon. Bending, creaking, and the crashing sound of breaking glass filled his ears. He was certain there would be no love-loss between the property and Amelia.

"I don't know how she's going to feel about this," he said, unable to turn away from the burning house.

Kyle coughed and wiped soot from his cheeks. "I think we should try to find her before her mother catches up to her. There's no telling what the woman will do."

"I'm worried about her. She could be in danger. The woman could hurt her."

Kyle twisted at the rope burns on his wrists, coughing one last, good cough. "Or try to barbeque her!"

"Are you able to go with me, or should I go by myself?"

"I can go. Do you want me to call the fire department?"

Caleb nodded, wiping the sweat from his brow. He had no idea how much heat a burning house generated.

"Call the police too. Her mom tried to burn you alive, and she took the money. Those are two very serious things."

Kyle dialed 911 from his cell phone, thankful that Amelia's mom hadn't thought to take it from him.

Chapter 14

Amelia tried in vain to break free from the entanglement of the barbed-wire, her arms and legs immovable against the deep cuts that held her tightly bound against the fence. Her energy spent, she could no longer move, nor could she escape.

She was defeated against the strength of her barbed-wire captor.

She would wait for Kyle to come and do his worst, and then perhaps finally, the ghosts of the past would be put to rest. Unable to run from her assailant, she waited, her heart barely beating.

She could hear the faint call of her *mamm* floating over the tops of the tassels in the cornfield. The voice whispered gently, calling her home.

Gusts of wind brought waves of memories rustling over the rows of dried cornstalks. She didn't want to think about the past at this moment, but a picture of her parents entered her mind—a happy time, when life felt safe, and the sun shined every day. It was a silly memory that fogged her thinking, but in her mind she needed safety, so she could face what would happen next.

She knew she didn't have much time, and all she could do was whisper a faint prayer, hoping that the current of air would carry her message along the fast-moving storm clouds, and up to heaven where it would be heard.

Blood drained from her wounds, and she shivered against the numbness and cold she now felt. It wouldn't be long, and all her ghosts would be put to rest.

"I'm here *mamm,*" she whispered faintly, answering the call from her mother. "I'm here, and I'm waiting for you to take me home."

Coming upon the clearing in the tall cornstalks, Abigail Graber gasped at the slip of a figure the lightning illuminated before her. The young woman resembled her daughter, and she cried out to her, lifting her only free arm, but then it dropped weakly to the ground.

"Melia?"

Her mother set down the bag of money and knelt down beside her daughter, gently unraveling the hem of her dress, giving her room to move more freely.

Unwrapping a slack wire from around her arm, she left the tines stuck in her wrist, knowing that to remove it would cause Amelia to bleed to death. So instead, she pulled gently away from the post to cause more slack, the tines cutting into her own hand.

"Come here, my little Melia," she cooed her daughter, as she pulled her into her arms. "I'm here."

Amelia spotted an unfamiliar figure illuminating in the flashes of lightning, and thunder cracked, causing her to jump slightly, her senses barely aware of what was happening to her, but she somehow felt safe.

Working quickly to free her daughter from the entanglement of the wire web, she knew she was losing precious time, for Amelia had already lost a lot of blood. She would die if she wasn't careful, and if she didn't get help soon. In the distance, Abigail could hear sirens, and she knew they would be coming to put out the fire she'd started.

Abigail looked into her daughter's nearly lifeless, pale face. What had she done? They had told her that her only child was dead, but here she was in front of her, and she was holding little Amelia in her arms. She wept, not for herself, but for her child, and the fear she must've felt growing up without her mother.

"Mamm, where are you?" Amelia called out weakly.

"I'm here. Hush my Melia. Help is on the way."

Holding Amelia in her arms, Abigail glanced down at the bag of money next to her leg. Tilting her head back, she lifted her chin toward the heavens and sobbed.

"Forgive me, Lord. Deliver me from the evil this money has added to my life. Please don't let my daughter suffer for my sins. I've lost my faith, dear Lord, and I pray you'll forgive me and help me to have faith again."

She gently rocked her barely conscious daughter in her arms, seeing her only child's life slipping away.

"What have I done, Lord?" she cried out. "My greed and anger, and my need for revenge has cost me my only child. Please change my heart, and spare my child from paying for my sins," she begged.

Amelia's lashes fluttered once more, and she looked up into her *mamm's* face and whispered, "I forgive you."

Then she went limp in her mother's arms.

Chapter 15

Abigail's screams rent the air. Caleb and Kyle, who had been following the trail through the cornfield, looked at each other at the sound of the woman's screams. They knew Amelia wasn't far off, but they also knew that the scream did not come from Amelia. Caleb's mind was whirling, and he wondered if Amelia had gotten into a scuttle with her mother.

"Do you think you can run?" he asked Kyle. "I think we should hurry."

Kyle nodded and the two took off running in the direction they'd heard the screams.

When they came upon the clearing in the cornfield, Kyle was suddenly faced with the woman who'd tried to kill him. He yanked Caleb's sleeve, and pulled him back into the shadows of the cornfield. "Watch it," he warned. "She has a gun!"

They both stepped cautiously out of the cornfield, the lightning illuminating the path. When Caleb saw how bloody Amelia was, and that she lay limp in her mother's arms, he could feel his throat constricting. He loved her more than anything. He'd loved her his entire life. And now, was she... *dead*?

They both stood there in shock, unable to speak for what seemed like a small eternity.

"What did you do to her?" Kyle accused.

"I found her like this," Abigail defended herself. "Help her! I think she's dying!"

Caleb collapsed onto his haunches in front of Abigail, pulling Amelia into his arms and sobbing. Her breath hitched ever so slightly, but that was enough to put a hopeful smile on his face.

"She's alive!" he said, rushing to his feet and pulling her closely.

"Wait!" Abigail shouted. "You can't move her. The barbed-wire is the only thing keeping her from bleeding to death. It has to be cut away from the post before we can move her!"

Kyle shoved his hand deep into his jeans pocket and pulled out a screwdriver and a small pair of wire cutters.

"I don't know if these'll work," he said. "But I'm gonna try."

He worked the barbed-wire, bending it back and forth with the wire-cutters until he finally snapped the section loose. Then he wound it up and tucked it into the hem of Amelia's skirts as Caleb carried her back through the cornfield and out to the road. Police and fire trucks had assembled there with an entire rescue crew at Amelia's house to put out the fire.

Kyle began to walk behind him, but Abigail stopped him with a gentle hand on his arm.

"Please," she said. "I want to tell you that I'm sorry for what I did to you, and I'm glad you're okay. If you hadn't been here with the tools to cut my daughter free, she might have died here. Now, she has a chance. Thank you for saving her after what I did to you."

"I didn't do it for you. I did it for Amelia."

"I really am sorry for what I did."

"Tell it to the authorities, lady!" he said. "Give me the gun."

She reached into her pocket and handed it to him. "I wasn't going to shoot you."

Kyle picked up the bag of money and stepped back.

"Do I have to point the gun at you now, or are you gonna go peacefully with me?"

"It isn't loaded!" she said.

"You managed to tie me up and leave me for dead in a burning building, and the gun wasn't even loaded?"

"I told you I was sorry," she said. "I'm ready to face whatever consequences I'm due. I don't know what I was thinking. I've been so stricken with grief for the past eight years that I didn't know what I was doing. I think I need to go back to the state hospital so I can continue to get treatment because I'm not a well woman."

Kyle looked at her skeptically.

"I wasn't really in Witness Protection. I've been in the state mental institution all these years, but as long as I know that my daughter is okay, I think I'll be okay now. Being able to see her a second time has really changed me. I've locked away all the past and it's not been easy, but now that I know my daughter is alive and she's going to live I just know everything else is going to be okay too. I know because I prayed for it and I have faith now."

Chapter 16

Amelia woke up hearing faint noises that sounded the same as when she'd had her appendix out. She'd stayed a couple days in the hospital, and this sounded the same.

She breathed in deeply, smelling fresh oxygen, the feel of the cannula tucked in her nostrils. If she wasn't in the hospital, perhaps she was dead? Did being dead smell and sound the same as being in the hospital?

She let her eyes drift open, her gaze traveling around the hospital room. Caleb slept in the chair next to her bed, and she was happy to see him, but then her gaze fell on the chair seated at the foot of her bed, and she began to scream.

Caleb jumped up, startled awake. "What's wrong?"

She tried to sit up in bed, but her bandaged arms wouldn't allow her too much movement without pain.

"What's he doing here?" she asked, narrowing her eyes at Kyle.

"Everything is going to be fine, Amelia," Caleb assured her. "Kyle isn't going to hurt you. I give you my word on that."

"But he… chased me through the cornfield and… I don't remember what happened after that, but if I'm in the hospital, I want to know what he did to me?"

"He didn't chase you; he admitted to getting impatient with you and trying to scare you a little, but you ran from the house, and he didn't follow you," Caleb assured her again, patting her hand gently.

In the meantime, Kyle excused himself from the room, rubbing the sleep from his eyes. "I'm going for a cup of coffee, Caleb. Do you want one?"

Caleb nodded. *"Danki."*

Then he turned back to Amelia and tried to calm her.

"My father put up barbed-wire fence between our properties so that you couldn't get through," Caleb said. "You ran into it and cut yourself up pretty bad. You've lost a lot of blood."

"Speaking of blood. What about the blood all over my porch and on your rug in the *dawdi haus*?"

Caleb lowered his head shamefully. "My dad did that to scare you away, and he's very sorry for it. He did it to cover up his involvement in the robbery. Turns out, my parents and your parents committed the crime when they were not too much younger than we are. They were on their *rumspringa,* but that's no excuse. My father figured that if he got you to believe that someone wanted you out of the community, you would actually leave, and he could continue to hide his part in the robbery. But he came clean and turned himself in. He's at home now waiting for the decision, but his lawyer said that he thinks he's going to get him just probation."

A quiet knock sounded at the door, and Amelia looked at the woman in the doorway, her breath catching in her throat.

"*Mamm,*" she whispered, a lump clogging her throat. "Is it really you?"

The woman at the door nodded.

Was she really seeing what she thought she saw? Was it possible her *mamm* was truly alive? She thought that she'd only dreamed of her, but now it seemed she was standing in the doorway.

"Is it alright if I come see you, my little Melia?"

Amelia began to sob, and she nodded her head. She'd longed to hear her mother call her by her pet name for so many years.

Abigail sat on the edge of her bed, and Caleb excused himself from the room.

Amelia looked up into her mother's aged face, searching for the familiarity that she'd missed so much. "What happened to you? I saw Bruce shoot you! I thought you were dead."

"I almost was," she said softly. "When I woke up in the hospital, I was told you were dead. I went to your funeral."

"I was there too, but they wouldn't let me get out of the car!" Amelia said. "They told me I had to watch from the car, and when it was over, they took me to the orphanage, and that's where I stayed until about a week ago."

Abigail placed her hand over her daughter's bandaged hands and held them.

"I was so distraught with grief after having to watch my family's funeral from a state car too, that I've spent all this time in a mental institution."

Amelia cried even harder. "Oh *Mamm,* I'm so sorry you had to stay there. I wish I'd known that you were alive."

"I wish I'd known too; it might have saved us both a lot of heartache over the past eight years."

"We have the rest of our lives to make up for lost time," Amelia said, wiping her tears.

Abigail's gaze lowered. "I'm afraid we don't," she said, holding up her right arm showing off a thick, locked bracelet on her arm. "At least not yet. And that's if you still want anything to do with me after you hear what I have to say."

"You sound so serious," Amelia said.

Abigail tucked her daughter's wispy brown hair behind her ear, trying to savor the moment before she risked it all with the truth. "I'd rather you heard this from me, so, here goes! I'm afraid I'm on lockdown for a little while. Like I said, I've been in a state facility for mentally ill patients, and I need to continue to stay there for a while. The only reason I'm here now, is because they're holding me over in the psychiatric ward here at the hospital while you're here. They think it'll be good for my therapy, and I agree with them. I've never felt better."

"Now that you know that I'm alive you should be okay, shouldn't you?"

Abigail couldn't even look her daughter in the eye.

"I'm afraid not," she said quietly. "I burned down the house—our house—*your* house."

"I don't care!" Amelia said. "That place is tainted with ghosts of the past. We need to start fresh. What's the problem?"

"The problem is," Abigail said shamefully. "Is that I tied Kyle up in the house and left him there after lighting a match, and setting the house ablaze. I left him there to die!" she said, sobbing.

Amelia sucked in a breath. "Why would you do such a thing, *Mamm?"* she asked quietly.

"It's not one of my prouder moments, but neither is robbing a bank when I was seventeen. I wanted to hurt Kyle because I hurt so much that I wanted revenge, and I felt his father was responsible. I wanted to avenge your death and your father's death. I wasn't thinking straight, and I know this now."

She held up the bracelet and smiled, grief still clouding her thoughts. "I'm going to get the right help, and now that I know you're okay, I'll be okay."

Amelia hugged her mother, savoring the moment, and making plans in her head to keep in close contact with the woman. She loved her *mamm,* despite her many faults, and there was nothing that would ever change that.

Chapter 17

"They're here!" Amelia said excitedly, as she positioned and repositioned the flowers on the table. She wanted everything to be perfect. She'd set out tea, using her best teacups, and she couldn't wait for her *mamm* to see the new house that her betrothed, Caleb, and his business partner, Kyle, had built for their future. Running a hand along her *mamm's* rocking chair—the only item that had survived the fire, she couldn't wait for her to see how nicely Caleb had restored it. She'd told her *mamm* about salvaging the chair from the yard amidst the rubble before the mess from the fire was cleared, and her *mamm* had told her she could have the chair to rock her future grandchildren in, and that she wanted the chair to create a happy memory for her. Amelia had to admit that it looked nice positioned next to the brick hearth that Caleb had tried his best to duplicate from her childhood home—only this one was devoid of ghosts from the past. She smiled, unwilling to let anything spoil this day for her.

Straightening the pleats of her newly sewn, blue dress, and tucking a stray tendril up underneath her prayer *kapp*, she pulled in a deep breath, determined not to let her nervousness show. Caleb's dad had been released from his ninety-day sentence a few days earlier, but he would be on probation for three years. He'd taken the buggy to go pick up her *mamm* from the bus station. Although yesterday was her release day, she decided to wait until today, her daughter's wedding day, to make her first visit. Amelia and Caleb, and even Kyle, had been to visit her several times at the facility, and had even sat with her during a few of her therapy sessions. It had helped Amelia a great deal with the nightmares that had plagued her.

Thanks to the sessions, and her new life, she hadn't had a nightmare in close to two months. They had slowly dwindled away after she'd left the hospital and all of the pieces of the past had been put together and finally laid to rest.

With the reward money they received for turning in the money from the bank robbery that their parents have been involved in, Caleb and Amelia had shared that equally with Kyle and the two men had become business partners and already had contracts to build three more houses now that their own home was finished.

Life was finally good for Amelia, and she couldn't wait for her new future to begin.

Looking out the window one more time at the snow that had made a fresh new blanket over the expanse of farmland, Amelia couldn't help but think it was the perfect day to celebrate both the New Year, and the beginning of hers and Caleb's life together.

Caleb stepped behind her, and watched out the window, dipping his head into the back of her neck to steal a few kisses.

"Save that for the wedding," Kyle said jokingly as he entered the room. "I think I'll go out and help everyone get into the house safely, and leave you two love-birds alone for a minute."

Caleb gave Amelia a little squeeze. "I'm thankful that God has brought you back to me," he said. "My life would not be the same without you."

She turned around and faced him with the biggest smile he'd ever seen.

He pressed his lips to hers, unable to wait for the wedding. She indulged him for a moment, and then pulled away when the front door opened. With warm cheeks, she greeted her guests into the home that she and Caleb would begin to share this very night—just as soon as she said *I do,* and she certainly would.

THE END

DON'T MISS Book 2 in this series!

ON THE NEXT PAGE!

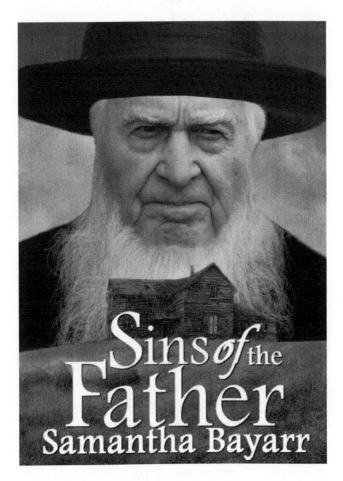

Sins of the Father

Book Two

Pigeon Hollow Mysteries

Samantha Bayarr

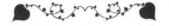

A note from the Author:

While this novel is set against the backdrop of an Amish community, the characters and the names of the community are fictional. There is no intended resemblance between the characters in this book or the setting, and any real members of any Amish or Mennonite community. As with any work of fiction, I've taken license in some areas of research as a means of creating the necessary circumstances for my characters and setting. It is completely impossible to be accurate in details and descriptions, since every community differs, and such a setting would destroy the fictional quality of entertainment this book serves to present. Any inaccuracies in the Amish and Mennonite lifestyles portrayed in this book are completely due to fictional license. Please keep in mind that this book is meant for fictional, entertainment purposes only, and is not written as a text book on the Amish.

Happy Reading

Ezekiel 18:19-20 New International Version (NIV)

19 "Yet you ask, 'Why does the son not share the guilt of his father?' Since the son has done what is just and right and has been careful to keep all my decrees, he will surely live. 20 The one who sins is the one who will die. The child will not share the guilt of the father, nor will the father share the guilt of the child. The righteousness of the righteous will be credited to them, and the wickedness of the wicked will be charged against them.

Chapter 1

Selma rose to her bone-chilled feet once more, her legs wobbly and weak, her energy nearly spent. She shivered, her stocking-clad feet and the hem of her long nightgown damp from the dirt floor of the cellar.

"Where did I leave my shoes?" she asked herself.

Did she even remember having shoes?

Her feet ached and throbbed, her toes numb from the cold floor, feeling as though she was standing barefoot on the frozen pond. Her teeth chattered as she wrapped the light quilt around her shoulders, working her way back up the ladder. Once again, when she reached the top wrung, her head pressed against the trapdoor. Bracing her shoulder against the thick wood, she pushed, putting her weight into it, but it was no use.

She was still trapped, still cold, and still alone.

"How many times do I have to do this, Lord, before you'll set me free?"

All traces of emotion had left her voice; she hadn't the energy for it. There had been a time when she'd been full of life, and her faith had been strong. Now, her faith had been shaken and tested, twisted and fallen to absence. There were days when she hadn't even felt human, much less, a child of God. Deep down she knew, but there had been no light at the end of this tunnel; no hope to hold onto, and no faith to carry her.

The stench from her makeshift chamber-pot in the corner was almost unbearable. It hadn't been emptied in the three days she'd been left alone. For the past two, it had nauseated her so much she had not been able to keep anything down. The linen cloth she kept over it was not enough to mask the odor.

Rats had rummaged through what little food she had left, and had eaten what she hadn't, which made her even more nauseated. She could hear them scavenging in the dark as she sat in the opposite corner.

"I'd rather die here, Lord, than for you to send him even one more time to release me!" she cried out into the dark. "Deliver me from this prison, Lord."

She curled up on the thin mattress in the farthest corner of the room, closing her eyes against the thoughts that plagued her. She'd lost all track of time, her health failing, and her spirit fading even faster. She laid there trying desperately to quiet the voices that crowded her mind. Anger and fear consumed her, but it no longer drove her to crave survival the way it once had. Giving up was easier. Each time she fought him, the punishment was greater, and the solitude grew longer.

The days in captivity had worn thin on her nerves and played tricks on her mind. Her son would likely no longer remember her, and she doubted she would recognize him. Surely he was a grown man by now, and had most likely given up hope of ever seeing her alive. Seeing his face again was the only thing that drove her anymore. She no longer cared anything about her own well-being; her only worry was for her child.

Unsure if she possessed the energy to fight, Selma laid in wait for that moment of weakness that would surely come. Her only bit of hope had come from the Mason jar she'd broken. It was the last canned peaches in the cellar, but it had spurred an idea. She prayed it was sharp enough to defend. It was her last resort, and if it failed to free her, she would use it to drain her own blood, having lost her will to live. She would take the desperate measure if need-be, just to put an end to her torture and imprisonment once and for all. He'd taken everything from her, but she would not let him take away her right to finally have peace.

Zebedee lifted the latch to the cellar in the barn at the edge of his property. With a shotgun in his hand, he felt he was better-prepared this time. He would not let the out-of-control woman ambush him again. Surely she would recognize the threat that the gun posed, and would not make another attempt at escaping. He had become just desperate enough to teach her a lesson the hard way, if necessary. He hated that things had to be this way, but she just couldn't be reasoned with anymore. He'd tried to make things easy on her, he'd even tried to be good to her, but she'd made it clear she would have no part of him.

Truth was, she belonged to him, and he would be sure she understood that no matter what the cost.

Lowering himself into the cellar, Zeb was pleased to see she was sleeping soundly. He went to her, crouching down on his haunches, and smoothed the back of his hand across her ashen cheek. She had aged considerably, and her face was not as plump and beautiful as it once was when she was young, but he still loved her.

"I love you my dear, Selma," he whispered. "Why do you fight me so?"

In a fit of rage, Selma rolled over, drawing the thick piece of glass across his wrist, piercing his flesh.

"You don't love me!" she said through gritted teeth. "You only want to own me."

Selma scrambled to her feet, the element of surprise at catching Zeb off-guard long enough to drop the gun and grab his painful, bleeding wrist.

Selma scooped up the shotgun and held it at his back, contemplating what she'd only dreamt about for too many days. Her conscience, however, would not permit her to kill him, and so with one swift motion, she used the butt of the gun to hit him on the back of the head, knocking him out. His head hit the cellar floor with a thud, and she dropped the gun, scrambling her way up the ladder and out of the cellar into the cold, snowy night.

Chapter 2

Kyle stood on the bank of the large pond in pigeon Hollow and skipped a stone across the glassy shallow plane of water, counting five skips. It was his highest count during the time since he'd arrived at the large pond with his mother. She'd left him at the water's edge, making him promise he'd stay there while she approached a strangely-dressed man who was busy fishing, and ignoring her from what Kyle could see.

He watched the sinking sun flickering amber glitter across the light ripples of water as the wind swept across the surface. An occasional firefly dipped down, alighting the layer of edible particles, creating perfect circles that expanded, interrupting the glittery pattern. He tossed in a handful of autumn leaves just to watch them float out of sight, ferrying some of the bio-life to the other side.

"Don't do that, boy," the man's angry voice hollered to him. "You'll scare away the fish."

Kyle watched the motionless bobber a few feet offshore for movement, but didn't see any. The man wasn't doing it right. That wasn't the way his dad had taught him to fish, but he hadn't seen his dad since he was too young to remember. He'd forgotten almost everything about the man—except how to fish—and this man was not doing it right.

"Sorry," Kyle mumbled, kicking a light spray of sand into the water. "But you're not doing it right. My dad taught me how, and you won't catch any fish that way!"

The angry figure approached him, towering over him, the sun to his back. It cast a shadow over the faceless man, but Kyle could still see the disdain there regardless.

"You'll address me properly, boy," he said as he grabbed the scruff of his shirt pushing him to the ground.

His mother came to his rescue, touching the man's arms. "Please don't be so harsh," she begged. "He doesn't know you."

"He needs to learn proper manners and how to be respectful of his elders," the man's gruff voice sounded. "You don't teach him anything."

"He's only seven years old, and I'm doing the best I can on my own," she said, defending herself. "The boy needs a father."

"I told you not to bring him here. I don't want him here."

The man's thunderous voice rattled Kyle's ears, causing him to flinch. He looked into the stern pair of dark eyes that were deep-set, and fixed between a permanently cinched brow, which showed his disapproval with the young boy.

Kyle sucked in his breath and held it there, knowing something bad was about to happen.

Kyle bolted upright, scrambling from beneath the heavy quilts that wound around his legs so tight they were suffocating them. His breath heaved and gasped as he focused on the small bedroom in which he'd been staying in Caleb's *dawdi haus*.

His thoughts righting themselves, he still felt a little disoriented. Kyle struggled to remember the dream that had rattled him awake, leaving him with a grave feeling he knew the old man who'd conversed with his mother at the pond—almost as if the event really happened.

Before he could gain his bearings, a loud boom and a flash of light caught his attention, startling him further. He peered out the window beside the bed watching what looked like sparks flying off in the distance. They popped and cracked, shooting sparks like fireworks across the night sky.

If he didn't know better, he'd swear it looked like a transformer had blown, but he knew there was no such thing on the Amish property. He pressed his nose to the glass, watching the sparks light up the night sky, and realized they were coming from near the Yoder's barn at the edge of the property.

He pulled on his trousers right over the top of his long-johns, shivering as his bare feet touched the cold wood floor. He knew the noise was not thunder and the sparks would not be lightning, because such things did not happen in the winter.

Stuffing his feet into his boots, he looked around the dark room for a sweatshirt. When he located a heavy enough one, he pulled it down over his head and grabbed his heavy Carhartt jacket. It was bitterly cold when he'd gone to bed, and he could only imagine how much colder it was now. Last he'd heard on his truck radio just before dark, it was only 17°. He imagined the wind chill was likely 10 below.

As cold as it was, he wasn't up for investigating the loud boom or the sparks flying, but he feared something out there might catch fire if he didn't. Plus, he knew he'd never be able to sleep unless he checked it out, not wanting Caleb to have anything to worry about. He wanted his friend and his new wife to have a good honeymoon in Florida. They weren't due back for another few days, and there would be no sense in worrying him needlessly.

Kyle shoved his hands into his leather gloves and shouldered out into the cold night air, the wind assaulting him with pelts of icy snow that stung his cheeks.

Knowing he could not get back toward the Yoder's barn without going through the cornfield that separated the barn from Caleb's new house, he contemplated going on foot, but when he heard a scream, he hopped in his truck and drove over the uneven, frozen soil toward the commotion, his truck dipping and bouncing over the tilled rows.

His headlights bounced off the barn and onto the ground, then, back up again as the truck rolled over the humps of tilled earth.

Was that a body in the snow?

Kyle pressed on the gas pedal, trying to push the truck faster over the dips and humps of frozen ground. He let off the gas when the front of the truck dipped hard, bringing the front fender down onto solid ground.

Stopping the truck short of the barn, he pulled around and aimed his headlights toward a figure lying motionless in the snow, sparks flying near the body.

Hopping out of the truck, Kyle left the door open and ran toward the figure he now realized was a woman. She lay there, face pushed into the snow, a blue, flannel nightgown clinging to her wet figure, brownish gray hair falling out from where it was loosely pinned at the nape of her neck.

He rolled her over, pulling off his heavy jacket to wrap her in. "Can you hear me?" he asked the older woman.

She groaned and looked up at him, her lashes fluttering open and closed. "Help me," she said weakly.

He tucked his arms under her frail frame to lift her out of the snow when she clenched his arm and looked him into the eye, a warm mist in her eyes.

"My baby!" she cried. "You came to rescue me."

"I'm here," he said to her, confusion clouding his judgment.

She'd obviously confused him with someone else.

Then her expression turned serious. "If you know what's good for you, son, you'll leave this place before it's too late!" she mumbled, then, she went limp in his arms.

Her warning sent shivers through his already cold body, as he lifted her up and cradled her against his sturdy frame. It was the sort of warning that was usually accompanied by an abundance of reasons behind it.

His gaze traveled to the area that shone brightly in the light from the headlamps of his truck that he'd left running. The transformer was attached to electric fence that surrounded the Yoder's barn, and he thought it odd. He'd thought it was strange when Amelia had run into barbed wire the night she'd run from him, and now Old-Man-Yoder had installed electric fence in its stead around his barn, with a voltage high enough to kill a herd of cows?

Why?

He looked at the woman in his arms, and noted the snow shovel she'd apparently used to break the voltage.

Was she breaking into the barn or *out* of it?

His mind filled with a million questions as he rushed her to the front seat of his truck and took the time to buckle her in for the bumpy ride back to the main road.

Whoever she was, she was in need of medical help, and he would not be able to give an explanation of her identity or her reason for being in the snow way out there without a coat or shoes.

Kyle hadn't planned on leaving the house on such a cold night, but now, it seemed, he'd be taking the strange woman to the hospital.

Chapter 3

Kyle rushed into the emergency room, the still unconscious woman in his arms.

"I need help!" he hollered.

A nurse rushed to his side with a wheelchair and helped Kyle lower the woman into it.

"What happened?" she asked.

"I have no idea," he said, out of breath. "I found her in the snow near a blown transformer. I'm house-sitting for a friend, and she was at the far edge of his property."

"Who is she?" the nurse asked.

"I have no idea," Kyle said. "I think she was trying to get into the barn back there, but it has electrical fence around it. I think she's homeless."

"We got a *Jane Doe,*" the nurse hollered. "She looks like she's suffered malnutrition and hypothermia. I'm gonna need a room and a team right away."

Two nurses jumped up from behind the large desk that looked to be the hub of the emergency room. They each grabbed supplies and a cart, then, followed her down the hall.

The nurse who'd taken charge turned around and hollered to Kyle. "Have a seat in the waiting room, and I'll come get you once we get her settled."

"But I don't know *her...*" he started to say, but they disappeared into a room.

He yawned and walked slowly toward the room she'd pointed to, his spirits lifting when he spotted the coffee station in the corner. He dispensed a large cup from the tall thermal decanter and then peeled back the lid of four creamers, dumping them in and stirring with a thin, red swizzle straw.

Lifting the steaming coffee to his lips, he sipped the hot liquid and cradled the cup with both hands to warm himself up. He glanced at the clock, having no idea of the time, staring in disbelief that it was four o'clock in the morning. No wonder he was exhausted.

Kyle lowered his tired bones down onto one of the chairs in the waiting room, unable to stop thinking about what the old woman had said to him. Who was she? She acted like she knew him, but he had no idea who she was. Did Caleb know? Or perhaps Old Man Yoder knew her. She'd warned him to get away from the place before it was too late. Too late for what?

The thing that nagged at him the most, was the fact she'd called him *son*. Did she really think he was her son? Perhaps she had a family out there somewhere that was missing her. Certainly it wasn't him or Caleb; both their mothers were long-since dead. But they'd recently discovered Amelia's mom alive when they'd thought she was dead too!

Kyle shook away the crazy thought. It was either too late at night or too early in the morning for that type of crazy thought, and he wasn't sure which one. It was one of those for sure, but he refused to entertain the thought again.

He'd attended his mother's funeral. He'd seen her body in the casket, and he'd never forget how cold and stiff she was, and how she just didn't look anything like herself. The life had gone from her, and she was nothing like the woman he'd known in his youth.

Sadly, they weren't particularly close in her last years, and he'd found himself regretting that as an adult. The woman certainly had her secrets. She seemed to have a whole other life that he knew nothing about. It was so full of mystery, and whatever it was, had caused her great pain.

He would always regret leaving home at the age of ten, but he'd found it too difficult to relate to his mother, and it'd been easier on him to stay with his uncle's family. His uncle didn't ask questions, and he didn't make any rules. What young boy wouldn't like that? Kyle certainly did. Suddenly, he was his own man, and he didn't have anyone to worry about, except himself. No more making sure his mother was dressed to go to the bank to cash her welfare check so they could eat. No more having to cut classes when the landlady would complain his mother was sitting outside on the front stoop in her bathrobe in the dead of winter.

Truth-be-told, this woman reminded him so much of his own mother, it scared him.

Kyle had too often regretted not growing up a little faster and taking on the responsibility God had dropped in his lap where his mother was concerned, but at ten years old, he was incapable of understanding the responsibility of caring for her. Not only was he too young, he'd become tired of having to be the parent, especially when the only time his mother seemed lucid was when she went on her special outings twice a week.

He'd seen his mother quite often just after he'd moved out, but as time wore on, she'd fallen into a deeper and deeper depression, and had even stopped going on her outings. He just couldn't understand her life at such an early age, and as a result, he didn't see her very often after that.

Her death had come as a shock to him, and he regretted not being with her when she died. After her funeral, he'd had no other choice but to be raised for the last four years of his childhood by his mother's brother. It had taken his mother's death to realize that she and her brother weren't even close, which made it easier for Kyle to stay away.

Now, twelve years later, the memories still haunted him.

If only he'd been there for her.

The nurse entered the waiting room and Kyle looked up at her.

"Your mother needs you," she said.

Kyle looked behind him at the row of chairs, but he was the only one in the room.

"If you're talking about the woman I brought in here," he said. "She's not my mother."

"I'm sorry, Sir, but she told us you were her son. She called you her son, and I guess we just assumed."

"I don't know who she is," he said. "But I aim to find out."

Kyle followed the nurse into the room, and thankfully, the woman was resting peacefully. He looked at all the tubes and wires attached to her, and the IV that would hydrate her again. Perhaps then she would begin to make some sense. He watched the monitor above the head of the bed, thinking that her heart rate seemed pretty normal.

"Hello son," the woman said, startling Kyle.

He looked at her for a moment, studying her face, but it was not familiar to him. Was she the one who was confused, or was it him? If it was her, he certainly didn't want to hurt her after all she'd been through. Did he have the heart to let her down easily?

He had to.

"You do know I'm not your son, don't you?" Kyle asked.

"How can you be sure of this?" she asked.

"Because I buried my mother some years ago," he said, his eyes down-cast.

"I see," she said quietly.

"Do you know what your name is?" he asked nervously.

"I don't think I'm going to tell you that."

"You know they have you listed here as Jane Doe, right?"

"I kind of like that name," she said.

"You need to know they won't let you out of here until they find out who you are," Kyle said. "I think you deserve to know that."

"But I have to get out of here!" she said with a sense of urgency that worried Kyle all over again.

"I don't want them to hold me here," she said. "Will you tell them I'm your mother?"

"I don't know that I want to lie for you unless there's a reason, and it better be a good reason."

She looked at him soberly, her eyes getting misty.

"Come on now, I don't want you getting all upset," Kyle said, feeling bad for her. "I just want to know what you were doing out there by the Yoder's barn in the middle of the night—without a jacket or shoes!"

She looked away, her jaw clenched, and she swallowed hard. Kyle could see that something was upsetting her. He also sensed she didn't want to tell him.

"I think you know you can trust me," he said. "I brought you here."

She turned to look at him, taking into consideration the sincerity in his eyes. She had to trust someone. If she was wrong, she would end up right back in captivity, but she knew she had to take a chance.

"Why should I trust you?"

Kyle sighed heavily. "Let's just say I owe it to my real mom."

"But you said your mother was dead," she replied.

"That has a lot to do with the fact that I let her down," he said soberly.

Her look softened. "I find that hard to believe," the old woman said. "You brought me here, and you helped me when you didn't have to. You could have left me out there to die."

Kyle smirked. "I suppose that's because I've done a lot of growing up since then."

She looked at him with seriousness in her eyes, a sense of urgency in her voice. "I need to get out of here immediately."

"Well, you're not going anywhere until they hydrate you. And I suppose I'm going to have to get you some shoes and a coat. Do you know where I can find any of that?"

She shook her head and wouldn't look at him.

Kyle sat down on the edge of the bed and took her hand in his. "If I'm going to help you, I need to know one thing," he said. "Were you breaking into the barn, or out of it?"

Her lower lip trembled, and the beeping of the heart monitor sped up.

"I'm not going to hurt you," Kyle said. "I only want to help. Were you breaking into the barn, or out?"

She parted her lips to speak, but hesitated, looking up into Kyles trusting eyes.

"Out," she whispered. "I was breaking out!"

Chapter 4

Kyle watched and waited for old man Yoder to drive his buggy out onto the main road before getting out of his truck and heading toward the man's barn. He just had to get in there and see if he could find any evidence that might shed some light on the truth about the mysterious woman. She'd refused to tell him who she was, but he had a hunch about her identity, and wouldn't know for sure unless he checked out the barn.

Knowing the only way he would find out was to go back to the scene where he'd found her, he would reluctantly investigate on his own. Not wanting to cause a stir and alert old man Yoder of his presence, he decided to walk down to the barn. The way he figured, his getaway would be easier on foot if the old man decided to come back.

As he walked out into the cornfield, stepping over the brown stalks that were nubs sticking up from the frozen earth, he wondered how Caleb would feel about him checking up on his dad. He knew the two of them were not close, so he reasoned that it was best for the sake of the woman to see if there was some truth to her story.

He walked slowly, keeping an eye over his shoulder for any sign he wasn't alone on the path. Even in the light of day, Kyle could feel his stomach churning at the thought of going near the Yoder's barn behind the old man's back—especially if he had been, in any way, holding the mysterious woman against her will as she'd suggested.

When he approached the barn, he noticed there was something different. The downed fence had been repaired, and the large generator that electrified it was gone.

It had snowed heavily from the time Kyle had taken the woman to the hospital up to now, and it covered over a lot, including the spot where the woman's body had laid in the snow.

Backing up to get a better look, he stepped on a twig, and the noise echoed loudly enough to make him jump. He took in a deep breath, chiding himself for suddenly being afraid of his own shadow. He had to keep his head if he was going to get through this.

Grabbing a long stick that had fallen from the tree, Kyle tossed it at the fence, cringing, until it hit the wires. Expecting to see sparks fly, he was surprised when nothing happened. Strangely, the fence was no longer electrified.

His gaze followed the span of the fence line, realizing the only way he was getting anywhere near the Yoder's barn would be to climb over the fence or break through it— neither of which would be an easy task.

Sizing up the fairly large tree in front of him, he decided to climb it and jump from the limb that extended over the fence line.

Kyle made quick work of shimmying up the tree, extended himself out onto the branch, and dropped onto the property, before thinking of how he was going to get back out of the enclosure.

I'll have to worry about that later, he said, blowing out a heavy sigh.

Checking around to be sure there was no one around, he slowly approached the barn. His heart sped up as he opened the barn door, thinking to himself he had no way of protecting himself should the need arise. He had not completely thought this through, and if the woman was truly in danger here, it could mean he was in danger as well. He closed the barn door behind him, scanning the unusually clean barn, looking for any shred of evidence that the woman had been there.

He walked slowly toward the tack-room, remembering what Amelia had told him about the Derringer being hidden under the work-bench in there. He didn't hold much hope that it would still be there, but he knew he'd feel better having it in his possession.

Crouching down, Kyle felt around under the bench until his outstretched fingers connected with a metal box. He pulled it toward him, and it was just as she'd described. He opened the lid, but found only a few stray bullets mixed with dirty straw.

That's funny, he thought, as he held one of the bullets up to examine it. *This is a 41 short, Rim-fire.*

It made sense to him, having a considerable amount of knowledge about guns, that it was one of the bullets that were loaded in the Derringer. He'd also read the coroner's report that listed the bullet that was extracted from his father's body, and he could've sworn the bullet that killed him was listed as a 41 long.

Making a mental note to check over the documents that he knew were tucked away in a box somewhere, he put the thought away for the time-being and stuffed one of the bullets into his pocket, then, replaced the box under the workbench.

Checking to be sure he was the only one in the barn, he listened intently until he was sure there were no noises other than his own. Standing up, he walked toward the back of the barn, when his eyes caught a flicker from a crossbeam of the rafters. The bright reflection of the winter sun streaming into the small window reflected off something shiny up there. From the barn floor he could not see exactly what the tiny object was, but he had to admit the shiny object piqued his curiosity.

Pulling out his phone, he opened up the camera on it, and then zoomed in to focus in on the object. His eyes darted from his phone screen to the cross beam, and back again, surprised to see that the object looked just like the bullet that was tucked away in his pocket.

Now he *had* to go up there to see exactly what it was. How could he let something that curious slip through his fingers? He snapped a few pictures and then stuffed his phone back into his pocket.

Climbing the ladder to the loft, Kyle walked over to where the object was wedged in the crossbeam and leaned over the edge to get a better look. Reaching down, he realized that it was indeed a bullet that matched the one he put in his pocket.

He wondered how it would've gotten there. Was it possible that was the bullet that dislodged from the gun the night Amelia shot Bruce? If that was the case, that would mean that someone else had killed his father.

He remembered hearing from Caleb and Amelia that the only place they had shot the gun was out in the field, using tin cans for practice. Surely no one would shoot the gun in such a closed space like this, with the exception being the night that Bruce was shot.

Knowing it was eight years ago and Amelia was just a child when it happened, he was eager to talk to her and ask her about the possibility of another shot being fired that night. For now, he needed to check out the rest of the barn before Old Man Yoder showed up. He left the bullet where it was, assuming he had been the only one to notice it there. He knew if he removed something that could be considered evidence, it could hurt the case if there was to be an additional investigation.

Again, he pulled his cell phone from his pocket, and took several pictures of the bullet where it was lodged in the cross beam, as opposed to removing it and risking tampering with possible evidence.

Kyle jumped down from the loft, his feet landing on the fresh straw on the floor, making a hollow sound rather than a solid one. Was it possible there was a space beneath the barn? He swished the straw with his feet, unearthing a small trapdoor.

His heart skipped a beat.

Why does there always have to be a trap door or a secret room? he asked himself half-jokingly.

This was the kind of thing scary movies were made of, and it set his nerves on edge. He looked around once more to be sure he was alone in the barn, relief washing over him when he was satisfied he was still the only one in the barn.

I need to get ahold of myself before I scare myself to death, he chided himself.

He took a deep breath and lifted the latch. He sucked in his breath upon seeing the ladder that led down into a dark room below ground.

Did he dare go down there?

It was obvious that Old Man Yoder was hiding something, and that made him nervous, but he knew if he didn't keep looking, he'd never find the answers he sought.

Grabbing a lantern from one of the support beams, where it hung from a nail, he lit a match from the little tin box that was nailed to the pole. He lit the lantern and crouched down on his haunches, lowering the lantern into the space, illuminating the room below.

It was certainly creepy, to say the least, but no matter how nervous it made him, he had to push from his mind the thoughts that filled him with so much terror, it made the hair raise off the back of his neck.

He shuddered at the thought of going down there, but forced himself to grab the lantern and lower himself down the ladder. When his feet connected with the dirt floor, he held up the lantern, turning all the way around and looking around the strange empty room. There was nothing but a dirt floor and four cinderblock walls. There was nothing in the room whatsoever, and strangely, not even cobwebs.

Fear crept back up his spine, feeling suddenly spooked. The last thing he needed or wanted was to be trapped in this room. He took one last look at the dirty walls that suddenly seemed to be closing in on him. His legs felt wobbly, and his breathing hitched at a noise from up above. His heart slammed against his ribcage when the latch door shut with a loud crash.

"Oh, God," he said with a heaving breath. "Don't let me be trapped in here!"

His legs felt weak when he heard footsteps on the floor above his head. The old man knew he was there!

His nerves jangling, he backed away from the trapdoor, looking around the room again for *anything* he could use to defend himself. In the far corner, he found a thick piece of glass that looked like it had come from a broken Mason jar. He held it up to the light, examining what looked like dried blood on it.

He dropped it to the ground. "I *have* to get out of here!" he said, not realizing how loud he was being.

The footfalls above him faded, and the barn door closed. Had the old man left, or was it a trick?

Kyle waited and listened, his eyes bulging in the dark cellar. How long did he have to wait before it was safe to try the latch? His mind reeled with the possibility that it wouldn't open, and he'd be trapped indefinitely.

"Lord, I know I don't talk to you as often as I should, but right now I pray you'll forgive me for that, and help me out of here. I'm scared!"

His prayer surprised him, but he had exhausted his own means of trying to stay calm. He needed a higher power to help. His faith was weak, but Amelia and Caleb had told him that was when God was there the most.

"I pray you were right, my friends," he said of Caleb and Amelia.

When several minutes had passed, and all was still silent, Kyle decided to try the trapdoor. Looping the lantern over his forearm, he climbed the ladder and pushed at the heavy, wooden door, but it wouldn't open.

Panic filled him as he slammed his shoulder against it repeatedly, grunting and pushing with everything he had in him. Working up a sweat, the latch began to wiggle loose, but Kyle kept heaving his weight against it over and over until it finally popped open.

Taking in a deep breath, he raised his head above the floor level just enough to look around the barn for signs of the old man. When he didn't see him, he hoisted himself up as fast as he could and slammed the lid shut.

After closing the latch, he quickly raked the straw back over the door, snuffed out the lantern and replaced it on its nail on the pole.

Listening for noises, Kyle had an uneasy feeling, but couldn't get out of that barn fast enough. He hurried out the door and made a running jump for the tree branch that hung over the fence line, adrenalin his driving force, he grabbed onto the limb on the first try. Hurling his legs up using every muscle in his abdomen, he shimmied back down the branch onto the tree trunk.

When his feet hit the ground, he took off running back through the open field, feeling vulnerable until he reached the *dawdi haus*.

He rushed into the door out of breath and leaned against the frame to steady his wobbly legs. His breathing was so labored he felt he couldn't get enough air. He walked over to the sink and looked out the kitchen window. Was the old man really someone to be afraid of, or had he been closed in the cellar by accident?

Pouring himself a cup of coffee with a shaky hand, he wasn't sure if finding nothing was good or bad, but he didn't intend to go back there again.

He knew he needed something to collaborate the old woman's story, but it wasn't worth all of this. What was it that the old man was hiding, and what did it have to do with that woman? Had she been a part of the bank robbery? The old man had come clean with his part in it, but not before he used pig blood to scare Amelia. Was he capable of much worse? Things that even his own son had no knowledge of?

Kyle shuddered at the thought of returning to the hospital empty-handed and with no answers to give her. He also knew he would be hard-pressed to get any more information out of her, and that discouraged him. He needed answers.

He was no closer to figuring out who she was, and she wasn't giving him the answers he needed.

Perhaps now was the time for him to rethink his involvement.

Chapter 5

"What do you mean she's in the psychiatric ward?" Kyle asked, raking his hands through his thick hair. "How could you put my mother in such a place?"

The nurse looked at him and raised an eyebrow. "You told us last night you had no idea who she was, and now she's your mother suddenly?"

He hadn't meant to say that, but he thought perhaps it might help to get him in to see her.

He needed to see her like he needed his next breath. She was the only one that could provide the answers he needed, and she was also the only one who could tell him if he was in danger. Certain that only family members would get in to see her in the psychiatric ward, he hoped he could convince the nurse enough to allow a visit with the old woman.

"I'm sorry, Sir," the nurse said. "But we found drugs in her bloodstream when we did the blood-work, and she became hysterical about an hour ago, screaming and rambling on that there was a man in her room who was trying to kill her, but when we looked, there was no one there."

Kyle had a hunch he knew who it was.

"What kind of drugs?" he asked.

"I'm sorry, but unless you can provide proof that she's your blood relative, we aren't at liberty to give you that information, because right now she's registered here as Jane Doe, and she'll stay that way until you can provide some ID for her. Until you can get that information for us, we're required to keep her privacy."

Kyle knew he didn't have any such thing, but he hoped that he could gain the sympathy of the nursing staff. If not, there was no way he would be able to help her.

"Did she describe the man she claims was trying to kill her?"

"She said he was her husband," the nurse said.

Kyle's blood went cold and he stumbled backward against the wall. He felt like he couldn't breathe.

"Are you alright?" the nurse asked.

He nodded.

It was obvious to Kyle that Old Man Yoder had been at the hospital and had paid the woman a visit, but now he knew the woman had to be Caleb's mother—his dead mother.

"Is it possible for me to visit her?"

The nurse sighed. "I don't see how it could hurt. After all, you're the only one that she seems to know, and she certainly looked comfortable with you. If you can help her put the pieces of her life back together, that would be the best thing for her. She's very confused. If you happen to upset her, we'll have to ask you to leave."

"I'll do my best," Kyle promised. "Please let me see her; I need to talk to her."

Kyle felt sick to his stomach. If she was truly Caleb's mother, he wondered how he would react when he found out. He'd described to Kyle how his father had *lost his mind* after being shunned from the community, but was a shunned Amish man really capable of all of this? Keeping a person—even a spouse, locked up was a crime, wasn't it?

There was no denying the old man was in the barn earlier and had closed the latch on the cellar door while Kyle was down there, but how did he manage to get to the hospital and back so fast?

So, he still had a few details to work out, but if it was not the old man who was here threatening her, who was it? One thing was certain; if the old woman was *frau* Yoder, he would have to believe her story.

If Old Man Yoder had been holding her down in the cellar against her will, he'd certainly done a fine job of cleaning up all the evidence, and Kyle would be hard-pressed to prove any of it. Still, he'd seen the two large generators he'd used to power the electric fence, but now they were gone, so perhaps he'd cleaned up all of her belongings while he was at it. Since she'd escaped, he'd have to hide the evidence—but where?

Kyle could not quiet his thoughts as he followed the nurse to the elevator.

Maybe it was best to report all of this and let the authorities handle it. But before he got the police involved, he wanted to talk to the old woman one more time.

The nurse led Kyle up to the third-floor, and into a locked-down area, and then to a room where she used her ID badge to open the locked door. Behind that door was the old woman, and she was resting quietly on the bed by the window staring blankly out the window

"What's wrong with her?" Kyle whispered to the nurse.

"We had to give her a mild sedative to calm her down. Like I said, she was just hysterical and screaming. You could hear her all the way down the hall. We put her in here for her own safety—on the off-chance that someone really was in the room with her. We've put in a call to the sheriff's department. They should be sending an officer soon."

Now his need to talk to her was even more urgent. He wanted to find out as much as he could before she talked to any police.

"Did you have to call them?" he asked.

"Since she has no idea who she is, or at least she isn't giving us any real clues except saying it was her husband in here earlier harassing her, we're required to file a missing person search. That way, if she has any family, they can come and claim her."

"But I told you *I'm* her family," Kyle said.

"I know what you said, young man, but I have to wonder what you're trying to protect her from."

"I'm not exactly sure yet," he admitted. "But I'm trying to find out."

"I know you mean well," the nurse said. "But maybe you should just let the police handle it. They do this all the time. They can protect her."

"They weren't there to protect her when I found her. I feel responsible. I have a feeling she's the mother of an Amish friend of mine."

"Amish?" she asked. "That would make sense. I can tell she's trying to hide her accent, but I can still detect it. I have a friend who's Amish, and I've come to know the way they sound. She sounds Amish—but kind of like she's trying to hide it!"

Kyle felt very sorry for the woman, realizing that it was possible she was beyond his reach, and beyond his capabilities to help her, but he would certainly do his best to try.

Chapter 6

Kyle looked at his watch as he outstretched his arms and yawned. Jerking his arm up to his face, he stared at the clock face one more time. It was almost 6 o'clock.

"Greta!" he said aloud. "How could I have forgotten about my buggy ride with Greta?"

He stepped off the elevator and walked down the long corridor. How was he going to be able to enjoy his time with Greta when he had so much weighing on his mind? Caleb had gone out of his way to introduce the two of them after Kyle had seen her on a couple of occasions when they were visiting with his cousins, and had become immediately infatuated with her. Caleb had managed to convince his older cousin to talk his neighbor into going out with Kyle, even though he was an *Englisher*.

He looked at his watch again, worrying. "If I hurry, I'll have just enough time to get back to shower and get ready for my date."

Before long, he was pulling the truck into the long drive to Caleb's and Amelia's new house. He could see the Yoder's barn when he pulled up to the *dawdi haus,* and it made his heart thump a few extra beats. Just thinking about being stuck in that root cellar made him sick to his stomach.

He momentarily wondered if he should even continue to stay at his friends' house, even though he agreed to stay so he could feed the horses and the cats. He could certainly do that during the day and go back to his apartment despite the lengthy drive back and forth. It had been the only reason it made sense to stay at Caleb's farm. Maybe he would go back into town just until all this blew over, and he figured out what was really going on, and if he was truly in danger.

For now, he had to assume it was a coincidence that he got closed in the cellar, but it didn't seem like a coincidence that he found the old woman where he did. Hysteria over the possible visit from Old Man Yoder, however, was not something to push from his mind. But maybe it was someone else who'd visited her—or no one at all, as the hospital staff had suggested. Maybe, just maybe, he found a homeless, crazy old woman trying to break into the Yoder's barn, and there was nothing more to come of it than that.

It frustrated him that his visit with the old woman had not gone well. Not only was she not completely awake from the medicine that made her groggy, but she certainly was not willing to give him any personal information that would prove her identity. So, for the time being, perhaps the nurse was correct in saying she was safer in a locked-down facility. It was possible she was a danger even to herself.

He hated leaving her, but the medicine had finally won, and she'd fallen into a deep and fitful sleep. He'd listened for a little while until she'd gone deeper into sleep, but while she was having nightmares it seemed she was deeply disturbed over something, and he could only make out a few words she'd mumbled in her sleep, but she'd said the same thing repeatedly; she kept saying she was sorry—to her son. Was it possible she had a son out there somewhere that was missing her? It even crossed his mind that the son could be Caleb.

Kyle stepped out of the truck, looking all around Caleb's farm, feeling suddenly very uneasy about being there. He would decide what to do about his living arrangement later. For now, he didn't want to be late for his first date. He really liked Greta, and he didn't want to mess this up. He felt lucky that she was willing to give him a chance, even though she'd mentioned his only fault was that he was an *Englisher!* He couldn't do anything to change the fact he was an *Englisher,* so he wouldn't chance ruining what might possibly be his only chance with her by being late. It was already bad enough that his mind was not on this date, and he would have a hard time keeping it there. If not for his extreme attraction to her and the fact he already felt he was falling for her, he would have rescheduled the date.

Kyle quickly cleaned himself up and put on the plain clothes that Caleb had suggested. He wanted to appear as Amish as possible. It wasn't that he was trying to change himself, but rather adapt to something that she was used to. Besides, if he could do anything else to appeal to her, it would be worth it to him. He felt a little odd wearing a pair of black dress pants and a navy dress shirt, but he had to admit he did look really nice, and the shirt complimented his blue eyes.

He certainly hoped she would find him appealing. Caleb had been kind enough to teach him how to hitch up the buggy to his horse, Chestnut. He and his bride had taken a Greyhound bus to Florida for their non-traditional honeymoon.

Kyle and Chestnut had gotten to know each other over the past week while he'd been there feeding him. Kyle was rather enjoying the horse's company. He was especially grateful for how cooperative the horse was when he was trying to hitch him to the buggy.

Once everything was fastened down, Kyle hopped up into the buggy, making sure he had enough lap quilts, and then picked up the reins and prompted Chestnut down the long driveway. He was so proud of himself for learning how to drive the buggy, and he hoped that Greta would look upon him fondly because of it.

Kyle steered Chestnut down the snowy Lane, feeling grateful he didn't have to drive the buggy far. He felt confident taking the horse down the quiet country road, knowing the likelihood of running into any cars was next to none. Even if he did, it was a straight, flat road, and he could see for miles. Drivers would be able to spot him easily, and that made him confident that his risk was minimal. It wasn't that he didn't trust the horse or his own ability to drive, but he'd seen too many haphazard drivers not being careful around the buggies, or drivers getting impatient around them, which seemed to cause a lot of accidents.

When he pulled up the lane to Greta's house, he was happy to see that she was waiting on the covered porch for him, on the porch swing. Her smile warmed his heart as she bound from the swing and down the steps to the driveway to greet him.

Kyle hopped down from the buggy and assisted Greta up; the warmth of her hand making his skin tingle. She'd removed her mitten to take his hand, and he had removed his glove. He couldn't help feeling her hand fit his perfectly.

Climbing up into the buggy, Kyle sat close to her and spread the lap quilt across both of their laps, feeling another tingle down his spine when their thighs touched. They rode in silence down the driveway, and out to the main road. It was a pleasant sort of quiet, but Kyle enjoyed the sound of her voice, and hoped he could mask his nervousness by getting her to talk. He was certain that, like most females, once she got to talking, she wouldn't likely stop, and that would ease the first-date tension a little. At least, he hoped it would.

"Tell me," Kyle said trying to steady his voice. "How long have you known Caleb and Amelia?"

Greta giggled. "We grew up together in the community, so I've known them both since we were born—with the exception of the time Amelia has been gone. But even then, we weren't supposed to see either of them after the shunning. But since two of his cousins are still in their *rumspringa,* they can see him. I can too, since I'm in my *rumspringa* too. It's really the only reason I can take this buggy ride with you—since you're an *Englisher.*"

"What is it like to have to shun people in the community? Does it happen a lot?"

"Not as often as most *Englishers* think it does."

"I'm not sure if being shunned has been good for Caleb or his dad."

"His *daed* has always been a strange man," she said.

Kyle chuckled. "He seems very angry."

"Before *Frau* Yoder died, he'd pulled away from the community. He stayed away, and we didn't see much of Caleb, and neither did my brothers, and they were all friends. Then, after everything happened with Amelia and the shooting, they were shunned, but I overheard *mei daed* saying to *mei mamm* that Zeb Yoder had gotten a little *narrish*—crazy. He said the man was not the same after his wife died, but some say he was not right since they were young—after he came back from his *rumspringa*."

Suddenly, Kyle had a million questions, but didn't want to worry Greta with all of them, so he picked only one.

"What was Caleb's mother's given name?"

"I don't know. The community would have referred to her as *Frau Yoder*, and I don't remember her, so I would have no idea." Greta said sadly. "I know she had an older *schweschder*. I don't think Caleb ever met his *mamm's schweschder*. I heard she left the community when she was on her *rumspringa*, and she never came back. There were rumors that she had a *boppli*—baby, out of wedlock, but no one knows for sure, or has ever seen her since."

"What was her sister's name?" he asked.

"I don't know that either. I really don't know that much, and can't offer more than I've already told you."

"I'm sorry for bringing it all up," he said. "I just don't know much about Caleb, other than the fact that our parents were involved somehow all those years ago, and I just had a bit of a run-in with his dad."

"What kind of a run-in?"

Kyle patted her hand. "It's not important. Let's enjoy the snowy night. Would you like to go down to the pond and look at the moon?"

Greta smiled. "I'd like that very much."

Even though Greta's information shed some light on a few things for him, it wasn't anything he could use to help solve the mystery woman's identity—unless she was *Frau Yoder*. For now, he would put all of that behind him, and concentrate on the lovely Greta, his Amish date.

Kyle steered the buggy down the gravel road toward the pond that overlooked the Yoder's property. From that distance, he could see the lanterns being lit on the sides of the old man's buggy.

Where would he be going at this time of night?

Kyle wasn't going to worry about it. He turned his attention to his date. Tonight was his night, and he was not going to let Old Man Yoder or the mystery woman spoil it for him.

"Did you know you have the same color eyes as Caleb?" Greta said. "When I first met you, I thought you were a relative of his."

Kyle chuckled. "You think we look alike?"

She smiled. "*Jah.*"

"They say everyone in the world has a *twin— or a double*—someone who looks so much like them that people say they must be twins from another lifetime. What is the word for it? Oh yeah—it's called *doppelganger,* but I don't think we look that much alike."

"I do!" she said. "Especially in that hat!"

Kyle swiped Caleb's black hat off his head, feeling a little embarrassed that he'd worn it. Caleb had told him it would make his *date* a little easier on Greta, but it seems he'd only made a fool of himself.

Greta took the hat from him and placed it back on his head. "I like that hat. It suits you. I almost forgot you weren't Amish for a minute."

"I can't make myself Amish," he said. "But I'm willing to dress this way if it makes it easier for you."

"I want you to be yourself. I like you despite the fact you're an *Englisher.*"

He chuckled. "I'm not sure if I should take that as a compliment."

She cozied up to him and looked him in the eye. "You can!"

They continued to talk, but about the weather, and what it was like for her growing up Amish. He could have listened to her talk all night, and the more she talked, the more he fell in love with her.

The bright light of the full moon shining on her pink cheeks made him forget everything except what was right in front of him. He wanted more than anything to kiss her, but he feared her reaction.

Kyle blinked away snowflakes from his lashes, suddenly throwing caution to the wind as he bent toward her and pressed his lips gently to hers. Surprisingly, she deepened the kiss, but she let out a little shiver.

"I should take you home," he said as he pulled gently away from her soft lips. "We've been out here for hours, and the wind is really picking up."

She moved in closer, and he wrapped his arms around her.

"I'm not too cold to end the evening," she said. "But it is getting late. I want to be able to see you again, and *mei daed* won't like you if you don't bring me home at a respectable hour."

Kyle smiled. She wanted to see him again, and he couldn't be happier. "I'd like to see you again too."

She pressed her lips to his, and this time, he pulled her close, kissing her like a man in love.

Kyle left Greta's driveway feeling happier than he thought he could. He'd forgotten all about his troubles with Old Man Yoder and the mystery woman, and could think of nothing except his date and the feel of her lips on his. He puckered his lips against the cold air, happy that they still tingled with warmth from hers.

Pulling the buggy up to Caleb's barn, he talked to Chestnut. "I'm sure you'll be happy to get back into the barn and see your new sweetheart too!" he said to him.

Caleb had purchased a mare for Amelia for a wedding gift, and even though Chestnut would not be able to mate with her, being a gelding, he still seemed to take a liking to her.

After rubbing him down and putting a blanket on him for the night, Kyle shouldered out into the wind toward the *dawdi haus,* when he noticed the door was open and the lights were on. How had he missed that when he'd pulled up, or had someone gone in the house while he was in the barn for the past half hour?

He walked cautiously toward his truck, pulling a crow bar from his toolbox across the bed. If someone was in the house, what would he do? A crowbar was not something to defend yourself with! The only thing he couldn't figure out was that there wasn't a vehicle around, and there were no fresh tire tracks— only the tracks from Caleb's buggy.

As he neared the porch, he noticed large footprints—likely from a man, that led into the kitchen. He stood at the door and listened. The puddles of water left would indicate the person had gone inside the house a while ago since the snow had melted, but there was something else.

Blood!

He cautiously stepped up to the doorway, shaking, and wondering if he shouldn't call the police instead of going into the home alone. He would feel like a fool if it turned out to be nothing, but if someone was hurt in there, they would need help.

He took a deep breath, and held the crowbar over his head, ready to strike at the first sign of trouble, and walked slowly, following the wet puddles and blood splatters to the small bathroom off the kitchen. He froze when he looked up into the mirror and saw the words painted on the mirror in blood that served as a warning to him:

Leave this place!

Kyle jumped and turned on his heels at a noise behind him, the crowbar raised. Walking slowly toward the kitchen, his heart racing, he kept the crowbar up and ready to swing at whatever was out there. Before he could even think about it, he felt a blow to the back of his head, and he was falling to the floor. The crowbar clanged when it hit the floor just before he did, and his last thought just before everything went black, was of the old woman and her warning to leave.

Chapter 7

Kyle tried to lift his face up from the linoleum floor, but he couldn't even move. His lashes fluttered as he focused on a large pair of boots standing in front of his face. There was someone there with him, but he couldn't get up.

"Bring her back," a gruff voice said to him. "Or you'll replace her!"

Kyle groaned as he closed his eyes against the pain in his head. He listened to the foot-falls fade as the person walked out of the house, but he was too weak to open his eyes to see who it was, but he had his hunches. He knew it could only be one person; Old Man Yoder.

Sometime later, Kyle's eyes opened slightly, the bright sun from the kitchen window warming his face. How had morning managed to come without him realizing? Had he been asleep on the floor the entire night? He groaned as he tried to move, the pain in his head quite intense.

Reaching back with his hand, he felt something warm, moist and sticky. Bringing his hand back down in front of his face, he could see that his fingers were bloody. He could barely move, but he needed help. Rolling on his side slowly, he cringed against the pain in his head, as he struggled to remember what had happened.

Pushing himself up, Kyle rested his back against the cupboards, unable to stand up just yet. He felt dizzy, and sick to his stomach, but he was awake enough to know he needed help.

Reaching into his pocket, he grabbed his cell phone and dialed 911.

"911, what's your emergency?" the person on the other end asked.

"I—I think I need an ambulance," Kyle said. "And maybe a police officer."

"What's the nature of your injury?" the person asked.

"I've been hit on the head, and my head is bleeding."

"What's your address?"

"I'm at, um, 25925 County Road 17, Pigeon Hollow," he said, trying to remember Caleb's address.

"Is there someone with you?"

"No, I'm here alone. Someone hit me last night, and I've been passed out all this time."

"Was it a male or female that struck you?"

"I'm pretty sure it was a man."

"Do you happen to know the person who hit you?"

"I can't prove it, but I have an idea," he said.

"Did you see the person's face? Can you identify him?"

Kyle thought about the pair of boots he saw, and realized he never actually saw the person who'd hit him.

"No, I didn't see his face. I was lying on the floor and only saw his boots."

"I have an officer and an ambulance on the way. Do you want me to stay on the phone with you until they get there?"

"I don't know," Kyle said. "I think I'm gonna be sick."

"I'll stay on the line with you, but you can put the phone down if you need to."

Kyle agreed, but he couldn't hold the phone to his ear any longer. He let his hand fall to his lap, his phone fell to the floor, and his eyes drifted closed a few times as he fought off the urge to vomit.

Within a few minutes, he heard sirens off in the distance and prayed they would get to him in time.

Before he realized, Kyle was being put on a stretcher and he woke up just slightly.

"Can you hear me?" a paramedic was asking him.

Kyle reached up and pulled the oxygen mask off his face so he could speak. "The mirror," he said weakly. "He painted a warning on the bathroom mirror—in blood."

The police officer approached him. "What are you talking about, young man?"

"Look at the mirror in the bathroom. He painted a warning to me in blood."

The officer held up a finger to the paramedics to wait just a minute while he checked out the bathroom.

Kyle turned his head and watched the officer walk down the hall and turn on the bathroom light. He stood there for a minute, but then came back.

"What are you talking about?"

"The writing on the bathroom mirror," Kyle insisted. "He wrote it in blood."

"Who did?" he asked Kyle.

"The man who hit me!"

"There's nothing there, young man," the officer said. "You must've hit your head harder than you think. Were you drinking?"

"Drinking? No!" Kyle said. "I don't drink. "I'm telling you, someone hit me in the head, and it was the same person who wrote the warning on the bathroom mirror."

"What did the warning say?" the officer asked.

"It said: Leave this place."

"I'm sorry, Son," the officer said. "But there's no writing on the mirror, and there isn't any blood anywhere that I could see. Where this chair is on the kitchen floor, it looks like you fell. You probably hit your head then. There's a half-empty bottle of vodka on the kitchen table. How much of it did you drink?"

"I don't drink! That isn't mine!"

"Well the empty bottle and lack of evidence points toward you having a little too much to drink and a big imagination."

"But I'm telling you he hit me!" Kyle insisted. "He must've cleaned up the mess and put the bottle on the table after I passed out."

"I'm sorry, young man," the officer said. "But there's nothing here that indicates foul play, so I have no evidence to go by. If you had a witness, I'd have a case, but right now, I have nothing more than the word of a young kid who looks like he had a little too much to drink."

Kyle sighed and closed his eyes in defeat as the paramedic replaced the oxygen mask back over his face and wheeled him out to the ambulance.

Chapter 8

Kyle watched the nurse draw blood from his arm; blood he'd insisted they take from him to prove he wasn't drinking. The officer had accused him of such, and he aimed to prove he hadn't been. He was so confused right now and so groggy, that he was beginning to doubt himself, and he prayed this blood test would set his mind at ease.

They'd already stitched him up, and recommend he stay for twenty-four hours, but he only agreed to do that on the condition that they let him visit the woman who was upstairs in the locked-down facility. He hoped she might be able to solve the mystery of what had happened to him last night.

He needed to talk to her more than ever. He needed to find out if she was Caleb's mother. If she was, she perhaps, held the key to stopping Old Man Yoder from going completely off the deep end, though he feared it was too late to stop the inevitable. He knew he wasn't the one who was crazy, the old man was behind all of this, and Kyle was going to do everything in his power to prove it.

He had to admit, he found it odd that the warning written on the mirror was the same exact warning the old woman had given him. If not for the fact he knew she was in lockdown, he'd wonder if it was her that had done it. The fact remained, though, that Old Man Yoder already had a reputation for using blood as a scare-tactic.

After the blood he spread around Amelia's front door, and the rug in his own *dawdi haus*, this newest mischief had Old Man Yoder written all over it.

Only problem was, if it was only mischief, he wouldn't feel so threatened. Truth was, Kyle was terrified of the old man, and didn't intend on going back to Caleb's house except to feed the animals, and even then he would be on his guard.

No sooner did the nurse finish taking his blood, than he was out of the room and entering the elevator—before she had a chance to stop him.

Kyle approached the nurse's station, and asked them to let him in the old woman's room.

"I'm sorry, but she said she doesn't want to see you."

"I *have* to see her," he begged the nurses. "I know who she is!"

"You know who she is?" the nurse asked, turning to another nurse. "He says he knows who our Jane Doe is. Should I let him talk to her?"

"Tell us her name," the other nurse said.

"I have reason to believe she's my friend's mother. Her last name would be Yoder."

"Yoder?" the nurse asked. "So, she is Amish?"

"Yes, I believe so." Kyle answered.

"How did you figure this out?"

"Because I was just threatened by her husband, and I happen to be staying in her son's home. I'm a friend of his, and he's away on his honeymoon. He's thought his mother was dead for the past ten or so years."

"This just keeps getting better and better," one of the nurses said.

"You said her husband threatened you?" the nurse asked. "Did you tell the police?"

"Yes, I did," he said, showing them the stitches in the back of his head. "He hit me from behind and knocked me out, and while I was passed out, he cleaned up all the blood, and he put a bottle of vodka on the table to make it look like I was drunk. I had the nurses downstairs draw blood from me to prove I hadn't been drinking."

"Maybe we should wait to get the results of those tests," one of the nurses said. "Before we let you see her."

"Please," he begged. "I need to see her now. Please ask her if she'll see me. Tell her I know who she is. Well, maybe I should tell her that. She's going to be afraid when she finds out I know her identity. She knows her own name, I'm sure of it, but she isn't telling because she's afraid of the old man—her husband."

"I suppose it can't hurt to ask her if she'll see you," one of the nurses said.

She picked up the phone and dialed the woman's room, and after a minute or so, she asked the woman if she would see Kyle, then, briefly listened, and finally hung up the phone.

"She said she'll see you."

He let out the breath he'd been holding in, relieved she would see him, but he couldn't shake the bad feeling he had no matter what.

Following the nurse down the hall, he rehearsed in his mind what he might say to the woman, and how he would approach the subject of her name. Should he blurt it out, or address her by her real name when he entered, or should he wait for the right opportunity? He decided waiting would be best, and he'd have to bring it up delicately. The last thing he wanted to do was to spook her.

"You know the routine, right?" the nurse asked.

"Yes, I know, you have to lock me in with her. Would you mind standing outside the door, though—just in case."

The nurse raised an eyebrow. "Just in case of what?"

He sighed. "In case she doesn't take the news well and she needs to be medicated to calm her down!"

The nurse slid her key in the door and unlocked it, the woman sitting on the edge of the bed, facing the barred window.

"Hello, Mrs. Yoder," the nurse greeted her with a pasted-on smile. "I have a visitor for you!"

Kyle cringed, especially when he saw how disturbed the woman looked, her eyes suddenly very sad.

The nurse left the room and locked him in with her. Even though he knew she would be standing outside the door, he didn't like the idea of being locked in there with her. He didn't know her well enough to trust her, and after everything that had happened recently, he didn't trust anyone anymore—not even himself.

She glared at him as he sat in the chair in the corner of the room, and he tried to calm himself before speaking to her, knowing his voice would shake, giving away his fear.

"I'm sorry about that," he said as calmly and steadily as he could. "But they wouldn't let me in to see you unless I could identify you. Are you *Frau* Yoder?"

Her lower lip trembled and she looked out the window, feigning interest in the snow.

"No, I'm not *Frau* Yoder," she finally said. "But that's a good guess."

He didn't know whether to believe her or not, but decided to take another approach.

"Did you know *Frau* Yoder?" he asked cautiously.

"Yes, we were very close," she said soberly. "But now she's buried in my grave!"

Chapter 9

Kyle stirred a few times, falling in and out of the same dream. He felt a cold rag to his head, and the sound of his mother's angelic voice, as she sang the lullaby he hadn't heard since he was a child. He knew the foreign words by heart, and the tune played in his head as if haunting him, but he never knew what the words meant.

Unable to move, the pain in his head bound his eyelids closed as if by an invisible force, allowing him to dream. It was a dream he didn't want to wake from; a dream he would hold onto as long as he could, knowing once he woke, his mother would be gone, and he'd lose her all over again.

The pain in his head assaulted his skull like a wrecking ball. Perhaps he shouldn't have been so hasty in leaving the hospital, but he couldn't stay there after his disturbing talk with the old woman.

She'd become silent and restrained the moment she'd let the unspeakable escape her lips. The most confusing point was when he went to leave, and she suddenly asked to hug him—almost as if mourning the loss of her own son. If not for the fact he knew her embrace would satisfy his own mournful loss, he'd have rejected it altogether.

Kyle tossed about, the sound of his mother's voice drawing near, comforting him back to sleep, but only for a moment. Sleep would not stay, the pain too great to bear. He felt the spinning in his head like a clock wound too tightly, and bile threatened to spill from his throat. A cold sweat drenched him like the down-pouring of rain on a warm, summer night, but his mother was there to comfort him.

Had he driven home in this state? He reached with an outstretched arm for the familiar alarm clock at his bedside, pulling it close to his face, and painfully lifting an eyelid just above a flutter to see the time. The room was dark, but the red numbers illuminated 4:27am. His hand relaxed on the device, unable to move it back, but a gentle hand swept it away, and then brought the cool rag to his warm forehead.

Kyle groaned against the pain, but his mother's comforting song lulled him just a little longer. Sleep overcame him finally, and his mother's gentle song left him.

Kyle woke to the distant sound of sirens, and as the sound drew near, he could hear rustling at his side.

"Get up, Kyle!" a woman's voice said. "I think the police are here, and we need to get our story straight!"

Kyle groaned, the pain in his head a little lighter than it had been. He was groggy, and could hear the sirens, but had thought he was dreaming them.

He tried to sit up, but he was still very dizzy. His mouth was dry and his eyes felt very heavy. He yawned and stretched, but the pain in his head kept him down flat on his back.

"Story?" Kyle asked as he focused on the old woman. "What? What are you doing here?"

"I brought you home yesterday, don't you remember?"

Kyle groaned as he wiped the sleep from his eyes and made another attempt to sit up.

"Do you even have a driver's license?"

She threw her hands up. "Not on me, no!"

He looked at her a little more closely, noting that she'd helped herself to his clothes. His sweat pants and t-shirt were baggy on her frail frame, but she looked a little healthier than the last time he'd seen her. In all fairness, anyone looked ill in a hospital gown.

"Did you break out of the mental ward at the hospital?"

She handed him a glass of water. "Not exactly. But we don't have time to discuss that right now."

"I won't go to jail for you!" Kyle said.

"No one is going to jail, but they could make me go back and I don't want to go back. It isn't safe there."

"It's not exactly safe here either! Or did you miss the sirens outside? I'm sure they brought an ambulance to take us *both* back! I broke out too!"

Hearing a car door, she jumped. "We need to tell them I'm your mother," she begged. "Please don't send me back there. It's just as bad as being locked in…"

She didn't finish her sentence, but Kyle had an idea what she was trying not to say.

"I've never lied to a police officer, but I'd be willing to bet it's against the law!"

"What if it's not a lie?"

He reached up and grabbed her arms and looked her in the eye, even though his vision was still a little blurry from sleep. The lump in his throat wouldn't let him speak until he swallowed it down.

"What do you mean, if it's not a lie?" he said, his eyes now wide with terror. "I went to your funeral!"

His heart raced, and his face felt like it was on fire. What was happening? Had he hit his head harder than he thought, and now he was dreaming this—or worse—was he dead?

"You might have gone to a funeral that day, but it wasn't mine!"

"I admit my mother didn't look right that day, but I hadn't seen her for a couple of years, and she'd been taking drugs, and…"

"No she wasn't!"

"How do you know this?"

"I don't have time to go into that right now. Just follow my lead, and we'll get rid of them."

Kyle shook as a knock sounded at the door.

"Can you *prove* you're my mother?"

"The only proof I have of anything is locked away in the attic at Zeb Yoder's house!"

Chapter 10

"We had a report ma'am, filed by Zebedee Yoder, and he states that you're his wife and that this young man is holding you against your will."

Selma practically choked on his words as she turned to Kyle. "*He's* not holding me against my will! I'm not that man's wife. There's a grave on the back of his land where his wife is buried. Perhaps you should ask him who's in that grave!" she challenged the officer. "Ask him if I'm his wife, then, who's in that grave. I can't very well be here standing in front of you, and be dead and buried at the same time, could I? Zeb Yoder is a very sick man. Perhaps you should turn your questions on him. As for me, I'm staying here with Kyle."

"She's my mother," he told the police officer, fully believing and praying she truly was. "I can vouch for her."

The officer tipped his hat and bid them goodbye.

After the police left, Kyle felt suddenly let down.

He turned to the woman, sadness rising up in him, causing his throat to constrict as he swallowed down tears. "You're Amish, aren't you?" he asked her.

"*Jah,* I'm Amish," she answered quietly.

He knew from her answer there was no way she was his mother, without even asking the question. He wouldn't ask her, because to do so would break his heart all over again.

Zeb looked up from hitching his horse to the buggy when two police cars pulled into his driveway. Searching for any sign that Selma was with them, he clenched his jaw and ground his teeth in anger. They were supposed to bring her back. After all, she belonged to him, and she didn't belong among the *English*.

"Good afternoon, I'm Officer Banks," the first officer said as he approached Zeb. "I understand you filed a missing person's report for your wife."

He clenched his jaw and looked at them sternly. "You were supposed to bring her back here! She belongs here with me."

"The woman says she isn't your wife, and she wants to stay where she is. I don't know what kind of domestic problems you're having, but we can't force a spouse to go back home if the person doesn't want to."

"This is not a matter for *Englishers* to decide. The Bishop decides, and she is *mei fraa.*"

"Perhaps you could ask your *Bishop* to help you with this matter," the officer suggested.

Zeb narrowed his eyes. "I cannot. I'm shunned!" he said through gritted teeth.

"I'm afraid we can't help you," he said. "But we do have a couple of questions we'd like to ask."

Zeb glared at them, and then turned his back to them as he checked the harnesses on the buggy.

"She mentioned you have a grave on a family plot here on your property. Can you tell me whose grave it is? A *first* wife, perhaps?"

"The grave is empty!"

The officers gave each other a warning look.

"Empty?" Officer Banks asked. "Did you say the grave is empty?"

"*Jah,*" Zeb said without turning around. "This is none of your business. It is a *familye* matter."

"I'm afraid you're wrong about that, Mr. Yoder!" the officer said. "If we suspect foul play, it becomes a matter of the law. We need you to tell us about the grave, or we're going to have to take you in for further questioning."

"*Mei fraa* left me," Zeb said through gritted teeth. "The grave was for the boy."

Officer Banks put a hand on his gun, the other, reaching for his handcuffs. "You have a boy buried in the grave?"

"*Nee*—no! The grave was for *mei* son's benefit, so he wouldn't know his *mamm* left him! I had a funeral for her so he wouldn't know she left us."

"Why go to all that trouble? Didn't you think about what it would do to your son if she was to come back? Your son might have wanted to see her again."

"I've forbidden her to see him."

"But you just told us she was here with you, and you wanted her to come back. Doesn't your son know she's here?"

Zeb would not face them. "*Nee,* he does not live here, and he does not know I still know her as *mei fraa*. But she ran off again, so you see, it was *gut* that I didn't tell him, or his heart would be breaking the same as mine is now."

The officer eased up a little. "I'm going to need you to show me the grave, Mr. Yoder."

Zeb jumped up into his buggy and picked up the reins. "Unless you are detaining me for something, you can go out there yourself," he said pointing in the direction of the grave. "I have business to take care of in town."

"One more thing, Mr. Yoder. If we need you to dig up that grave to prove that it's empty, are you willing to do that?"

"My son has forgiven me for my shame, but now he will have another burden from his *vadder* if you open that grave," Zeb said angrily.

"You can do it willingly, or we can get a search warrant," the officer warned him.

Zeb slapped the reins, and set his horse in motion without answering the officer. He knew to agree to such a thing would bring further ridicule and shame on his head, and he wanted no part of it.

Chapter 11

Feeling discouraged, Kyle knew there was something he needed to take care of; something he'd put off for too many years. He felt more than ever it was time to face his past once and for all.

He offered to drop the woman off at a few shops downtown so she could pick up a few things for herself. He felt bad that she didn't have proper clothes to wear. She mentioned she'd like to get some material to make a couple of things, and he offered to pay. He even offered to let her stay in his spare room in his apartment, having felt responsible for her safety. In exchange, she offered to cook for him, and he was happy with that arrangement until she could get on her feet and be out on her own.

He didn't know why, perhaps because he missed his own mother so much, but he just couldn't turn her out into the streets or put her up in a women's shelter—especially if she was Caleb's mother. Surely he would want him to care for her until he returned from Florida.

On the drive into town, Kyle shared with her about Greta, and how she'd agreed to see him even though he was an *Englisher.*

"If she's smart," she said. "Greta will let you court her!"

"Don't the Amish believe that courting is like being engaged?"

"*Jah,* they do in a way."

Kyle chuckled nervously. "So if I'm taking her for a buggy ride, does that mean she expects me to marry her?"

"It's possible," she agreed. "Amish girls take courting very seriously."

"I don't want to hurt her," Kyle said. "I like her a lot. I may even be in love with her, but I never planned on getting married."

"Why not?"

Kyle shrugged as he turned off County Road 17, and onto the parkway. "I didn't really have a good sense of family when I was growing up. It didn't make me want one. I would never want to put a kid through what I went through."

"What do you mean?" she asked.

He shrugged again and sighed. "Well, my dad went to prison when I was only four years old, and I didn't have a great relationship with my mom after I left home at the age of ten. I went and stayed with my Uncle—well, I knew he wasn't really my uncle. I took on my mother's maiden name after my father was killed—at least, I think it was her maiden name—I never really knew if anything she told me was the truth. I think she was trying so hard to manage her own bad decisions, that she didn't make the best ones where I was concerned."

"Do you think your mother loved you?"

He smiled. "I know she loved me. There was never any doubt about that. She loved me more than she loved herself, but she didn't love herself much at all. I felt bad for leaving her, but I just couldn't take care of her. She had a sadness in her I just couldn't help her with. I was too young, and I didn't understand what she was going through. I deeply regret leaving her—now that I'm an adult, I really regret that."

"I'm certain she knew you loved her."

"I pray you're right about that."

Kyle put his blinker on and merged onto the off-ramp for Hartford.

"Why are we going here?" she asked.

"I have a little unfinished business to take care of, and I thought it would be safer for you to shop here—away from Old Man Yoder."

She suppressed a smile. "Why do you call him that?'

"Because he's a mean old man! For the short time I've known him, he's never said a kind word to me. He's harsh with his own son, and I've never seen anything other than a scowl on his face."

"He's a very troubled man. You should have some grace for him."

Kyle shook his head as he pulled in front of the downtown area and parked at the fabric store. "That man did something to hurt you, so why didn't you tell the police what he did?"

"It isn't my place to decide if he is punished for his sins. The Amish ways teach us to forgive the transgressions of others. We are not to judge or condemn."

Kyle put the truck in park and turned to her. "Here you are, ma'am. Curbside service. I'll be back to pick you up in about an hour, and we'll get a cup of hot cocoa and pie at the diner. Go there when you finish, and I'll meet you there."

She opened the door to the truck and turned to Kyle, and smiled. *"Danki."*

"By the way, if you and I are going to be roommates for a while, what should I call you? I still don't know your name. Do you even know it?"

"Ma'am is fine for now."

Kyle smirked. "Have it your way. But sooner or later, you're going to have to trust me!"

She smiled.

"I'll see you in an hour," he said, just before she closed the door.

Chapter 12

Kyle stood outside his old apartment building, looking up at the window his mother used to hang out of when she'd call him inside from playing stickball in the street with the neighbor kids. He closed his eyes and listened to the street noises. They hadn't changed much since he was a kid; sirens that could be heard for miles, kids playing…he was back home in his element.

"Kyle Albee!" a familiar voice yelled from up above. "What are you doing down there in the snow? Get up here and give me some sugar!"

He smiled, as he looked up at his old landlady, who was hanging out of the third-floor window and frantically unpinning pink, foam curlers from her hair.

"I'll be right up, Mrs. Haverty."

She pushed down on the window and shivered, wrapping the same terrycloth robe around her that should have been tossed in the rag pile years ago. He chuckled to himself, thinking nothing had really changed—except for him.

He stomped the slush off his boots and walked up three flights to visit a woman who was so much a part of his childhood. Before he had a chance to knock, the door swung open and he was greeted with a pair of chubby arms that pulled him into a squishy hug there was no way out of except to wait for it to end.

"Oh, it's so good to see you," the older woman cried. "I thought I'd never see my little Kyle again."

She rocked him back and forth as she cried and laughed at the same time. She'd always been the emotional type, but she was a good woman. She'd always get after him when he needed to be gotten after, and she looked out for his mom in her own way—mostly by making sure he took care of her.

"Take care of your momma," she would reprimand him. *"She took care of you when you were a baby, and now it's your turn to care for her."*

He'd never forgotten the look of shame she'd given him when he left, but apparently, all was forgiven now, as her hug would suggest.

She pulled him away from her and swatted him in the arm.

Alright, perhaps not!

"Why haven't you come to visit sooner?" she said, tears streaming down her ample cheeks. "I'm an old woman, and I'm not going to be around forever, you know!"

"I'm sorry, Mrs. Haverty. I guess I just needed to sort some things out."

She pushed him into her apartment, which covered the entire third floor of the building she and her husband owned.

"And have you sorted them out, or have you come to me for answers?" she asked, ushering him into the kitchen.

He sat down in the chair she pointed to, and she immediately had a glass of milk and a plate of cookies in front of him—just like when he was younger and he would go up there to pay the rent.

"A little of both," he admitted, stuffing a cookie into his mouth and chasing it with a gulp of milk.

"Would you like the box of her things I have up in the attic? It isn't much. I donated most of it, but I kept a few things that were too curious to get rid of—just in case you had questions later about her, mind you."

"What sort of things?"

"Well, for one thing, the Amish clothes she wore when she first arrived on my doorstep."

Kyle swallowed down hard a chunk of cookie, coughing to keep from choking on it. "Amish clothes? Are you sure? Why would my mother be wearing Amish clothes?"

Mrs. Haverty shrugged. "I didn't ask, and she never told. From the time she moved in until the time of her death, I never saw the clothes again, so I'd forgotten all about them."

Kyle's eyes grew wide. "What are you talking about?"

"When I found her—when she died—she was wearing Amish clothes then, too, but it was a different dress than what she'd worn when she first came here. She was just a young girl then—pregnant with you."

"What about my father?"

She stood from her chair and went to the refrigerator and pulled the carton of milk out and refilled Kyle's glass automatically.

"You mean the one that went to jail? What was his name again?"

"Bruce—Albee."

"Oh yes, Bruce. They got married just a few days before you arrived into this world, but you sure were the apple of his eye."

"He didn't marry her *before* she got pregnant for me?"

"No, but I don't know the whole story about that. I would hear them arguing sometimes. I could hear them all the way up here from the ground floor. I suppose that's why she didn't marry him at first. He never wore Amish clothes, but he had Amish friends. They used to come over, and then one day stopped— about the same time he went to prison. But then one Amish man started coming around again to see your mother. About a week before I found your mother when she'd overdosed from the pills, the man came to see her and brought an Amish woman with him. After that, I couldn't get your mother to open the door. She stayed in the apartment and didn't come out. One day, I decided to knock to see if she needed anything when I went to the market, and I heard a crash and glass breaking. I used my master key to open the door, and she was lying on the floor in the Amish clothes. She'd fallen on that glass table she had in the living room, and her face was cut badly. I called an ambulance, but she didn't make it."

Kyle ran a hand through his thick hair. Hearing about her death put a lump in his throat, and a heaviness in his heart.

He'd forgotten about the slash in her face. They'd tried to cover it up when they'd made her up for the funeral, but she just didn't look very much like herself. He'd used his pocket knife to steal a lock of her hair at the funeral home when the director's back was turned. It was the only thing he had left of her.

"That isn't the strangest thing I found in your apartment when I was cleaning out her things."

Kyle stood up, wishing he hadn't eaten so many cookies because they were now souring in his stomach. "What else could be stranger than that?"

"The strong-box at the back of her closet with the key stuck in the lock. It had a lot of money in it and a note to you! I've been waiting for you to come back and claim it."

Kyle shook the anxiety from his head. "How much money?"

The woman's eyes grew wide and dramatic. "Twenty-five-thousand dollars!"

"How did she get her hands on that kind of money? We were poor!"

Kyle fell to his knees, his heart breaking. "The robbery!" he whispered.

Chapter 13

"Start from the beginning," Kyle said. "I want to know how you know Old Man Yoder!"

He paced the floor of his townhouse apartment, while the old woman sat on the floor with her back against the sofa, cutting navy blue material for a dress.

"I suppose it all started when we were young," she said, resting the fabric on her lap, and looking off in the distance as if reflecting another time. "I was very much in love with Zeb Yoder. He was a fine young man and very handsome—back then. There was a time when he smiled all the time, and I was in love with him. But I wasn't his first choice. My younger sister, Rose, was his first choice. I was very envious of her at the time. I was older than she was, and I felt she was too young for him. While we were on our *rumspringa*, I decided I would have Zeb with wild abandon. I thought I could take his heart from my sister, but all I did was end up pregnant. I knew he didn't want to marry me, and so I ran away and I left the community."

"And yet he now calls you his wife?" Kyle asked angrily.

"I replaced her, because she rejected him, but I'll tell you about that in a minute. But at the time, he married Rose. I never got over him. He was my first love. I still continued to see him behind my sister's back and I'm ashamed of that, and when she found out, she left him."

"That would make you Caleb's aunt!"

She nodded, biting her bottom lip.

"So that's why there's a grave out back of the Yoder's property," he asked.

"*Jah*," she answered.

Kyle held his head. "If you ask me, I think you didn't tell the police what you know because you're afraid of the old man—not that I blame you. He's a pretty disturbed man. Why did you go back with him?"

"With Rose out of the picture, I thought I'd won, but instead, Zeb made me pay for leaving him the first time. At first, things were *gut* between us, and I thought we could be happy together. But as time went by, I realized he was keeping me hidden like a dirty secret. He became angry one day when Caleb saw me across the pond. Caleb thought I was his mother—back from the dead! He became so irate, in fact, that he decided he would tie me up and put me in the cellar in the barn. I was never allowed outside again."

"He tied you up?" Kyle asked.

"Jah," she said. "But that wasn't the worst of it."

"How could it get worse than that?"

She lowered her head averting his gaze, feelings of shame rising up from her spirit.

"That first night he tied me up, was the night Bruce Albee was killed in the barn."

Kyle's eyes widened, his attention gripping her every word. "So then you saw Amelia shoot him?"

"*Jah*, I saw him get shot," she said, tears in her eyes. "But I saw Zeb shoot him and kill him."

Kyle couldn't breathe. He paced the floor in front of her, wringing his sweaty hands. "What are you talking about?" he asked. "Amelia confessed to the shooting. She shot him with the Derringer she found in the barn. She said she pulled the trigger by accident, but the gun went off, and the bullet went straight through his heart."

She set aside her sewing, too agitated to concentrate on it.

"*Nee*," she said, correcting him. "It was the bullet from Zeb's gun that killed him. The shot from the gun in Amelia's hand went up above his head and missed him completely." She demonstrated by raising her arms and pivoting them backward really fast to show that her arms jerked upward when Bruce lurched toward her.

Kyle thought about the bullet he'd found lodged in the crossbeam in the barn, thinking it was all starting to make sense.

"I saw the whole thing," she continued. "The two of them shot the guns almost at the same time, and it was so close, that it sounded almost like one shot, with a bit of an echo. I knew the truth, but only because I saw it with my own eyes."

Kyle raked a shaky hand through his hair, fighting the bile that was threatening to come up.

"Because of this, Zeb left me in the cellar for nearly a week—that time."

"I wish you would tell the police all of this. I know you're afraid. I am too, but he needs help. Help we can't give him."

"I only want to break free from him."

"But he belongs in Jail!" Kyle insisted.

"Nee, I already told you, it's not my place to pass judgement. I must forgive him. It is my Amish wisdom that gives me peace to forgive. Any man can lose his way and go apart from *Gott*—even an Amish man."

"But this is different," Kyle argued. "He killed a man. He killed my father!"

"It is not for you or me to judge. *Gott* will do that in *His* timing, not ours."

Kyle was seething with anger. Bruce's death was more than eight years ago, but the pain was rising in him as fresh as it was when he was just a young boy and had lost both his parents in the span of a few days. He hadn't even had a chance to see his father after he'd gotten out of prison. He'd forgiven Amelia for shooting him, but if she didn't shoot him, he'd have to forgive the offense all over again.

"Did you even know Bruce Albee?"

She lowered her head in shame. "Yes, I knew him because I knew about the robbery. I didn't play a part, other than keeping quiet about it, but I was there the night Zeb shot him!"

"All this time, Amelia thought she'd shot him with the gun she found in Old Man Yoder's barn! The guilt almost ruined her life."

"I'm sorry for her, but that's not how it happened. Zeb was there that night, tying me up in the barn when Bruce walked in after Amelia. Zeb shot him to get revenge."

"Revenge for what?"

"Mostly because of the money, but there were other reasons too."

"There isn't ever any good reason for that kind of revenge," Kyle said.

The woman sighed, tears pooling in her eyes. "I'm afraid I feel drained. I can't talk about this too much without it causing me anxiety."

Kyle looked at her, feeling like a heel when he saw how much she was shaking.

"We can talk more about this later," he offered.

She looked at him, her eyes softened. "Perhaps the journal will shed some light on it."

He shook his head and wagged his finger at her. "Oh, no! You're not going to talk me into breaking into Old Man Yoder's house and getting you that journal."

Chapter 14

Kyle's heart raced and his sweaty hands shook as he went to the door and turned the knob, opening the kitchen door at Old Man Yoder's house. He didn't dare second-guess himself, for fear he would have too much time to talk himself out of it. He couldn't believe she'd managed to convince him to follow along with such a crazy scheme, but if it meant proving the old man's guilt in some way, he would do it for the sake of putting this nightmare to rest once and for all.

He'd promised the old woman he would do this one last favor, but only after she promised him a full explanation, claiming she owed him that much. Admittedly, he agreed with her on that account. But she'd all-but-threatened to go fetch the journal herself if he didn't go after it, and so he'd reluctantly allowed her to talk him into going in her stead.

Kyle had watched from the window of Caleb's house until he'd seen the old man drive off in his buggy, but that didn't mean he'd stay away. Remembering the last encounter with the old man when he'd gotten locked in the cellar made him shiver. But the possible violence he'd experienced in Caleb's *dawdi haus* a couple of nights ago was enough to set his teeth on edge.

Admittedly, he was nervous about leaving the woman in a home so close to the Yoder farm, but he figured having her where he could see potential danger was better than having her across town.

As he walked through the old man's house, he followed the path the woman had instructed him to take, and he wondered if he would serve time for breaking and entering, even though the door was unlocked. He supposed since he hadn't gotten an invitation, the law might consider it breaking in regardless of the door being unlocked. Those were all technicalities he couldn't afford to think about right now, especially since he'd made the decision to go ahead with the old woman's plan. She had assured him that she had rights to the home, and he assumed that was because she was living there for the past several years. With her permission to enter the home, he could hardly think he'd be held accountable for breaking and entering.

So why did he get the feeling she was leaving out a vital piece of the puzzle—perhaps purposefully, in order to get him to do her bidding? He didn't exactly feel manipulated, but he'd been talked into a caper he thought certain was a bad idea.

He cringed from every little creek in the stairs. Though he knew no one was home, it didn't stop him from trying to be quiet. His only goal was to retrieve the woman's journal she claimed was tucked away behind a loose brick in the fireplace up in the attic. To her, it was her entire life. To him, it would answer the myriad of questions that plagued him about the Yoder family.

Once he entered the attic, he immediately suppressed a sneeze. A thick layer of dust coated everything that didn't have a sheet draped over it. Even the floor was dusty, and it didn't take him long to see his footprints from the sunbeam that sprayed light across the floor, illuminating the undisturbed room now littered with his tracks. Regardless of whether he made it out of this predicament safely, his footprints would surely tell on him, and the old man would come looking for him; there was no doubt in his mind about that.

Since there was nothing to do now but follow through with the plan, Kyle forced himself to move toward the back of the room where he could see the red bricks of the chimney. He was so close; he could taste his freedom from this nightmare.

When he reached the chimney, he located the area the woman had instructed him and began to feel around for loose bricks. When he found the one in the back that jiggled, he craned his neck around to see between the bricks and the wall. Pulling the set of bricks from their place, he blindly pushed his hand into the opening, trying not to think of the spiders or mice that could be inhabiting the space. Thankfully, his fingers made contact with a thick book with a soft leather cover, and he pulled it free. Mortar dust covered it, so he tipped it and blew it off. Seeing the cover, he realized the book was not a journal, but a record-keeping book.

Was there another book in there?

He reached his hand into the space and found nothing. Curious, he opened the book to be sure he had what she'd asked for. He wasn't about to attempt this caper again.

Moving into the sunlight from the window, he could see there was writing in the book instead of figures that would measure book-keeping. He flipped through several more pages to be sure, when his gaze fell on his father's name within the pages. He read the sentence, which spurred him to read further, until he realized he was reading the passage that explained the events of his shooting that night. There it was, written in ink, the record of his father's murder—at the hands of Zeb Yoder.

Anger rose up in him as he stuffed the book in the waist of his jeans behind his jacket. If he should run into the old man, the last thing he wanted was for him to catch him with the evidence he needed to put the man in jail where he belonged.

Quickly replacing the bricks with shaky hands, Kyle wanted only to leave the man's house and take the book directly to the police instead of the old woman. He didn't intend to betray her, but he wanted justice for his father's death, and if that meant forcing her to answer for the words she'd written in the *journal,* then that's what he would do.

Tiptoeing back to the door, Kyle listened for a moment to be sure he wouldn't be met with any surprises on the other side. Turning the handle slowly, he opened the door, aware of every creak that echoed so dramatically, it caused him to cringe.

Once outside the door, he closed it behind him and let out the breath he'd been holding in.

"That's far enough," Zeb's gruff voice echoed from the end of the hall behind him.

Kyle could feel his heart beating double-time, the sound of the man's heavy foot-falls muffled only by the blood rushing to his head from his over-active heart.

He turned slowly, and the old man stopped just short of him. Shotgun in hand, Zeb's gaze narrowed on Kyle, the furrow in his brow cinched and unyielding.

"You're trespassing!"

Kyle had no good explanation other than the truth, which he thought might appease the man. "I was looking for something for Caleb's aunt. She said she left some of her things in your attic, and she sent me to fetch them."

Zeb chuckled madly. "Caleb's *aenti?* Is that who she told you she was?"

Kyle nodded, not understanding the way he'd asked the question. As if she was not who she claimed to be. Had the woman lied to him? No! She didn't seem capable of such a thing. But yet, here he was, breaking into a man's house at her request, and he really didn't know who she was.

"I told you boy, if you didn't bring her back here, you'd be replacing her!" he said, aiming the shotgun at him.

"I'm not going to hand her over to you so you can keep her here like she's your property. She's not going to be your prisoner anymore!"

Kyle's rasping breaths increased with anger. "Are you going to shoot me like you did my father? Amelia didn't shoot him—you did! You killed my father!"

"Your father?" the old man asked, throwing his head back and laughing madly. "I didn't kill your father—I *am* your father!"

His words shook Kyle to his very core.

"It isn't true!" he said, backing away from him.

"It's true, didn't your *mother* tell you?"

"Bruce is my father, and you killed him!"

"Turn around and walk out to the barn. I warned you boy. I told you if you didn't bring her back you would take her place. Move it!" he said, keeping the shotgun trained on him.

Kyle couldn't move. His mind was numb thinking about this man being his father. He refused to believe it.

"I said, turn around, or I'll shoot!" the man growled.

He turned, but only slightly, giving himself enough room to see any fast movements. "Is that thing even loaded?" he asked lightly, remembering his encounter with Amelia's mom.

He pumped the barrel, engaging the bullets in the chamber of the gun; that sound unmistakable.

"You care to find out?"

Kyle shook his head, his eyes bulging.

He was trapped, and he would be hard-pressed to get away unless he used his wit. He feared if he fought the old man, he'd get knocked out again. Cooperation was his only chance of survival. Perhaps keeping him talking would make a difference.

"If I'm really your son like you say," Kyle said with a shaky voice. "Why would you shoot me?"

"You betrayed me!" he said, marching Kyle out of the house and through the field toward the barn. "Just like my dear Rose did."

"I haven't betrayed you," Kyle tried reasoning with him.

Feeling the barrel of the gun press between his shoulder blades, Kyle struggled to think of a way out. The man had obviously lost his mind, and was capable of anything. But with a gun to his back, he was powerless. It would seem that since he was planning on holding him in the old woman's stead, perhaps he would ride this out, and find a way to escape after the man cooled down. Besides, she knew he was there, and if he didn't return, he'd instructed her to call the police. Could he count on her for that? He supposed he'd have to; he had no other choice.

Once inside the dark barn, the old man ordered him to light the lantern he'd lit once before. Then he ordered him to open the cellar door and go down inside.

"Don't do this!" Kyle begged. "If I'm really your son, how can you do this to your own flesh and blood?"

"Your mother betrayed me!" he said. "She kept you from me and made another man your father."

"I had no idea," he said.

"Everyone betrays me, and I can't let you get away with it! Rose didn't get away with it. She wouldn't listen to reason. I *had* to poison her with the pills," he rambled on.

Fear consumed Kyle, his blood pumping his heart to a speed that made him gasp for air. The pressure rose in his head, making him dizzy with terror. He steadied himself against the pole the lantern hung from.

He killed his wife. He's going to kill me, and the woman too when he catches her.

Rage filled Kyle with adrenalin. "You're not my father; I had a father and you killed him!"

"If you don't believe me," he said calmly. "You can ask your *mother*!"

Kyle felt the twinge of fear pour through him at the realization of his statement.

The old woman was his mother, and they would both die at the hands of this bitter and sick man if he didn't do something to stop him.

Grasping the lantern with his fingers, Kyle lifted it swiftly, without a second thought, and flung it against the floor, spilling out the oil.

Startled by the sparks that quickly ignited to flames, spreading over the fresh layer of straw on the floor, Zeb rushed at Kyle, tackling him to the ground. As his head hit the wood floor, his eyes closed, and his world went black.

Chapter 15

Selma peeked out the kitchen window nervously when a car pulled into the driveway of Caleb's house. She watched a young couple exit a taxicab, and realized she recognized him as her nephew.

She smoothed Kyle's baggy shirt and pants over her tiny frame, realizing it didn't matter what she looked like; she was going to have to give an explanation to the nephew she never really knew, and he'd likely be more worried about having a person in his house he didn't know than what she looked like. She had to admit, though, she felt like she looked homeless, which in a way, she was.

Caleb sniffed the air when he exited the cab. He smelled smoke, and it was the wrong season to be burning leaves. He promptly handed the driver the money and retrieved his luggage.

"Do you smell that?" Amelia asked.

He nodded. "Let's get you inside, and then I'll check it out. I'm sure it's nothing."

Before he could reach the door, Selma came running from the house and approached the couple out of breath.

"Your father's barn is on fire, and I think Kyle is over there. He's in trouble. I don't have time to explain, but you need to help him!" she said.

"Who are you?" Caleb asked.

"I'm Kyle's mother! Please help him!"

"Kyle's mother? I thought you were dead!"

"I was—sort of, but he rescued me. It's a long story, and I don't have time to go into it right now. I think he's in danger and I need you to help him!"

Caleb looked at her familiar face and the realization hit him all at once. "You stay here," he said to his wife and the woman claiming to be Kyle's mother. "I'll go see what's going on."

He took off running through the field toward the burning barn, his thoughts reeling. How could that woman be Kyle's mother? Was she the same woman he'd seen on too many occasions wandering his own property as a child?

He ran faster, seeing the flames licking the top of the barn roof, smoke billowing out from it. When he approached, he nearly ran into the electric fence that stood between him and the burning barn.

When and why had his dad put that up?

Admittedly, he hadn't gone near the barn since Amelia got hurt when she was caught in the barbed wire he had put up. Caleb hadn't known about that either. But electric fence? How was he going to get to the barn— especially if Kyle was in there like the woman claimed? And what did his father have to do with Kyle being in danger?

He didn't have time to run all the way up to the main house to get in through the yard. Looking around for a way in, he realized the only way in would be to climb the tree that hung over the fence.

When he jumped to the drifted snow under the tree branch, it wasn't as soft as he'd hoped it would be, and his feet throbbed from the high jump. He hobbled over toward the barn, calling out to Kyle.

From inside the barn, Kyle could hear someone calling his name. He coughed and drew in a breath, his lungs and throat burning from the smoke. Crawling toward the voice, he could see the barn door opening.

It was Caleb.

He ducked his head against the billowing smoke and rushed to Kyle's side, grabbing his shirt and pulling him toward the door.

Once they were out in the yard, Caleb dropped him in the snow, and collapsed next to him. They coughed and he patted Kyle on the back.

"How many times am I going to have to pull you from burning buildings?"

Kyle coughed and wiped soot from his face. "I'm praying this will be the last time!"

"What happened," Caleb asked. "Why were you in there?"

Kyle struggled to his feet, still feeling a little disoriented.

"Your dad! It's my fault. I started the fire, and your dad's still in there!"

He ran toward the barn and Caleb followed him in, the two of them pulling their coats over their faces to shield from the smoke. They stayed together, keeping low.

Kyle went toward the middle of the barn where he'd smashed the lantern, and found him lying on the floor. They both grabbed him, but he fought them.

"Leave me in here," he growled. "I need to burn for my sins."

"I'm not leaving you in here, no matter what you've done!" Kyle yelled at him.

Dragging him against his will, the two of them struggled, while the fire crackled and the roof creaked.

"We need to get out of here before the roof collapses!" Caleb hollered above the roaring of the fire.

Grabbing a support beam, Zeb tried to fight the two of them, until Caleb peeled his fingers from the pole, while Kyle grabbed his legs.

"Let—me—die!" he yelled between coughs, still struggling and fighting the two who were trying to rescue him.

Finally, they got him out of the barn and onto the snowy ground several feet away. As they collapsed in the snow beside their father, they looked up and watched the barn roof start to give-way. They both jumped up fast and pulled the old man further away, while he yelled at them.

"Leave me alone," he said, yanking his arms free. "You should have left me in there to die!"

Off in the distance, the sound of approaching fire trucks brought relief to Caleb.

He turned to his father. "Why do you want to die?"

He sat there silent.

"Tell him!" Kyle said angrily. "Tell him how you shot Bruce Albee and blamed it on Amelia! And how you poisoned his mother, and locked mine away for the last several years. Tell him that you're *my* father too!"

The old man remained silent, his eyes cast down.

Caleb looked at Kyle, who was breathing hard, anger clenching his jaw.

He turned to his father, tears welling up in his eyes. "Is this true?"

The old man just sat there, staring at the snow, but he wouldn't say a word.

Chapter 16

Caleb paced the floor of the hospital's emergency room waiting area, waiting to hear from the doctor who was examining his father.

Amelia stood and met him, interrupting his path.

"Come sit," she urged him. "All this pacing isn't going to make the doctors hurry, but you're going to wear yourself out."

He pulled her into his arms and leaned down to kiss her cheek. "In all this excitement," he whispered to her. "I forgot to tell you something."

She looked at him, worry in her eyes. "What else is there? Is there more to this story than Kyle being your brother?"

He sighed. "My father is the one that shot Bruce Albee. Your bullet was stuck in the rafters of the barn. Kyle told me he has pictures of it. My father confessed it to Kyle, Selma saw him shoot Bruce that night. She said your bullet shot up into the rafters over Bruce's head."

Amelia buried her face in his chest and began to weep quietly. "All this time, I've tormented myself over this. I'm relieved my bullet is not the one that killed that man, but I'm sorry it was your father who did it."

He hugged her tightly. "Me too!"

Kyle leaned in to talk quietly with his mom. "I think we still have a lot to talk about," he said to her. "But I need to talk to my brother about a few things too. Right now, he's too concerned with the old man, but I'm going to have to tell him about his mom. But first, I need you to tell me how she ended up in *your* grave."

Tears filled her eyes. "I never meant to hurt my sister—or you for that matter. I'm ashamed that I was still seeing Zeb even while he was married to my sister, Rose. I just never got over him. When she found out, she threatened to go to the Bishop with his indiscretion, and then told him she was going to leave him. He brought her to my apartment and told her she could stay there, and asked me to come back with him. I thought I was going to live in the house with him, and could eventually bring you back there with me."

"So the two of you switched places, and I never knew because I just didn't come home. I was having too much fun with my cousins."

"I would never have left her there if I'd known Zeb would go back and poison her. He confessed to me that he gave her tea with the sleeping pills in it. I didn't know whether or not what he said was true, but I didn't want to take the chance of it happening to me. After all, I depended on him to feed me all those years. As long as I didn't fight him, I wasn't locked up. So when I found out my sister was buried as *me,* I was trying to escape. We'd had an argument that day, and he showed me the obituary from Caleb's mother, but they named *me* as the deceased. That's when I tried to get away from him, but he locked me in the cellar, and I'd been there for about a week before I hit him over the head and escaped—the night you found me. When I threatened to expose him for his lies and abuse, he laughed and told me no one would believe a dead woman; that they would think I was crazy. After all, there was a grave with my name on it, and you'd had a funeral for me. To the world, I was a dead woman. I couldn't fight that."

Kyle pulled her hand into his and squeezed it. "I'm glad I found you."

"I am too," she said. "I'm sorry I wasn't there for you as much as I should have been. I know it's no excuse, but I suffered a lot of anxiety after leaving the community, and I went to doctors that gave me medicine that made things worse, so I didn't take them. I was sad all the time without my parents and the community. I was lost, and didn't know how to take care of a child on my own. Bruce was good to you, I don't know if you remember him, but when his friends came to him about the robbery, he was too quick to take the easy way out. Prison obviously turned him bitter, Zeb had blamed the entire thing on him, and witnessed against him as revenge for marrying me, and then eventually killed him for the same reason."

"If you weren't his first choice, and he didn't marry you, why did he care that you married Bruce?"

She sighed, fidgeting with the sleeve of the coat Amelia had given her to wear. "I don't know, other than he took it personally when I rejected him—after he'd rejected me! He is a very possessive and territorial man, but he's also very dangerous—to himself, and those he claims to love."

"What about the money? Is that from the robbery?"

She nodded. "We need to turn that money in. I'd wanted you to have it, but turning it in is the right thing to do."

"I was afraid you'd say that," he said with a chuckle.

The doctors finally returned to the waiting room to talk to them, and the two brothers sat together to support each other.

"Your father suffered from mild smoke inhalation, but he didn't have a stroke like we thought when you first brought him in," the doctor explained. "We've sent him upstairs to be evaluated, as it seems he may have suffered some trauma, and he's in a catatonic state. He hasn't spoken or responded even once since he's been here. He's in the psychiatric ward on the third floor. I think they'll hold him there twenty-four hours, unless a family member admits him for therapy, but we might also suggest putting him in a nursing home."

The two of them sat there, unable to make a decision, and so the doctor excused himself, and referred them to the third floor nursing station.

"What should we do with him?" Kyle asked after the doctor left them. "We need to decide if we should turn him in."

"He's committed crimes," Caleb said. "I understand this, but it is not our place to judge. I think he needs help, but I believe he needs prayer more than anything."

He patted Kyle on the back. "I have to say, I still can't get over the fact you're my brother!"

Kyle smirked at him and punched him playfully. "Half-brother! But I'm glad too. It's nice to have a family."

Caleb smiled. "I have an *aenti* and a new brother. Hey, do you realize this makes you Amish, Kyle?"

He sat next to his mom and leaned his head on her shoulder. "I hadn't even thought about that. I guess that means I can marry Greta!"

Selma nudged at her son. "I thought you said you were never getting married."

"That was before I found out I had a family. Besides, I think I'm in love with her. I know we only had one date, but it was a wonderful date, and I think I'm going to ask her to court."

"I'll make you a proper Amish shirt and trousers to wear so you can court her proper-like!" his mother said.

"But how can I court her *proper-like* if I don't have a proper Amish name? I know Jack Sinclair was not your brother, who was he?"

"He was a *gut* friend of Bruce's, and his *fraa,* Miriam, was my very best friend growing up. She and I both ran from the community when we became pregnant. It was something we had in common, and we leaned on each other. You and her oldest, Seth, were like cousins. How could I tell you anything different? I'm sorry you took on their name because you felt so lost."

"I know Zeb is my *father,* but I have no desire to carry on his name. I feel like a man without a country!"

"You can always take my *real* maiden name. It was Graber."

"Graber; I like that. Now that's a proper Amish name!"

Selma giggled and kissed her grown-up, baby boy on his cheek.

He leaned back and took in the reality of having a brother, but getting his mom back was almost surreal.

"Boy, won't Greta be surprised when she finds out I'm Amish!"

THE END

Blood
Brothers

Book Three
Pigeon Hollow Mysteries

Samantha Bayarr

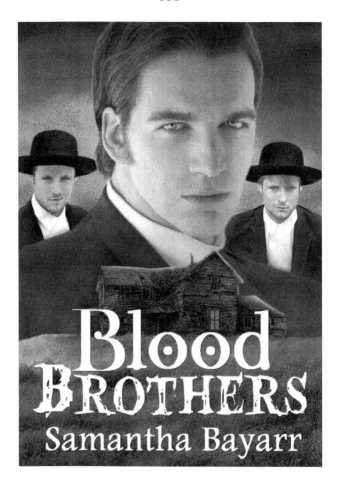

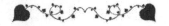

A note from the Author:

While this novel is set against the backdrop of an Amish community, the characters and the names of the community are fictional. There is no intended resemblance between the characters in this book or the setting, and any real members of any Amish or Mennonite community. As with any work of fiction, I've taken license in some areas of research as a means of creating the necessary circumstances for my characters and setting. It is completely impossible to be accurate in details and descriptions, since every community differs, and such a setting would destroy the fictional quality of entertainment this book serves to present. Any inaccuracies in the Amish and Mennonite lifestyles portrayed in this book are completely due to fictional license. Please keep in mind that this book is meant for fictional, entertainment purposes only, and is not written as a text book on the Amish.

Happy Reading

Chapter 1

"He asked to see the Bishop," Caleb told Kyle.

"Do you trust him?"

"I think we have no choice. I believe he wants to confess to the Bishop before he turns himself in. He told me he knows he needs to pay for the crimes he committed."

"Do you think it's wise to take him back home? I'm not sure any of us are safe," Kyle said nervously.

"I know he's done wrong, and he agrees he needs to turn himself in, but he's our father, and I think we should let him speak to the Bishop first."

"I suppose you're right," Kyle agreed. "But do you really think he should be around my mom and Amelia?"

"They're safe and sound at your house with the doors locked, and we removed all his guns from his house. Besides, it's only for an hour while he meets with the Bishop."

They waited outside the same locked room Kyle's mom had occupied only two days before, while the nurse slid her card in the lock to release him.

Zeb Yoder took his time in meeting them in the hallway, not seeming interested in leaving the hospital psychiatric ward.

"We have a search warrant to search the premises, and we brought a crew to dig up the grave your father buried some years ago. He's claimed it's empty, but there are laws against this sort of thing, whether the casket is empty or not."

Kyle and Caleb looked at the five-man crew wearing reflective vests and toting shovels, who stood behind the two police officers.

"We're going to need your father to go with us out to the grave site."

"He's in the middle of a meeting with our Bishop right now, can you wait a few minutes?"

"I'm afraid we're on a schedule," the officer said. "The city is paying these men to be here, and the city won't pay for your father to finish his visit."

"I'll get him," Caleb said.

Kyle's nerves jangled while he listened to the men grumble about the Amish thinking they are *above the law.* He leered at them, wishing he could blend away from the scene that was about to unfold, but even he was curious about the casket that was buried at the back of the old man's property.

When Caleb returned with his father, the Bishop agreed to go with him for support, and

Caleb thought it was more out of curiosity than anything else. Surely the rest of the community would hear about all of this before it even hit the newspapers.

One of the officers asked Zeb to step outside on the porch. "Are you Zebedee Yoder?"

He nodded. "*Jah.*"

The officer pulled out a pair of handcuffs and proceeded to read him his rights.

"What are you doing?" Kyle asked.

The officer ignored Kyle until he was finished. "Do you understand these rights?"

Zeb nodded again.

"Your father is under arrest for unlawful and improper burial, and for violating the city and county ordinances regarding placement of graves."

Knowing Zeb had committed far worse crimes than this, Kyle still wanted to make sure the man was being charged fairly. "But the grave is empty!"

"That doesn't matter!" the officer said. "There are codes and regulations regarding burials of anything other than house-pets, and your father broke the law."

"But he didn't bury anything other than a casket!" Kyle continued to argue. "What's the harm in that?"

Why was he defending the man? Did his blood-tie to the man suddenly shift his thoughts to have compassion for him even after all he'd done?

"Let's go dig up the casket so we can be sure it's empty," the officer said, ignoring Kyle.

After everything that had happened, Kyle had to admit he was just as curious to see if it was empty.

"Is that *really* against the law?" Caleb whispered to his brother.

Kyle shrugged, as they followed the officers out to the site. "I've heard of some strange laws on the books, so who knows. But I'm thinking they should have brought a back-hoe to dig it up. They're going to have fun cutting through the frozen ground with those shovels."

When they reached the site, one of the men removed the grave marker, a nice cross Caleb had carved for his mother, and tossed it to the ground. Upset by this, he went over to retrieve it, and was told to leave it since it was evidence. This angered him since he'd planned to have a proper burial for his mother, and that cross would serve as a grave marker wherever they put her.

The men began to dig, and everyone else stood by and watched. The tension was thick, anticipation making everyone's nerves stand on edge. The men made light work of digging up the shallow grave, each man taking his methodical turn as if they did this all the time.

When the primitive box was unearthed, they brushed it off and pulled it from the shallow grave.

"It's heavy," one of them said, turning to Zeb. "I thought you said this casket was empty!"

"I had a funeral for my wife—for my son's sake, so he wouldn't know his mother had chosen to leave him," he protested.

Caleb cringed.

More lies.

Aenti Selma had told him that Zeb had forbidden his mother to see him again. Did his father even know the truth anymore?

"Open it up!" the officers ordered the men.

Two of them used their shovels to pry open the casket. When they flipped open the lid, they all cringed and backed away, holding their hands over their faces and groaning, but Kyle and Caleb were not close enough to see what the problem was.

As the wind shifted, the stench of death consumed them.

All eyes peered in to see the deceased, fully clad in an Amish dress and *kapp*.

Chapter 2

Kyle felt his legs buckle underneath his six-foot frame.

What kind of man was this who shared his DNA?

He blew out a hard breath, watching the icy puff of air crystalize and evaporate, as if that was all he could concentrate on at the moment.

Did he dare look at the body? Did it even matter?

She was there no matter if he looked or not. Nothing was going to change the fact that his own father had committed such an unspeakable act.

His gaze traveled to Caleb, his *brother,* who had collapsed, and was sitting in the snow. He reached a shaky hand to him, but the muffled chaos around the grave switched his thoughts toward the men.

He felt his brother's hand in his, but he didn't turn. He couldn't turn away from the sight of the open casket, despite the tugging from Caleb's hand as he struggled to his feet.

With his brother beside him now, the two walked slowly toward the open casket, and the crowd of men who'd gathered there. Pictures flashed; orders were barked. One of the officers stepped away and radioed for the coroner and backup officers to come to the scene.

A perimeter of bright yellow tape was wound around two adjacent trees, roping off the *crime scene.*

Kyle couldn't think straight. His mind reeled with the possibility that the woman in that casket could have been his own mother. He wondered what Caleb must be thinking, knowing they were about to unearth his mother's grave as soon as the warrant was signed. Surely it would be signed now that a new *body* had turned up unexpectedly.

More pictures flashed, and Kyle shuddered at the thought of what the newspaper headlines would say. His name would be linked to this crime, now that Old Man Yoder had confessed to being his father.

He watched in horror as the old man protested, claiming he had no idea how the body had gotten into the casket, while they read him his rights again.

Accused of *murder.*

It held a certain stigma Kyle wasn't certain he would ever be able to shake. No one ever thinks such a thing could happen in their own family, but now he'd been grandfathered into this family and all of its problems.

He silently wished he'd never come back to Pigeon Hollow looking for answers. Wished he'd never made that delivery to Amelia and Caleb that day.

But that wasn't fair. It wasn't fair to them, since he cared so much for them both. Not to mention the fact that he'd have never found his mother if he hadn't come back. He certainly would never have known he had a brother. But at what price had all that come to him?

Kyle turned to Caleb, who was weeping.

Swallowing down the lump in his throat, he felt the warmth of a tear that rapidly froze against his own cheek, and it startled him.

How could he be so happy to have a brother, yet feel so miserable to be related to him? It confused him how both feelings could consume him all at once.

Kyle peered into the casket, unable to fight his curiosity any longer. His blood ran cold when the realization hit him. Though she was mostly unrecognizable, due to decay, the frozen earth had preserved her enough for him to know exactly who she was.

But how?

"Aunt Miriam," he whispered.

Chapter 3

Caleb turned to Kyle, horror spread across his face. "You know that woman?" He asked.

Kyle focused on his brother's face, his heart racing, dizziness overcoming him. He felt the bile rise up in his throat, and tried to swallow it down, but it was determined to escape. He turned his head and stepped to the side, leaning over and retching up the contents of his stomach. He coughed and choked and sputtered, until his stomach was empty. Then, he used his foot to kick fresh snow over the mess, and quickly grabbed a handful and wiped it across his mouth, not caring just how cold it was. He flicked the ice and water from his hand and then drew his sleeve across his mouth to wipe it dry.

Caleb approached him and placed a hand on his brother's back just to let him know he was there. Kyle turned a half turn toward him, feeling a little embarrassed.

"Are you alright, big brother?"

Kyle sniffled and nodded, wiping his eyes with his palms. If not for the crowd that still remained at the gravesite, he would have walked away, but his aunt awaited identification, and right now he was the only one who could identify her.

He had to pull himself together for her sake. Then there would be the task of calling uncle Jack and his cousins—a family it turned out he wasn't really related to.

Did they even know she'd been gone?

He hadn't seen his *cousin,* Seth, in the six years since he'd left their home to go out on his own. He'd seen the twins, Ellen and Elizabeth, but both had families of their own now, and he'd fallen away from the entire family.

His mother and his *Aunt* Miriam had been friends, and she'd mentioned them leaving home together during their *rumspringa.* What he couldn't wrap his mind around, was the connection to the old man, or why they'd found her buried on his property. Kyle was determined to find out the sordid details, no matter how much worse things got for them.

One of the officers approached Kyle, while the other closed Zeb in the back of the patrol car. Strangely, the old man was emotionless—as if he lacked a conscience. Kyle had very little faith in his father. But even after all the old man had put him through, he still felt a twinge of sadness at having never known him.

He shuddered, swallowing down the thought.

Blood ties did not make him feel any less estranged from his father, but those ties came with the burden of bearing a certain amount of responsibility; a responsibility he did not want.

"Did I hear you say you know this woman?" the officer asked Kyle.

Kyle blew out his breath, trying his best to understand what the officer had said to him. The pounding of his heartbeat had muffled the question, and drowned out everything around him.

"Young man," the officer said, placing a hand on Kyle's shoulder.

The action startled him, bringing the foreground to life.

"I asked you a question. Can you identify this woman?"

Kyle nodded methodically, finding it difficult to concentrate. "I—I think I do. I think she's a woman I've known all my life as my aunt."

He knew his mother would not be the best one to identify her, since they hadn't seen each other in so many years. But even if she was, he would spare his mother the gruesome task.

"My *Uncle* Jack," Kyle found himself saying. "Or maybe one of my *cousins,* would be the best ones to tell you for sure."

"Where can I find these family members?"

"I don't know for sure," he said, trying to remember their new address. He'd only been there once, but it was possible he could find it again. When he'd last seen the twins, they were out shopping in downtown Hartford, and had told him briefly about the trouble Seth had been involved with, and his drinking and gambling problems, but they had been in a hurry that day, and they'd each promised to keep in touch. Sadly, it hadn't happened.

"It's been a few years since I've seen any of them, but they're over in Hartford."

"That's still part of Raven County," the officer said without emotion. "So we can look into it further. Give me their full names and the approximate location, and we can track them down for you."

Kyle felt sick again.

"Maybe—I should be the one to talk to them," he said.

"I'm sorry, but this is a police matter now. We'll handle it."

After giving the officer his own information, Kyle and Caleb went up to the old man's house to get some coffee, and to get out of the cold that had numbed them both beyond the reality of the unearthed body.

They walked past the Bishop, but he lowered his gaze, and that was enough to let them know the ban would never be lifted for their family.

Chapter 4

Kyle rang the doorbell of his Uncle Jack's home, shaking uncontrollably at the words he'd rehearsed, but had suddenly left him. He struggled to remember just what it was he was going to say, and how he was going to say it. That wasn't something you blurted out on the street. He'd have to wait until he'd had a chance to be welcomed in by his uncle, and made sure the man was sitting down when he gave him the news.

Lost in thought, he suddenly realized the door had opened, and an older woman he didn't know was standing on the stoop, staring at him. Her brow furrowed over her dark eyes, and the gray, disheveled hair matched her complexion.

"Do I have to call the police," she was saying to him. "Or are you going to get off my porch willingly?"

She swatted at him with the broom in her hand, and he took a step back, almost falling backward off the icy slab of cement.

He grabbed onto the iron, stair rail to keep from toppling down the steps. "I'm looking for my Uncle Jack—Jack Sinclair," he said, finally finding his voice.

"I bought this place fair and square," she said, narrowing her gaze at him. "And not you, or that other man, is going to run me off!"

Horror spread across his face. "What *other* man?" he asked.

"That old, Amish man!" she answered.

Kyle could feel bile rising up in his throat again, but pushed it down. "Did he have a long white beard?" he asked, demonstrating the length with his hand. "And a constant angry look on his face?"

She nodded vigorously. "Yeah, that's the one! You kin to that crazy man?"

Not on purpose! he thought.

"I just happen to know who you're talking about. He's done some things—well, that's why I'm looking for my Uncle. I need to tell him my aunt is, um—dead."

Her face grew more ashen. "That old man killed her?"

Kyle swallowed hard. "Maybe—um—I don't know. I just need to know where I can find my Uncle Jack so I can tell him. Does my family still live here?"

"I told you I bought this place fair and square—from Jack Sinclair."

"How long ago?"

"Just before the first snowfall," she said with a far-off look. "I remember it because I was glad I got everything moved before it got too cold and slippery for the movers. I didn't want them to drop any of my things and break them."

"Back in November?" he asked impatiently.

"Yes," she said, nodding her head. "The first day I was in here, that Amish man came looking for him. He accused me of hiding him in my house! He pushed right past me and tracked mud all over my floors. Funniest thing, too—it wasn't even raining that day!"

Probably the day he buried my Aunt Miriam!

"Did he say why he was looking for my Uncle Jack?"

"No! And I didn't ask. I just wanted him to leave, but he showed up again the next day, so I called the police. By the time the police showed up, he was long-gone. He's a scary, scary man!"

I'm aware of that!

"Did my Uncle Jack leave a forwarding address?" he asked the older woman.

"No!" she answered curtly. "I've told you all I'm gonna tell you; now it's time to get off my property."

"Well, thank you for your time."

Kyle walked away, feeling more discouraged and more worried than ever. Things were certainly pointing toward his flesh and blood being a murderer at least two times over, and the very thought of it made his stomach churn.

Hopping in his truck that he'd left parked in front of the building, he looked up one more time at the place in which he'd resided with people he thought were his family. His whole life has been one big lie after another, and he'd hoped that finding his mother alive would be the beginning of good things, but it just wasn't. Having a father who'd committed crimes had opened up a new and bitter world for him. A world he wanted no part of at the moment.

By tomorrow, the news would be smeared all over the papers, and embarrassment would come down on his and Caleb's heads. It certainly wouldn't help their new roofing company at all, but that was the least of his troubles.

Now, he worried what Greta's family would think of him, and if her father would forbid him to continue courting her.

Kyle pulled up to the ranch-style home he'd last known his cousin, Ellen, to live in, and parked his truck close to the door. The place looked abandoned for some time; tall, brown grass poked through the snow, and the door hung from its hinges, the front window broken clean out.

Regardless of the condition of the property, he shouldered out into the wind, and walked carefully over the patches of ice to reach the front door. He knocked loudly on the door, causing it to swing open.

Seeing that the house was empty, except for a bit of trash, and a torn and soiled corduroy recliner in the corner, Kyle felt his hope dwindle. Had the police run into the same roadblocks trying to find his family? For all he knew, they hadn't even begun their search; the old woman he'd just talked to in town would have mentioned if the police had been there.

He looked around the room and blew out a discouraging breath. A small trash can over-flowed with papers in the opposite corner of the room, and Kyle didn't see any harm in looking for a clue to his family's whereabouts.

He made fast work of smoothing out wadded pages of old bills; final notices, and shut-off threats from electric, gas and phone companies took up most of the pile. At the bottom, he found and opened letter with a return address in Florida.

He examined the post-mark, finding it odd that the letter had a cancelled stamp on it from Pigeon Hollow. He read the address again, wondering why the two didn't match. Flipping up the flap of the envelope, he pulled the short letter from inside and read the words that made no sense to him.

"Florida?" he shouted. "She's in Florida?"

He read the short letter once more, thinking there had to be some mistake. There was a return address on the envelope, and he could Google it to see where it was. The post mark was from November, but he couldn't read the exact date.

One thing was certain; the police needed to know this before they told any of his family she might be dead.

Was it possible she was alive in Florida, and he'd mistaken the identity of the woman in the casket?

Chapter 5

"Let go of me!" Seth barked at the officer who was pushing him into the patrol car. "I didn't do anything wrong!"

"For the hundredth time, Mr. Sinclair, it's against the law to drive while under the influence of alcohol."

"And I told *you* at least a hundred times I wasn't driving!" he hollered back. "My friend dropped me off at my car, and I knew I wasn't fit to drive so I decided to call a cab. But I guess I dozed off and I missed him."

"If you hadn't been sleeping in the car, I probably wouldn't have stopped here, but there isn't any overnight parking here. Your car is in a metered zone, and I'm afraid I'm going to have to call a tow truck and have the car impounded too."

"C'mon," he begged. "Please don't do that. I went to a birthday party tonight and celebrated a little too much, but I wasn't driving! You can call my friend *and* the cab company to check out my story. What ever happened to being innocent until proven guilty?"

"You can tell it to the judge when you see him on Monday."

"You mean to tell me I gotta stay in jail all weekend?"

"Unless you can get someone to bail you out before then, but you'll have to wait to make your phone call until after I process you."

"Couldn't you save a little bit of tax-payer's money and let me call the cab company back?"

Before the officer could answer him, a taxi pulled up beside Seth's car.

"There's my cab!" he said. "I told you I wasn't lying!"

The driver jumped out and looked at the officer. "Did one of you call for a cab?" he asked, glancing into the back of the patrol car at Seth. "I would have been here sooner, except that there was a bad accident a few miles back, and traffic is backed up for miles. Looks like about twelve cars involved."

"I told you I called a cab!" Seth said excitedly, as he turned to the officer. "Can you let me go now? You can see I called a cab."

The officer's mouth formed a thin line. "I can see that, but it still doesn't explain how you got here. I arrested you on the suspicion that you were operating the vehicle while intoxicated."

He wanted to ask the officer if that was even legal, but he figured he'd better keep his mouth shut.

"But you looked me up and saw that I've never been arrested before," Seth pleaded with the man.

"For some, that just means they've never been caught!"

"I hate to be rude," the cab driver said. "But if you're going to let him go, I've got a schedule to keep, and I'm sure they could use you down the road at the accident."

The officer turned to Seth and then motioned for him to step out of the back of his patrol car. "I'm going to let you go this time with a warning, but make sure you're better prepared the next time you do a little too much celebrating."

He took the handcuffs off Seth, and then gave him back his license.

"What about my car?" he asked. "Will you give me time to get my friends to pick it up for me. I'm sure it won't take them more than an hour."

He nodded. "As long as it's gone by the time I return from helping with the pile-up back there, then I won't bother with it."

"Thank you, officer," Seth said in his most polite tone. "I'll get them on it right away."

"Have a good night," he said as he got into his patrol car. "Be careful on these icy roads."

"I will," the cab driver said as he waved to the officer.

When he was out of sight, he turned to Seth and waved a finger at him.

"Boy am I glad to see you, Frankie!" Seth said to his friend. "And thanks for not blowing my cover."

"I told you being a cab driver would come in handy one day!"

Seth chuckled as he opened the door to his BMW and grabbed his phone. "I like you better as my *bookie,* but I have to admit, that cab *front* of yours did come in handy!"

"That was pretty slick sending me that text message while the cop was looking up your license!"

"I knew from the look in his eyes he was going to arrest me for something. They see a young guy in a car nicer than what they drive, and they automatically think I've stolen it, or I'm a rich, spoiled punk!"

"Well, I can vouch for you that you're a dirt - poor dude with a good eye for counting cards," he said with a chuckle. "B'cause we grew up on the same side of the tracks!"

"Can I help it if I'm one of the luckiest poker players around?"

"Your luck almost ran out tonight. Don't forget who saved your butt tonight!"

"No chance of that, Frankie, b'cause if I know you, you'll be reminding me for a lot of days to come."

Frankie pulled out his phone and looked up a number. "You should take that act of yours to Vegas and make the two of us some real money, instead of taking these poor suckers around here for a ride all the time."

"You know I can't do that. They'd know I was counting cards, and I'd be arrested for sure," he said, grabbing a cigarette from the pack with his teeth. Then he flicked open his Zippo, striking it with his thumb to light it in one smooth motion.

He held the flame to his cigarette and lit the end, drawing in a smooth stream of smoke and closing his eyes, feeling immediately subdued.

"I thought you said you wanted to quit smoking!" Frankie barked at him as he held his phone to his ear.

"I am," Seth said. "But I need one to calm me down. That cop nearly arrested me—say, who are you calling?"

Frankie looked up. "I'm calling the boys so we can get your car out of here. When that cop gets down the road and figures out that twelve-car pile-up is nothing more than a fender-bender, we might *both* be arrested."

Chapter 6

Frankie hung up the phone and shivered, blowing out a warm breath into the cold night air. "The boys will be here in about ten minutes. Let's sit in the warm car until they get here. I'm freezing!"

"I hope they hurry," Seth said. "Because I want to get out of here before that cop gets back here."

A lone pair of headlights lit up the dark highway just as they were about to get back into the cab.

Frankie looked up. "Too late for that!" he said. "Here he comes now."

"What are we going to do?" Seth asked. "He warned us to get the car out of here before he came back here, and since we didn't, he's going to arrest me!"

Frankie held up a hand hoping to calm his friend. "Now, just give him a chance. He might've come back here just to check up on you. The fact that you didn't get back into your car and drive off should score some points with him. He's not going to arrest you if you're not doing anything wrong."

"I wasn't doing anything wrong the first time!" Seth complained.

"If you keep acting all fidgety, he's going to think something is up, and you *will* get yourself arrested. So calm down."

"Fine," Seth said.

He was already irritable, and the thought of dealing with the police officer again set his teeth on edge.

"What am I supposed to do?" Seth asked with a chuckle. "Act casual? I'm not sure I know how to do that, and I'm not up for going to jail and having to sit there the whole weekend."

"No one's going to jail, if you'd just calm down," Frankie said. "So, yes, you should just act casual."

They watched the officer get out of his car slowly, and Seth could feel his heart racing, his mind reeling with thoughts of how to talk his way out of this one.

"I see you're still sitting here," the officer said as he approached, pointing his question toward Frankie. "I thought you had a schedule to keep."

Frankie chuckled. "Well, when you've got a fare paying you double, you agree to sit wherever that person asks you to."

The officer looked over at Seth. "Double, huh?

Seth nodded methodically.

The officers mouth formed a thin line, and Seth could see he was irritated with the two of them.

"I won't go into the fact that you sent me on a wild goose chase," the officer said calmly. "That twelve-car pileup was nothing more than a little fender bender between two cars. Now, before I get into why you lied to me about that, I'm afraid I'm gonna have to let you know that I need to take you in after all."

Seth's heart slammed against his rib cage. The thought of going to jail didn't sit right with him. He'd been walking the fine line of the law for a while now, but he never thought his actions would land him in jail.

"Why are you arresting me?" he tried to protest. "I didn't do anything wrong. I swear to you I wasn't driving the car. I've been sitting here waiting for my friends to come get it because I didn't want you to take it to the impound yard."

"I'll wait for your friends," he said. "But I'm not arresting you."

"Then why are you taking me in?" Seth asked.

"I'm afraid Son," he said. I'm gonna have to take you in so you can identify a body."

Seth threw his hands up in defense. "A *body!* Wait a minute; I didn't kill anyone!"

"No one said anything about you killing anyone," the officer said. "We've got a Jane Doe, and your name came up as a possible relative to identify the body."

Seth collapsed against his car, his mind reeling with thoughts he didn't want to entertain.

"Are you sure?" he asked. "One of *my* relatives?"

The officer looked at his notes, and then looked back up at Seth, a mournful look clouding his expression. "We have reason to believe the body is that of a Miriam Sinclair".

Seth felt his knees buckle. He couldn't believe it. He refused to believe it.

"That's my mother, but she's alive!"

"The body has been in the ground for some time. When's the last time you spoke to your mother?"

Seth felt heat rising up the back of his neck. "My parents got it in their heads that they wanted to sell the house and get an RV so they could do some traveling. They went to Florida for Christmas."

"The body of the woman has already been identified as possibly being Miriam Sinclair."

"Who identified her?" Seth asked, anger overcoming him.

"Kyle Sinclair—Graber".

"Kyle?" he asked. "Since when is Graber his last name, and what does Kyle have to do with any of this?"

"Do you know him?" the officer asked.

"He's my cousin. At least I think he is."

The officer flashed him a sympathetic look. "The body was found on his father's property."

Seth shook his head. "None of this makes any sense," he said. "Kyle's dad is dead."

The officer shook his head. "Not according to my notes. It says here, we arrested Kyle's dad as a possible suspect."

"Are we talking about the same Kyle?" Seth asked.

"We arrested a man named—just a minute, let me be certain," the officer said, pausing to look at his notes again. "Yes, we arrested Zeb Yoder, Kyle Graber's father."

Seth smirked. "That solves your whole problem right there!" he said. "The Kyle I know is a Sinclair, just like me, and his father's name was Bruce. That man sounds Amish. My cousin is anything *but* Amish."

"Not according to the notes," the officer said. "But if you come with me to the station and fill in some of the gaps, I'm sure we can sort all of this out. If you're unable to identify the body, then you won't be needed any further."

"I can tell you right now you're wasting your time. My parents are in Florida!"

Chapter 7

Seth found it hard to breathe as he followed the officer down a long, lonesome corridor. When they approached the morgue, one of the fluorescent bulbs buzzed and flickered, setting his teeth on edge.

The darkness that shrouded him weighed down his conscience.

If only he'd been able to convince his father to use the cell phone he'd presented them with when they'd gone off on their adventure. The stubborn man had resisted instruction, and had even managed to convince his son they were better off without the use of the modern device.

If only he'd insisted.

Now, he paced down the eerily quiet corridor, and the only question that plagued him was; where was his father now if his mother was truly lying dead behind the cold door of the morgue?

He knew he hadn't been the best son that two parents could have, but he always thought they were proud of him. He'd shamed his parents with the trouble he'd gotten himself into; trouble that had become all too common-place in recent years.

He rubbed at his eyes.

They wouldn't stop twitching.

His hands shook at his sides, as he lifted a shaky limb to wipe the sweat from his brow. Blowing out a worrisome breath, the buzzing of the florescent bulbs overhead filled him with an irritation he couldn't rid himself of.

The whole ride over, he'd tried to reach his sisters, but it was already late when he'd first encountered the police officer. And now, that encounter seemed so far away and so insignificant compared to what he was about to face.

He'd never attended a funeral before, let alone been close to a dead body. The possibility of the woman being his own mother made him sick to his stomach, and his knees felt a bit wobbly.

The door to the morgue opened with a click that echoed through the empty corridor. He flinched at the sound that reverberated against his eardrums like a bolt of lightning, sending a current of electricity through his veins until it reached his brain with a stabbing pain. There, it brought him instant grief he could hold in no longer.

His throat swelled and his breath hitched as he followed the officer into the brightly lit room that smelled of formaldehyde. Bile rose up in his throat, and he feared he might vomit, but he was determined to stay strong.

It wasn't his mother that was dead. They'd made a mistake—Kyle had made a mistake.

He was stronger than this. He'd take a look at the body, and he'd laugh it off when it was over, because that's who he was. He wasn't a weak little boy—he was a man, and men didn't break down.

Get ahold of yourself before you embarrass yourself. Tough it up! And when it's over—walk it off.

Seth allowed the officer to lead him to a stainless steel slab that had been pulled from a wall filled with latched doors—like a big freezer. A body draped in a sheet lay on that slab, a pair of dainty feet poking out, a manila tag hanging from one toe. He shuddered and paused. This was like watching a TV show—except it was happening to him!

This was real.

He stopped.

He wasn't up for seeing a dead body. On the off-chance it *was* his mother lying there, he didn't want to know.

"Look," he said with a shaky voice. "I'm not the guy to do this. That isn't my mother. You need to get her family to identify her, and that ain't me!"

"I'm not going to force you, Son, but she's going to remain a *Jane Doe* until we can get a positive identification on her, and that could take months of searching through missing person files. It might even be impossible if there's no record of her because she's Amish."

"Amish!" Seth said with a raised voice. "My mother wasn't Amish! Now I *know* you've got the wrong guy."

Seth stormed out of the morgue and came face-to-face with Kyle. He paused, not saying a word.

"I'm sorry," Kyle offered. "I didn't want you to find out this way!"

Chapter 8

Zeb sat in the cold room with the two-way mirror staring straight ahead. He knew why he was there, but he had nothing to say to these *Englishers.* They had no idea how hard he'd worked to keep the sins of his past hidden, hoping that one day he'd be welcomed back into the community he'd felt lost without. They didn't care about him or what he needed. They'd interrupted his one chance at seeking the forgiveness he desperately needed, and now he would be forever banned. There would be no more chances, and no peace for him.

"Let me begin by informing you that we found your DNA on the body, but we don't believe you killed her," the detective said to Zeb. "I think you already know we found someone else's DNA on her body too. Most of it was under her fingernails—probably from scratching the person who strangled her. I think you know who did this. We have reason to believe you were present at the scene of the crime, and possibly helped to bury her body in your back yard!"

He'd been read his rights. He knew he had the right to keep silent, and he intended to exercise that right.

"You can tell us the truth and help us catch the person who killed her, or you might end up having to stand trial alone, and face murder charges."

His threats meant nothing to Zeb. He no longer cared what happened to him. The only thing that mattered to him was hearing the words he longed to hear from the Bishop—the words of forgiveness the man never got a chance to speak to him. Zeb desperately needed those words in order to have peace. His very soul depended on them.

"We've done the autopsy, but we still don't have a positive ID on the body. Perhaps you want to tell us who she is so we can contact her family."

Zeb looked beyond the officer and stared at the dark, mirrored wall, wondering who was watching him from behind the glass.

He remained silent.

"Have it your way, Mr. Yoder," the officer warned. "Just understand the more you're able to tell us, the easier things will go for you. Especially since we have a new report of another grave with the wrong woman lying in it—a woman we understand you may have poisoned."

Zeb thought of his beloved Rose. She'd betrayed him—threatened to tell the Bishop and their son of his infidelity and indiscretions. He knew it was only a matter of time before she drank the tea he'd brought her. He'd read in the newspaper they'd not only mistaken her body to be that of his mistress, Selma, but they'd also ruled her death as accidental. The blow to her head when she'd hit the glass table had been the cause of death on record. He knew better. He knew she'd fallen because of the tea. At the time, it had been the perfect crime of passion, but now, it seemed that Selma had spoken out, and there would be no explanation that would keep suspicion from linking him to the crime.

Chapter 9

Seth pushed past his cousin, not willing to entertain his foolish notions. Not only did he look ridiculous, but he wasn't about to engage in a confrontation with him right now. He was angry, there was no doubt about that, but he had some things to sort out, and his foolish cousin would only be in his way.

"Wait a minute Seth," Kyle said, calling after him as he followed closely on his heels. "I want to talk to you about this."

"I have nothing to say to you, *Cousin,*" he said angrily over his shoulder. "We have absolutely nothing to talk about!"

"What about your mother?" Kyle started to ask.

Seth turned on his heels and leered at Kyle. "That woman in that morgue is *not* my mother!" he said through gritted teeth. "And I don't appreciate this game you're playing with me."

"I'm not playing any game," Kyle pleaded with him. "This is serious."

Seth turned around and stopped suddenly, his breath coming out in ragged blows. "If you're not playing games with me," he said. "Then why are you dressed like an Amish man? Is this some sort of sick, April Fool's joke? You're celebrating a little early for that, don't you think?"

"I can assure you, Cousin, this is no joke!"

"Not a joke, huh? Then why did I have a police officer telling me that your *father*," he said, holding up his fingers to make air-quotes. "Is an Amish man?"

Kyle hung his head and looked down at the freshly-buffed square tiles of the floor, and blew out a heavy sigh. "It's a very long story, and I didn't want you to hear about all of this—not now—not like this. I was trying to find you so I could break the news to you gently."

"What news, Kyle? What news could you possibly have for me? That you decided to be Amish? That you like playing tricks on people and making them think their mother is dead? Or do you just get pure joy from ticking me off?"

"I don't even know what to tell you first," he said, discouragement clouding his thoughts. "Honestly, I just found out that my mother was really Amish."

"And how did you come to such an idiotic conclusion, *Cousin?* And I use that term lightly!"

"Because my mother has been alive all this time," he began.

"And mine isn't?" Seth interrupted, his jaw clenched.

"I don't know," Kyle said quietly. "I have a lot to tell you, but things are a bit of a mess right now."

Seth threw his head back and chuckled angrily.

"Such as you being Amish, and your mother being alive? I went to your mother's funeral with you, do you remember?" he said, wagging his finger at Kyle. "I saw her body in the casket with my own eyes."

"I did too," Kyle said, swallowing a lump in his throat, remembering how he'd felt that day. "It turns out it was her sister that died, and we mistook her for my mother, but that doesn't change the fact that you need to see if that woman in there is *your* mother."

"Let's not talk about that right now! Let's talk about you and this Amish get-up," he said, flicking Kyle's black hat with the back of his hand.

"This is all because I'm embracing my mother's Amish heritage. That, and I'm in love with an Amish girl. But none of that is important right now. What's important, is *your* mother."

"*My* mother is in Florida right now with my father, and they're both alive and well. My mother is not that woman lying on that cold slab wearing a toe tag!"

"Did you even look at her?" Kyle dared to ask.

"Why would I look at the dead body of a woman I don't know?" he said, as he began to walk away. "Let her family take care of her!"

"But *we* are her family," Kyle said around the lump in his throat. "Don't you want to know what happened to her?"

Seth bit back tears. "It's not my problem what happened to that woman! And for the record, *you* are not my family—especially if you're Amish!"

"But what about your mother?" Kyle argued.

"If that's my mother in there, maybe I don't want to know. But I do want to know more about the man who killed that woman. I hear it was your *father*. Funny, but did your father come back from the dead too?"

"No, actually," he said with downcast eyes. "It just so happens, I found out recently that my father is also an Amish man."

"The same one who killed that woman in there?" Seth accused.

Kyle sighed. "Quite possibly," he said, feeling embarrassed. "I wanted to tell you everything, but so much has happened recently that I just haven't had time to contact you. But I was trying to find you to tell you this news."

"Again, Cousin," Seth said coldly. "What news could you possibly have for me? If it has anything to do with that dead woman lying in there, I don't want to hear it."

"Seth, I'm sorry," Kyle pleaded with him. "I didn't want to hear it when I found out my own mother was gone, but it turns out she wasn't the one that had died. It's a long, sordid story, and I don't have time to go into that now. I'll tell you all about it later. Right now, that woman in there deserves to be identified."

"Not by me!" Seth said angrily.

"Not even if it turns out she's your mother?" Kyle asked.

Seth narrowed his gaze on his cousin.

"Especially if she's my mother!"

Chapter 10

Seth stood outside the morgue and lit his cigarette, closing his eyes and inhaling deeply, holding it there for a moment to calm his nerves. Kyle exited the building, following closely on Seth's heels. He'd allowed him to ride down the elevator alone, hoping it would give him a moment to calm down, but now he needed to talk to him and try to reason with him.

"What was that all about, Cousin?" Kyle asked when he caught up with Seth.

"I don't know," he replied angrily. "All I do know, is that we're not cousins!"

"You've known me your whole life," Kyle argued. "I might call you friend in addition to *cousin,* but we're as polar opposite as two guys can be. We always have been, but that doesn't make us any less family."

"I think it's finally obvious you and I are *not* family," he said, letting his gaze travel over Kyle's attire.

Kyle shook his head with disgust. "I've known you my whole entire life, Seth, and I'd have to say that walking out of that morgue before making sure that woman was not your mother, was the most selfish thing you've ever done."

"Kyle, you look ridiculous. Really, you're embarrassing yourself."

"Never mind about me; we're talking about *you* right now."

"No, Cousin, we're talking about you, and how ridiculous you are," Seth said with an angry chuckle. "I can't even take you seriously in that Amish get-up!"

"I might look ridiculous to you, but for the first time in my life, I know who I am, and I'm embracing it. My mother hid from me and the world, who she was. She was Amish, and there's no shame in that."

"And what of your new *father*? He's a murderer, and he's Amish. Are you proud of the heritage that a murderer passed down to you?"

"I'm not responsible for his sins. There are bad people all over the world, and being Amish doesn't make you immune to sin. But it's not up to us if he's forgiven; his judgment will come from God, not from us. I'll admit it doesn't sit well with me to have a blood relative who's in this kind of trouble, but in all fairness, you've been quite troublesome yourself for a while now, and I still care what happens to you."

Seth took an aggressive step toward Kyle and gritted his teeth. "You dare compare my harmless mischief to the crimes of murder?"

"No one said anything about comparing you, but a sin is a sin, no matter how big or small."

"So now you're calling me a sinner, Cousin?"

"We're all sinners, but each of us is equally entitled to the forgiveness that God offers, no matter how big or small our sins are."

"Don't preach to me, Cousin," Seth said bitterly. "Until you can convince me that you're perfect, you've got no room to talk."

"I *don't* have any room to talk, but the difference between you and me is that I'm willing to admit I'm a sinner. But we're getting off track. Whether we're blood relative or not; in my heart, you'll always be my cousin. But above all, you're my friend, and I loved your mother as my aunt. I, for one, want to know what happened to her. I hope you're with me on that, because I'd hate to think I have to deal with this all alone, just because you want to bail every time things get a little too uncomfortable for you. When you're part of a family, you do whatever it takes for those you love. In family, there's no room for selfishness of any kind. If it affects you, it affects me. I've got your back, but I hope you've got mine if things get rough."

Seth rolled his eyes. "You say that now, but where were you all this time I've needed you. I'm not sure if you realize it, but I've been without a family life for quite some time."

"Honestly, Seth, you really have only yourself to blame. I've been here all along, and you've made the choice to hang out with people who are walking the thin line of the law. I imagine you're walking that fine line yourself a little, or you wouldn't have gotten here the way you did," he said, gesturing to the building where the woman was waiting to be identified.

Seth pulled his collar up to keep out the snow.

"What are you talking about?"

"I'm talking about the police officer who brought you here. I got a phone call explaining to me that you almost got carted off to jail, but instead, he brought you here on my insistence."

"So now I should be grateful to you for doing me a favor?"

Kyle gestured to the dark sky against the soft glow of the lamps that illuminated the light snow flurries.

"You may not be aware of the time, Seth, but it's the middle of the night! I wouldn't be here, except I made the officers who unearthed that woman's body promise me that if they found you or your sisters, or Uncle Jack, that they were to call me—day or night. I was *that* worried my family would have to go through this alone. I wanted to be here to explain the best I could about this because I didn't want any of you to have to hear it from strangers."

Seth scoffed. "In case you hadn't already noticed, we *are* strangers. Go back to your perfect, Amish world where people get away with murder, and leave me alone. I'm going home to get some sleep."

"No one is getting away with anything, Seth. He's been arrested, and he'll stand trial the same as anyone else, but the outcome will be up to the justice system, not you or me."

"What about—*her?*" Seth asked. "Where was her justice?"

"You're right, there was *no* justice for her, but she certainly has the right to be identified."

"Let's get something straight, *Cousin.* The *only* reason I'm here is so I could avoid jail. That officer caught up with me a second time, and I had to cooperate with him, or get myself arrested. So, I agreed to come look at a dead body. Turns out, my stomach is weaker than I thought it was, and I couldn't go through with it. I think I'd rather go to jail than to go in there and face the possibility of that dead woman being my mother."

Seth bit his lower lip and turned away from Kyle to keep him from seeing the emotion that overcame him. He would not break down in front of the *Golden Boy.*

Everything had always come easy for Kyle. From school, to making friends—the right kind of friends. Kyle had a way about him that made him always rise to the top, no matter what. He was smart in a way that Seth couldn't grasp. He was everything opposite from Seth. He, himself, was by no means unintelligent, but he seemed to use his smarts for the wrong things—things that seemed to bring him nothing but trouble. He was certain Kyle had never been in the slightest of trouble.

"You don't have to go in there alone," Kyle offered. "I'll be right there with you. And no matter which way it turns out, I'll be here for you."

"We've come a long way from becoming *blood brothers* when we were kids, Kyle."

He nodded. "It's true; we aren't boys anymore, but the pact I made with you still remains. We may not be cousins, but I'll always honor that blood brother pact I made with you when we were just kids."

Seth nodded slowly and agreed to go with Kyle back into the building. The only thing that would drive him back to the elevator was remembering the last words he'd spoken to his mother. He'd made a promise to her the day she and his dad had left for Florida.

He'd promised to straighten out his life, and he'd let her down.

Chapter 11

Seth took one last drag of a cigarette before snuffing it out with the toe of his boot. He paused, wondering if there was a way to avoid what he was about to do but nothing came to him. His mind was too cluttered with fear of the possibility that his mother was dead. Kyle would not let him out of his obligation no matter how much he protested. Deep down, he knew he owed his mother that much and more, but that didn't make it any easier.

Seth counted the floor tiles as he walked over each one along the long cold corridor that led to the morgue. He knew if he didn't keep his mind occupied on something that mattered very little, he feared he might go mad just from the terror that he felt deep within his gut. The clack of his boots kept time with Kyle's, the sound echoing like wild horses thundering across wide-open country.

He tried to reason with himself that Kyle had mistaken the woman's identity, and he'd hear from his parents any day now. He'd make the changes he'd promised his mother, and his family would be together again the way they were when he was a young boy.

His mind flashed to the last Christmas they'd spent together, and the strain of his condescending sisters and their perfect lives being shoved down his throat. He'd been glad his parents had packed up and left on their cross-country trip. It had meant he no longer had to be accountable for his actions—despite the promise he'd made to his mother to change his ways.

There would be no more empty promises over a piece of her molasses pie that he loved so much. What was it she'd called that pie?

Shoo-fly pie.

They'd come to the end of the corridor, and the end of Seth's aimless thoughts. There was no turning back now.

Kyle flashed him a look of compassion as he pushed open the heavy door to the morgue, where the coroner was closing the woman's body back into the freezer. Glancing back at them, he pulled the drawer back open and pulled back the sheet without saying a word to either of them. He took a step back and busied himself in the corner as Kyle moved further into the room, Seth in his shadow.

Kyle glanced over his shoulder at his cousin, who seemed to be cowering near the door. His look of disappointment sent his cousin across the room toward the body on the slab.

There, he stood frozen, just like the body.

Seth stared with unseeing eyes at the woman on the slab. He didn't dare feel; didn't dare think, lest he would break down. He'd been brought up to be strong; he was taught that only girls and the weak cry. Swallowing down the lump that formed in his throat, he clenched his jaw against the emotion that threatened to bring tears; tears that would show weakness.

Anger filled him as his gaze traveled to the look of unrest on her decayed face. He'd been told that her body had been mostly preserved due to the cold weather conditions at the time of her burial. Regardless, he'd know his mother, and this woman was certainly her, but how?

"My father," Seth managed quietly without turning away from her. "Has anyone told him yet, or has he known all this time and didn't tell me? Where could he be all this time? Why isn't he here?"

"The police are following a lead to an address I found," Kyle said. "It was from a post office in Florida, but the letter was post-marked Pigeon Hollow."

"What sort of letter?"

"It was a letter from your parents to your sister, and it claimed they'd arrived in Florida, but it was post-marked here. Like I said, it doesn't make any sense."

Seth stared at his mother's face. Her hair was smoothed back, and lacked the luster it once had. Her skin was grey, and looked almost rubbery—like the dolphins at the aquarium.

"I'd say she's proof they didn't make it out of the county, and they certainly never made it to Florida."

Kyle swallowed hard the lump in his throat at the realization of Seth's confirmation.

The coroner stepped forward. "Can you confirm her identity?"

He nodded coldly as he took in a deep breath and blew it out slowly, trying to control his emotions.

Kyle put a hand on his shoulder. "Do you need a moment?"

He shook his head slightly. "There isn't anything I can do for her here."

"I have some paperwork I'll need you to fill out," he said with a clinical sort of automation.

Kyle supposed the man had become immune to the emotions of the loved-ones who would have to do the identifying. Still, his lack of compassion was a little unnerving.

"Where's that letter?" Seth asked. "I need to see if it's my mother's handwriting on it."

Chapter 12

Kyle stared out the kitchen window, washing his hands for dinner. He turned back to look at Caleb, who was putting a pot of stew on the table for his wife.

"Hey," he said. "There's a light on at the old man's house."

Caleb crossed the room and stood at the window with his brother. He turned to Kyle, his face flushed. "You don't suppose he's holding someone else hostage over there, do you?" He asked half-jokingly.

Kyle reflected for a moment on the terror his mother had suffered at the hands of Zeb Yoder, and his heart beat hard against his chest wall.

"Well, I think we can pretty much rule out the old man since he's in jail, but I had no idea he had electricity in the house."

"He doesn't," Caleb said matter-of-factly. "Which means, whoever is in there probably flipped on the switch to the gas lights without knowing they were gas."

"Do you think it could be a prowler? Maybe we should go check it out." Kyle said.

Caleb looked at Amelia, and she shooed him with her hand. "Go ahead," she said before he asked. "I'll hold dinner for you. I know if you don't go check it out, you'll be getting up every five minutes and looking out the window out of curiosity."

Caleb smiled and kissed his wife on the cheek.

"We won't be long, I promise."

The two men put on their coats and shouldered out into the cold, dark night. Once outside, Kyle unlocked the doors to his truck and they hopped in, both shivering. After starting the engine, Kyle reached under the seat and pulled out a black box and set it on the middle armrest.

Before Caleb could ask what was in the box, Kyle opened it and pulled out a large handgun. He checked the chamber and then loaded the clip. He put it back in the box without a word.

"You really think we need a gun to go over there?" Caleb asked him.

"Yes, brother, I do think I need a gun to go over there. After all the dead bodies and hostages that have turned up, I think we need to start protecting ourselves. There's no reason for anyone to be over at the old man's house, and I don't plan on being ambushed."

Caleb agreed he had a point, but having a gun in the mix made him feel a little uneasy. Had it really come to this?

They drove the short distance in silence, the tension thick between them. When he reached the driveway, he turned off his headlights and rolled up the driveway slowly. When they reached the barn, he shut off the engine and they opened the doors quietly. Kyle stuffed the gun in the back of his pants and pulled his coat over it as they walked carefully toward the house, the snow crunching beneath their boots.

As they approached the house, Caleb realized they hadn't discussed what they planned on doing if they encountered the intruder.

Kyle crept under the kitchen window where the lights were on, ducking close to the house as he slid in next to the frame. He motioned for Caleb to stick close to the house so he wouldn't be seen.

Then he pulled the gun out from the back of his pants and peered up into the window.

The kitchen was empty.

His heart did a flip-flop behind his ribcage, anticipation raising the hair on the back of his neck.

"Anyone in there?" Caleb whispered.

Kyle shook his head, and then listened to a noise that seemed to be coming from the next room in the house.

The lights went on in the living room, and Kyle advanced to that window to get a better look.

As he peered inside, he let out his breath and lowered his gun, shaking his head.

"I don't believe it," he said, walking toward the front porch.

"What?" Caleb called after him in a loud whisper. "Who's in there?"

Kyle was already on the porch, fast approaching the door, when he suddenly burst through it.

The dark-haired man dropped the stack of papers he was holding, and looked up at Kyle and Caleb as they entered the house.

"What are you doing here?" Kyle demanded.

"Are you planning on shooting me, Cousin?" Seth asked.

Kyle furrowed his brow as he stuffed the gun in the back of his pants. "Never mind that! I want to know what you're doing here."

Caleb got between the two of them. "I'd like it if someone would explain to *me* what's going on here. You know him?" he asked his brother.

"He's sort of my cousin."

Caleb nodded. He'd heard the story of the Sinclair family, and how they'd taken Kyle in when he and his mom were having problems.

He extended his hand politely. "You must be Seth; I'm Caleb Yoder."

Seth's lips formed a thin line. "Yoder?" he said through gritted teeth. "You're kin to this murderer too?"

Caleb held his hands up and shook his head. "Not by choice—no more than Kyle."

"That makes you both just as accountable for what happened to my mother—just by your association with this murderer."

"That's not fair!" Kyle said, raising his voice. "We didn't do it. We were just as surprised as you were!"

"You still haven't answered my question," Kyle continued. "What are you doing here?"

Seth blew out a sigh and motioned to the mess he'd made of the old man's house. "I'm looking for clues."

"Maybe you should let the authorities handle the investigation," Caleb advised him.

Seth took an aggressive step toward him. "What have they done to help any of the old man's victims so far?"

Caleb had to agree he had a point, but he didn't like the idea of Seth snooping around, and perhaps messing with evidence that could be used in the investigation.

"How'd you get in here, anyway?"

"The same way you just did—through the door!"

"Did you break in?" Caleb grilled him.

"No! The door was unlocked."

Caleb thought back to the Bishop's visit, and realized they had been so wrapped up in unearthing the body of the Amish woman, they had probably left the door unlocked.

"Say, how do you explain the Amish clothing she was wearing when—you know…" Caleb stammered.

"When your father murdered her?" Seth accused. "Maybe he has some strange fetish with Amish women, and he made her wear the clothes before he did the deed!"

"You're not Amish?" Caleb asked.

"No!" Seth said with a chuckle. "You can't see that just by looking at me?"

Caleb shrugged. "I thought perhaps your mother might have been. Kyle didn't know his mom was Amish until recently."

Seth leered at him. "Let me just stop you right there. My mother wasn't Amish, and there was no deep dark secret involved with her death. I think your old man just likes to…*hurt women!*"

"I'm not going to argue with you there, but don't lump us in with him," Kyle said. "We're just as invested in finding out what happened as you are."

"No you're not!" he accused his cousin. "Your mother is alive!"

"Mine isn't," Caleb stepped in. "He poisoned *my* mother!"

Seth's look softened a little, and he lowered his gaze. "I didn't know that."

"Now that you do, perhaps we can all work together."

"Why don't you come back to the house with us and have a little dinner," Kyle offered.

Seth looked around at the mess he'd made. "I am a little hungry."

"It's settled then," Caleb said. "My wife made enough beef stew and biscuits to feed an army, and she'll be happy to set another place for you."

He nodded and grabbed his coat.

"You want to get the lights?" Caleb asked.

Seth shook his head. "I plan on coming back after we eat!"

"I'm not so sure that's a good idea," Kyle said.

"Look here, Cousin; I plan on camping out here until I find something solid that explains why the old man did what he did!"

"I don't think anyone but him knows why he's done the things he's done," Caleb said soberly.

"I'm not sure if the old man can do anything about you being here, but…"

Seth held up a hand to interrupt him. "The old man is never going to know. He's in jail, right?"

"Yeah, but what about the police? What if they think you're interfering with their investigation?"

He smirked. "They don't have a choice!"

Chapter 13

Seth tossed his cigarette out the car window as he turned into the long drive that led to the Amish farmhouse. He'd followed Kyle back to Caleb's home, who had turned out to be his half-brother. His cousin's life, it would seem, had become even more complicated than his own, if that was possible. He was numb, and needed some time to think. He certainly wasn't in the mood for socializing, but his growling stomach betrayed his need for solitude.

His sisters had turned him away the last few times he'd spoken to them, and so he'd decided to allow the authorities to break the news to them. He knew it was the coward's way out, but he just couldn't face them after the last conversation he'd had with them.

They'd both complained he wasn't a good influence on his young nephews and nieces. They were right, and he wondered if things would be more estranged between them once they learned the news of their mother. He felt guilty for not being there when the news was broken to them, but he feared he wouldn't be well received.

Anger raged inside him at the thought of the anguish his mother had suffered at the hands of the man who'd killed her. And now, he was about to break bread with the descendants of the murderer. How could he possibly explain his association with this family to his sisters? It would only perpetuate their distrust for him. They likely wouldn't accept Kyle's connection to the man, nor his close relationship with the son who'd grown up with the murderer.

Things were becoming more complicated by the minute, and he wasn't sure he was ready for all of this acceptance just yet. He couldn't look the other way and become friends with Caleb, and he certainly couldn't account for his cousin's blindness to the situation.

He pulled his car in behind Kyle's truck, wondering if he'd be able to desensitize himself to the death of his mother long enough to be cordial during dinner. He couldn't help but feel that he'd traded his loyalty to his mother for a home-cooked meal.

Suddenly feeling sick in his gut, he took a deep breath of the damp, wintry air and blew it out slowly. He hoped it would make him feel better, but it didn't. He was certain his mother would be rolling over in her grave— that is, if she was in a proper one yet.

He worried about the arrangements, even though he knew his sisters would take over the situation and handle things *their way*. He wasn't looking forward to facing his family at the funeral, especially since he'd not done as he'd promised and set his life on the straight-and-narrow path.

It was too late for all of that anyway. He'd failed to make his mother proud in her last days on this earth, and it weighed heavily on his heart.

He exited his car and pulled out a cigarette, flicking his Zippo to light it, and suddenly changed his mind, realizing he no longer had the stomach for it.

Stuffing the cigarette back in the box, and the lighter in his pocket, he followed his cousin into Caleb's house, the wonderful aroma of food momentarily clouding over the feeling of unrest that plagued him.

As they entered in through the kitchen, introductions were made, and Seth robotically greeted each of the women with feigned interest.

All, except for one—Kyle's mother.

He was more than a little interested in how she managed to escape the old man's captivity, and come out of it alive. Especially since his own mother had failed to do so.

Seth intended to grill her for information about the old man. He wanted to know all he could about the man, and what made him tick. He would study the man's character through his victim's eyes if need-be in order to prove his guilt for the crime. Though he wasn't wild about the idea of getting into the mind of a murderer, he knew that learning his character traits would help solve what happened. After all, he'd watched enough of those forensic shows that he figured he was smart enough to figure it all out.

How hard could it be?

Chapter 14

"Seth, you can't be serious about staying at the old man's house, could you?" Kyle asked.

"I was really hoping your mom could give me some information I could use to figure out why this happened, but all she did was confuse me by telling me how much she missed me, and what good of friends she and my mother were when they were young," he complained. "So, yes! I'm absolutely going to stay at his house. I figure he owes me that much."

"Are you homeless?" Kyle caught him off-guard with the remark.

He shifted his weight from one foot to the other, and looked off in the distance.

"Not exactly. I lost my condo in a poker game, and I've been living in the rat-infested loft of the guy who won it. I've been there for the last two weeks," he admitted. "But as soon as Frankie sets up the big game for me on Saturday, I'll get my condo back from that hustler!"

"Isn't that what *you've* become? A hustler?"

"Don't judge me, Amish boy!"

"I personally don't care if you stay there, but I can't answer for Caleb."

"How does it feel to find out after all these years that your old man is a murderer?" Seth accused.

"What he's done has nothing to do with me— any more than my choices in life would affect him!"

"Whatever," Seth grumbled.

"Just be careful," Kyle warned his cousin. "I'm not sure how well it would go over with the detective if you mess up his investigation."

"He isn't doing his job fast enough for me!" he said snuffing out the cigarette he'd taken only one drag from.

"I'll come over there tomorrow afternoon and see if you've come up with anything. I think I'm going to sleep in a little tomorrow. This stress has caused me to lose a lot of sleep. You could stand to get some yourself. Don't stay awake all night."

"I'm a grown man, Cousin," he growled. "I think I can decide for myself when I need sleep."

With that, he hopped in his BMW and backed down the driveway. He had nothing more to say to his overbearing cousin. His only thoughts were of his mother, and finding out exactly what happened to her.

Within minutes, he'd pulled into the driveway of the Yoder farm, realizing the lights were off. Had Kyle gone behind him and turned out the lights? Strangely, he couldn't' remember. The only thing he could remember was the remark about turning them off, but now he couldn't be sure if they were on or off when they'd left the house.

He grabbed a flashlight from the trunk and proceeded into the house. If, for some reason, the gas lights weren't working, he'd have to locate the lanterns he'd seen scattered around the place earlier.

Once on the porch, he stomped the snow off his boots and went inside, trying the light switch.

Nothing.

He flicked the switch of his flashlight, but the batteries were low, and only a dim light glowed from the end. He tapped the end of it, knowing sometimes it would make the bulb brighter, but this time it failed him.

The familiar, metallic click of a pump-action shotgun from the other side of the room stopped him dead in his tracks. He raised the short beam of the flashlight with a shaky hand, aiming it on an old man with a long, white beard.

"You're trespassing!" the old man barked.

"Who are you?" Seth asked, backing toward the door.

The man pointed the gun at him. "I should be asking you that question since this is my *haus,* and you're trespassing!"

Seth could feel the blood draining from his head. He was dizzy, and breathing was suddenly difficult for him.

"You killed my mother!" Seth accused, as he charged toward the old man, adrenaline making him fearless of the danger.

With one quick motion, Zeb jerked the gun to the left and shot toward the wall, and Seth felt a sting penetrating the flesh of his shoulder.

His flashlight hit the floor, and the narrow beam went dark.

"Are you completely crazy, Old Man?" Seth shouted. "You shot me!"

The old man chuckled. "I just winged you with a stray pellet. Next time it'll be a gut-shot. Now get back real slow, and keep your hands where I can see them while you explain to me why you're trespassing on my property!"

"Why don't you tell me how you escaped from jail!" Seth demanded.

"They can't hold a man on suspicion," Zeb said, striking a match and lighting a lantern.

"Suspicion?" Seth accused. "You're a murderer!"

"They don't have any proof," he said with a chuckle. "All they have is hearsay!"

"What about Kyle's mom? She can testify to you kidnapping her!"

"She isn't going to press any charges against me!"

"How can you be so sure of that?" he asked, gazing around the room for anything he could use to overpower the man with the gun pointed at him.

"Amish ways are forgiveness," he said, calmly.

"Well, I don't forgive you for murdering my mother; I'll press charges against you!"

"You must be Seth," Zeb said casually. "And you're wrong. I didn't kill your mother, her husband did!"

Chapter 15

"You're insane! My father wouldn't do such a thing!"

"Your father?" Zeb asked casually. "Now that's where you're wrong."

Seth's heart sped up, but he couldn't resist asking the question. "What am I wrong about?"

"Jack Sinclair isn't your father!"

"Yeah? Who do you suppose is my father? You?"

Zeb chuckled. "Now you're catching on, boy!"

"You're a liar!" he shouted. "My mother was in love with my father, and she wouldn't take up with the likes of you!"

Zeb looked him in the eye, his expression twinkling with delight over Seth's reaction to the news. "We were young then, and she was acquainted with Jack at the time. As a matter of fact, she married him only two short weeks after spending the night with me in my parent's barn."

Seth could feel his torso weakening, his knees wobbling at the very thought of it. He clutched his middle, wondering if he would lose his dinner. He cringed as he set his gaze upon the old man.

It wasn't true. It couldn't be.

Sweat formed on his brow, the sting of the shotgun pellet fading in comparison to the words the old man spoke. Kyle had described the same situation with the old man. He'd said the same words to him, but why would he be saying them now?

It was absurd to even think about.

Still, it had turned out to be the truth for Kyle.

Unable to stand any longer on his wobbly legs, Seth dropped to his knees, tunnel vision threatening a total blackout.

His thoughts reeled.

Being the son of a murderer was not something he could live with. Was his relation to the old man the reason behind his rebellious streak that Jack could never seem to tame?

"Did my father—*Jack,* know about—what you're saying?"

"Your mother had deceived him all those years," the old man reflected. "I agreed to keep her confidence as long as she came to *visit* me on a regular basis."

Seth could feel the bile rising in his throat at the old man's statement.

"My mother wouldn't have betrayed my father like that."

"The day she died, she came to see me. She came to tell me goodbye; that she was leaving for Florida with her husband. Naturally, I couldn't let her go."

"So you killed her!" Seth accused weakly.

"I loved her; I wouldn't kill her."

"You didn't love her! You might have sewed some wild oats with her when the two of you were young, but you did *not love* her!"

Zeb smiled. "*Jah,* the days during our *rumspringa* were quite joyful."

Seth had only just found out what that term meant at dinner, having discussed the old man being Kyle's father.

And now he was claiming to be Seth's father!

That would make me Amish—and a brother to Kyle and Caleb, he thought.

"Those days might have been joyful for you— sewing your wild oats all over the community, but if it was so great for the young girls you took advantage of, they would have stayed with you instead of marrying other men."

"Well, I can't deny that Rose was my true love."

"Isn't she Caleb's mother? The one you poisoned?"

"She was going to expose my sins to the Bishop!"

Seth held a hand over his mouth, sure he was going to vomit.

"So you killed her to keep her quiet?"

"I merely banned her from my presence, and that of Caleb. She knew there was poison in the tea. I told her! It's not my fault she chose to drink it."

"Why don't we get back to *my mother,* and how you murdered her!"

Zeb raised the gun angrily. "I already told you, boy; I didn't kill your mother. Jack killed her."

A sudden feeling of dread made him sweat.

"Why do I get the feeling you know where my father is? The police can't find him, but I'd be willing to bet you know."

The old man smirked. "Your mother told me you were a betting man. What do you suppose the odds are that Jack is here?"

"I'd say pretty high," Seth said. "But I get the feeling the odds of him being alive are about zero!"

"I'd say you guessed that one right!"

Seth let out a strangled cry. "Oh, you didn't?"

"That was an accident—like the shot that hit you."

"That was no accident!" he sobbed. "It was deliberate. You pulled that trigger; the gun didn't go off by accident."

Zeb turned up the lantern. "I suppose you have me on that one, boy."

"Sounds like you're admitting you killed my father deliberately, too."

"Let's get something straight, boy. I'm your father—not Jack Sinclair. And the shot I took at him was just to scare him like I did to you just now, but I was a bit groggy still from being hit on the head by him. I told you he followed her that day, and when he overheard the truth, he had a breakdown and came at me with a shovel, ironically."

Seth found it hard to breathe. "What do you mean, *ironically?*"

"Because it's the same shovel I used to bury him," Zeb said gruffly.

Chapter 16

Seth remained doubled over. He was certainly exposing his weakness to the old man.

He stood and crossed the room, aiming the gun at Seth. "Get up!" Zeb ordered him. "Now that you're here, you're going to help me move Jack's body. If they find his grave, they'll take me back to jail, and I'm not going to let that happen."

Seth rose to his feet, contemplating whether or not to charge toward the old man. He knew the likelihood of him getting shot was pretty high, but he had no intention of helping him cover up murder. Now he understood what his mother meant all those times she tried to get him to change his ways. It all made sense; she didn't want him turning out like the man who shared his DNA.

Zeb ordered him out the door, and Seth remained quiet while he thought of a way out of his dilemma. His mother had instilled one good trait in him, and that was to remain silent when the situation called for it, which this one did.

If he resisted anymore, the old man would certainly shoot him. He also knew that the man was not dumb, and would know better than to let him go when he knew too much.

Seth concluded the only thing he could do was to cooperate. It was his only chance at staying alive.

They walked out the door, and Seth wondered if he could make it to his car before the shotgun went off. His shoulder still stung from the pellet lodged there, and the old man seemed like the type to shoot an unarmed man in the back.

Though he wasn't wild about digging up his father's grave, he knew he probably needed to see it for himself to believe it. He also knew, from watching cop shows on TV, that the likelihood of a killer turning on you was less if you could keep him talking. He knew it was foolish to put his trust in anything he'd ever seen on TV being true-to-life, but he had nothing else to hope for at the moment.

"Tell me what happened that night when my mother came to meet you."

"You really want to know the details of her death?"

"Yes!"

"Jack overheard our conversation and accused me of soiling your mother. He threatened to kill her so neither of us would have her," Zeb said from behind him.

They walked past his car, and he knew that even getting the old man to talk was not enough of a distraction to get away. He was certain he'd dropped his car keys on the floor when the old man had surprised him with the gun, so it was really a moot point anyway.

"You can get a shovel and a pickaxe out of the shed right there," Zeb told him. "And don't get any wise ideas about hitting me with it. I've already warned you I'll put a hole in your gut."

"You still didn't tell me how my mother died," Seth questioned him as he walked toward the shed.

Zeb stood behind him and held up the lantern so he could see to get the tools he'd need for digging.

"We got into a fight, and he hit me on the head with the shovel. When I came-to, he was choking your mother."

Seth turned sharply. "You expect me to believe that my own father strangled my mother? He loved her."

"I believe the *Englishers* called that a *crime of passion.*"

"How did my father die?"

Zeb pushed the gun between Seth's shoulder blades. "We need to get something straight, boy. I'm your father, and you better get used to saying it."

Seth swallowed hard and clenched his jaw as he lifted the pickaxe from its hook, contemplating the risk of swinging it at the old man and missing his target.

"Okay, how did *Jack* die?"

"Like I said, when I came-to, he was hunched over her and choking her. I picked up my gun and shot toward him. I was still a little wobbly from the blow to my head and I suppose I overshot. It killed him instantly. I didn't mean to, and I only did it to defend your mother. But when I went over to her, she was already dead."

His quivering voice when he mentioned her death didn't go unnoticed by Seth.

So *that* was the old man's kryptonite!

"Why did you lie to the police and say you had no idea how she'd gotten in the casket?"

"I didn't want them to take her away," Zeb admitted.

And there it was again! His weakness—the women in his life. It was all beginning to make sense to Seth. He loved them all. He may have had his favorite—Rose, Caleb's mother, but he actually loved them all—in his own sick way.

The real question was, how many more sons had the old man fathered? How many more would turn up? Would there be casualties attached to each of them?

Seth had to put his worries aside for the time-being and concentrate on not getting shot by the unstable man. Just because his first shot had only winged him, didn't mean he wasn't capable of shooting his own flesh-and-blood. He'd threatened it, and Seth figured he'd better take the old man seriously. After all, he'd held Kyle's mother captive, and had offered Caleb's mother death as an option to betraying him.

Seth remained silent as he walked the path to the edge of the Yoder property to the site where his mother had just been unearthed.

"That's far enough," Zeb barked at him. "Dig right there, next to the other hole."

He felt a shiver run through him. It wasn't the cold, night air that was to blame. The very thought of digging up his own father's grave filled him with enough terror, he worried he might lose consciousness. The only thing that kept his faculties intact was knowing he needed to stay alert if he was to stay alive.

His nerves jangled, and his hands shook. He needed a cigarette, and he needed one badly.

Reaching into his pocket, he pulled a cigarette from the pack and flicked his lighter.

Zeb motioned to him with the gun. "You put that out or I'll shoot you right now! You should quit. It's a disgusting habit."

"So is murder," Seth said as he tossed the lit cigarette down and snuffed it out with his boot. "But I don't see you quitting that!"

"Stop talking and dig!" the old man demanded.

After setting the shovel against a nearby tree, Seth swung the pickaxe, the pain in his left shoulder escalating. He groaned against the pain, but continued to swing. Every time it came down against the frozen ground, he wanted to yell, but he knew to do that could draw attention from the farmhouse across the field. He was surprised they hadn't heard the crack from the shotgun. Being inside when he got shot, it was possible the house muffled the sound just enough they wouldn't hear it from there, and if they did, they would likely not know what it was.

As much as he could use Kyle's and Caleb's help about now—especially his cousin's gun, he didn't want to put them in danger. Was it possible he had grown that mature in the last half hour? Perhaps getting shot by a man who claimed to be kin to him was enough to wake him up and *scare him straight!*

He continued to hack at the dirt until he hit something that made a dull thud. He was less than three feet down, thinking how careless it was of the old man to dig the graves so shallow. He supposed it was due to having done the digging himself to bury the bodies in the first place.

"How did you manage to dig both of these holes without help?" Seth asked.

Zeb jerked his head up from watching him dig, and looked Seth in the eye. "Who said I had help?"

"No one! It's just that I'm sure you have at least thirty years on me, and I'm struggling."

The old man furrowed his brow. "That's because your mother never made you work an honest day in your life. That's why you're lazy and take the sinner's way and gamble."

Like you have any right to be calling me a sinner, old man!

Seth had to admit the old man had a point, but he wasn't about to agree with him because he was acting smug and judging him when he had no right to.

"I don't know what information you *think* you're going to get out of me with all these questions, but you need to be quiet!"

"Being the gambling man that I am, I don't think you're going to shoot me now, because you need me to do the digging. It's obvious you can't do the digging yourself, or you'd have done it this time too! And since I don't think my chances of coming out of this alive are that great, I'd be willing to bet my father wasn't dead when the digging was done the first time, was he? Were you holding the gun on him then?"

The old man made an aggressive move toward him with the gun. "You shut your mouth," he said through clenched teeth. "Just shut your mouth."

Seth dropped the shovel, emotion clogging his throat at the sudden realization his father had been shot in cold blood. "Oh crap! You made him dig his own grave, didn't you?"

"I said shut up!" Zeb said, stepping toward him.

Tripping on a tree branch, the old man fell to the ground and the gun fired another shot.

Chapter 17

Seth hit the ground when the gun went off, but it wasn't enough to keep the fear from overtaking him. Before he could do anything to stop it, he began to lose consciousness. The last thing he remembered was light rain hitting his face.

"Was that thunder?" Caleb asked as he looked out at the rain.

"It sounded more like a shotgun to me!" Kyle answered. "But deer season is long over. Even so, the only farm within twenty miles is the old man's."

"You think it's possible Seth is over there playing target practice?"

"No! The Seth I know wouldn't have a shotgun. He might talk real tough, but when it comes right down to it, he's the exact opposite of tough, if you know what I mean!"

"Maybe we should go check it out," Caleb said.

"In this rain? It's coming down in buckets now, and the river is already so high because of all the rain and snow we had this year, this rain is probably going to cause a washout on the road."

Caleb thought for a moment about the risk of a washout, knowing his brother was right, but he had a bad feeling. "I still think we should check it out."

Zeb lifted himself from the rapidly melting snow and went over to Seth, who'd fallen face-first into the mud. The hole was rapidly filling with water, and he'd be covered in a matter of minutes. He knew he'd drown if he left him there, and to him, it was the perfect crime. It would be ruled an accidental death, and he wouldn't have to worry about the boy knowing his secrets that could put him in jail for the rest of his days.

He wasn't about to go back to jail willingly.

A light from the road caused him to look up at a pair of headlights coming from the direction of Caleb's farm. It would be a matter of minutes before the two boys would be here, and there was not enough time to make a rational decision about Seth. By the time they found him, he'd be drowned in the mud he was lying in, but Zeb knew if he didn't leave the scene, he'd be caught and blamed for his death too.

The only place to hide was the cellar. Beneath the rubble from the barn fire, the latch still remained, and the cellar was still usable. He walked fast, slipping several times in the slush, heavy rain drenching him.

When he reached the latch, he pulled it open quickly and put his foot on the top rung of the ladder going down. It gave-way under his weight, and Zeb plummeted to the bottom of the cellar, the wind knocked from his lungs.

He struggled to draw in air, panic filling him at the pain it caused. Even in his struggle to breathe, he knew he'd broken a few ribs on impact.

He wheezed and coughed, trying to get enough air in his lungs, but it was a struggle. Forcing himself over on his other side brought some relief, but he still didn't feel he was getting enough air. He'd broken ribs before, after being thrown from a horse he was trying to break, and he knew if he propped himself up, his breathing would be easier.

He slowly and painfully reached an arm toward the center beam in the cellar and dragged himself the three feet to reach it, sliding in mud the entire way. After propping himself up, he looked up and could see rain water pouring into the cellar at an alarming rate.

He chuckled to himself, figuring that he would suffer the same fate as young Seth in this storm. He knew the river was high, and with no barn to keep out the water, the washout would drain into the cellar, and he would probably drown.

Trapped, with broken ribs, there was no way he would get out. He couldn't help but think that it almost seemed like poetic justice to perish in the very same spot he'd held his loved-ones hostage, as he closed his eyes against the darkness that had already claimed him.

Kyle and Caleb jumped out of the truck and headed up the porch to the old man's house. They found it odd that the front door was wide open, but they hollered for Seth anyway.

Caleb tried the light switch, but nothing happened. Knowing the gas had to be turned off outside somewhere, he opted for lighting a lantern he found on the table.

Looking up at his brother, who still stood near the door waiting on the light, he pointed behind him at the hole in the wall.

Kyle went over and examined the spray of buckshot around the hole. "That's from a shotgun. We need to find Seth!"

They searched the house and found nothing.

"You don't suppose he's out there in this weather, do you?"

"His car is here and the door was open. This shotgun hole in the wall suggests he might not be alone."

Off in the distance, the sound of sirens filled their ears, and they were moving closer to the main road at the foot of the long dirt drive leading to their father's farm.

Caleb looked out at the line of police cars pulling into the driveway. "What do you suppose this is all about?"

"My guess is that the old man escaped!"

"No! How could he?"

"Not sure," Kyle said. "But I think we're about to find out what happened."

The two walked out to greet the police, but one of them stopped them abruptly.

"Stop right where you are!" he said, holding his gun out toward them. "Hand over Zebedee Yoder, and no one will get hurt."

"We don't know where he is," Kyle said. "What makes you think he's here?"

"He faked a heart attack, and when he was being transferred to the infirmary, he knocked out the guard and escaped."

"We think my cousin is here somewhere," Kyle said. "But we can't find him. Someone shot a hole in the wall inside the house with a shotgun, but there isn't any sign of the old man or Seth. Can you help us find them?"

"Let's search the grounds," one of them said.

The officers turned on their spotlights on their cars, aiming them out toward the acres of land behind the house.

"I have a million, candle-power spotlight in my truck we could use to go out and look around the property."

He was already at his truck retrieving it before anyone could protest. His only goal was to find Seth—hopefully alive.

Seth picked his head up out of the mud once more. Several minutes before, he'd watched the old man running away from him, and couldn't figure out why, but now he knew. He coughed and sputtered, trying to get the water he'd inhaled out of his lungs as he listened to the sirens coming closer. Muffled voices filled his head, but he was too weak and disoriented to yell out to them.

He tried to move, but his leg was stuck, and he was certain he'd slipped in the mud and was trapped between a thick wall of mud and his father's casket. He knew he'd hit his head pretty hard when he'd fallen, and he felt the sting most likely from an open wound on his scalp.

The voices neared him, but he wasn't certain he was dreaming them or not, and so remained in the mud-hole up to his neck now. The river water had washed in so fast, he was trapped pretty tightly against the heavy box that was still half-buried. Finding it increasingly hard to hold up his head, he gave in to the weakness and darkness that faded in and out, his head fully immersed in the muddy pool that surrounded him.

"I want you to stay here and let us handle this. We believe Mr. Yoder is armed, and he's dangerous," one of the officers warned them.

"You don't have to tell us how dangerous he is," Kyle said. "He's our father, so we know!"

"All the more reason for you to stay here and let us handle things."

"Yes, Sir," Kyle said.

Caleb turned to his brother once the officers were scattered along the property.

"Why did you tell him we'd stay here?"

"I just wanted him to leave us alone so we could go look for Seth," he answered.

"Then let's go!" Caleb urged him.

As soon as the last officer was out of site, the two grabbed Kyle's spotlight and went out to the opposite end of the property. They sloshed in the wet earth, rain still pouring down in thick sheets.

Kyle blinked away the rain, squinting against the heavy drops that blew sideways against them. "I hope we can find him out in this mess before the river rises too high."

He shone the flashlight toward the back of the property as they walked past the shed.

"The door is open!" Caleb remarked.

"I can see a shovel stuck in the ground out there, and it looks like someone might be out there too."

"Let's go!"

Terrible thoughts reeled in Kyle's head as they ran to the back of the property, trying not to slide in the slushy grass. The last thing he wanted to find back there was Seth buried where his mother used to be.

When they came upon the gravesite, they both grabbed Seth out of the muck and laid him face up.

"Is he still alive?" Caleb shouted above the rain.

Kyle collapsed to his knees at his cousin's side and swiftly pressed his head to his chest. "I can hear a heartbeat, but I can't tell if he's breathing."

Seth coughed up muddy water, and struggled to pull in air. They turned him on his side, and Kyle pounded on his back with enough force to help him cough up the rest of it so he could breathe.

He looked up at Kyle with a fading look. "My brother, you saved me."

"He's delirious!" Caleb said. "Should we call an ambulance?"

"No, he's not," Kyle said. "I think he's making perfect sense."

At that point, Kyle knew he'd had a run-in with the old man, and he'd heard the same frightening words he'd heard from him.

Seth was no longer just a blood brother from a childhood pact, he was a true blood brother who shared his same DNA.

Chapter 18

Seth tried to speak, but Kyle hushed him. It was important that he conserve his energy until the ambulance could arrive.

"The old man ran that way," Seth said weakly, barely lifting his arm to show the direction.

"He'd run into the barbed wire fence if he went that way," Kyle said. "It makes no sense for him to go that way. It isn't like the barn is there anymore."

"The barn might not be there anymore, but the cellar is!" Caleb said, as he took off running toward the rubble of the barn.

"Hey," he hollered, as he ran toward the officers. "I think I know where he is!"

He pointed to the hatch from the cellar door. "I think he might be down there."

One of the officers lifted the door and shone his flashlight down in the cellar. "Looks like this rain filled it with water. There's no telling how deep it's gotten, but judging by the flow we can see here, we might not find him alive if he's down there."

Caleb looked at the water draining into the cellar like a sewer on a city street.

The officer hollered into the hole, but Caleb noticed the top rung of the ladder looked freshly broken since the center shade of the wooden step was lighter than the charred outside.

He pointed it out to the officer, and they asked for a volunteer to go down there and look for Zeb.

"I'll go," Caleb offered.

"No, Son," the officer said. "I admire your bravery, but we have special training in emergency situations like this. With all this rain, the walls of that cellar could cave in, and we're better equipped to handle that stuff. Besides, that water is so cold, you could die of hypothermia if you're down there too long."

He motioned for his men to get a cinch collar and straps from the fire truck that had just arrived on the scene.

If he was down there, they might even need to extend the ladder over the opening to pull him and his rescuer out of the flooded cellar.

"I think I found him," the man below shouted up to the others. "No telling if he's alive or not; his face was half in the water, but I think he suffered hypothermia."

The fireman attached the cinch collar around Zeb and yanked on the straps. "Pull him up!"

The officers and fireman pulled on the straps to hoist him out of the cellar, while the fireman in the cellar hung on long enough to get to the ladder that was half-immersed in the cold water from the flooded river.

He watched as they pulled him out and began to revive him. Although Caleb was emotional, he felt a certain numbness to the idea that his father might not survive this. He'd done so much damage to everyone he loved, including himself. He'd probably harmed himself the most by putting more concern on acceptance from the community than he had on doing the right thing.

"We have a pulse," one of them said.

He's breathing on his own, but it's shallow," the other said.

They placed an oxygen mask on his face, but he didn't seem to be conscious. Sadly, Caleb had to wonder if it had been better if they had not tried to revive him.

Chapter 19

Paramedics lifted Seth into an ambulance, an oxygen mask on his face, and a splint on his leg.

He pulled the mask down and looked at Kyle. "I need to tell you something."

"The old man killed my father—Jack. He's in a casket where I was digging. He's also the one who shot me in the arm! I know he's confessed to being my real father, but I'm not like the rest of you. I intend to press charges against him!"

"Let's just concentrate on getting you better first—*brother!*"

"I like the sound of that!" he said, as he replaced the mask on his face and laid back on the stretcher, allowing the paramedics to close the door of the ambulance.

Caleb caught up with him just then, as they wheeled Zeb up on a stretcher.

"How is he?" Kyle asked.

"He's suffered hypothermia from being in the icy water so long, and he may have drowned. They didn't have to jump-start his heart, and he's breathing on his own, but he hasn't been conscious the whole time. How's your cousin?"

"Turns out my *cousin* is our *brother!*"

"You're kidding!"

"Nope! Makes me wonder how many more will turn up."

Caleb slapped Kyle on the back. "I went from being an only child to being part of a baseball team real fast!"

"Except poor Seth looks like the old man!"

"As long as he doesn't act like him, I'll be happy to welcome him into the family. I guess we're going to have to build another house."

Kyle chuckled. "I'd hold off on those plans. Seth is kind of a loner. It might take him longer to get used to the idea than it took for me!"

"Let's go tell the police they have another body to excavate, and then we'll go to the hospital. Seth should be out of surgery by the time we get there."

"We should say a few prayers for him—for both of them."

"I agree," Kyle said. "But let's get the hard part over first."

Caleb couldn't help but think that none of this was going to be easy. Life had certainly thrown them a few curve balls. But really, even that was an understatement.

When they caught up with the officers, they were driving stakes around the property, using trees where available, and even marking off certain areas with yellow tape that read: *Crime Scene Do Not Cross*.

"I'm afraid we have some more evidence you need to be aware of," Kyle began. "Where we found our brother, our old man was making him dig up another body—in the back."

He pointed to where they had just come from.

"I have to warn you that you need to stay off the property now. This is a crime scene, so let us handle everything from here on out. When we showed up here, it wasn't just to arrest Mr. Yoder for escaping. That hair sample you gave us from the funeral of the woman you thought might be the mother of one of you...well, it turns out the DNA doesn't match, which means we have another random murder on our hands."

Caleb felt his world fall out from under him all over again. "If the woman in that grave wasn't my mother, then that means my mother's body is out there missing somewhere."

Kyle patted him on the shoulder. "Or—it could mean she's still alive! Let's try to think positively."

Caleb could feel his heart beating double-time. "With three bodies turning up now, what do you think is the likelihood of her being alive? If she is, why hasn't she tried to contact me all this time?"

"It's possible she could be terrified of the old man, and doesn't dare come around—even if it means losing her son."

Caleb couldn't think about that. He didn't dare hope; didn't dare dream. He'd had to give that up as a child, and he wasn't about to pick it up again now.

Chapter 20

"I know what they told me is probably true," Seth said soberly. "I mean, that's their job to find out the truth, but I find it hard to believe that Jack strangled my mother. They called it a crime of passion."

"Let's not worry about that today, Brother," Kyle said. "Let's give your parents a proper funeral and burial."

The three brothers lifted the handle on one side of his mother's casket, ushers from the church on the other, and brought it to the front of the little white church she used to frequent. Then, they did the same with Jack's casket.

At the back of the church, a woman with short, red hair and dark sunglasses sat in the last pew.

Seth greeted her, introducing her as Rosa, who waited tables at the diner in Hartford.

Caleb shook as he looked at the *English* woman; her short, black dress and long, black coat making her look like a stranger, but he knew her as his mother, Rose.

He flung himself in her arms, and she pulled him close, the two of them sobbing.

"Why did you leave and become *English?*"

"Your father put me under the ban—from you! I'm only dressed this way to keep him from recognizing me. He likes plain, blond women, and this is the exact opposite of what he would pay any attention to. I've kept an eye on you from afar, but I stayed away to protect you. Then, when I read in the paper about all the bodies, and the fact he may never wake up, I figured it was safe to see you. I'm so sorry it had to be this way."

"I understand," he said, sniffling. "I've missed you. I have a lot to tell you. I'm married now, and she's expecting!"

"You mean I'm going to be a *grossmammi?*"

"Jah," he said chuckling. "Come with me, I'd like you to meet Amelia. Do you remember her?"

"I've seen you with her," his mother said. "I'm pleased you and Amelia found each other again after all these years, and I'd love to see her again, but I have to face my sister first. You understand, don't you?"

He kissed her on the cheek and nodded, escorting her to the front of the church, where her sister, Selma, sat with Amelia and her mother.

Chapter 21

The doors at the back of the church burst open suddenly, followed by a lot of gasps and hushed voices, as several police officers walked up the aisle toward the caskets.

"I'm sorry," one of the officers Seth recognized said to him. "But we're going to have to take the woman's body into custody for further investigation."

Seth felt anger rise up in him as he tried to stand between the officers and his mother's casket.

"Why are you doing this? Why would you take my mother's body when I'm about to bury her so she can finally rest in peace?"

The officer laid a hand on his shoulder. "I'm taking the body, because she's not your mother."

Seth felt his legs wobble. Was it possible for the bottom to fall out of his world more than once in the course of two days?

"I can explain," a familiar woman's voice called from the back of the church.

Seth thought he might pass out if he looked at her, but he had to confirm his suspicion. But how? Was this some sort of trick? He'd seen her body with his own eyes.

The sound of her footsteps as she made her way up the aisle filled Seth with a morbid sense of dread. He was too frightened to look; in case it wasn't true.

A soft hand rested on his wounded arm he still had propped in a sling. "I was told he shot you," she said in her soothing, gentle voice. It was the same voice that had calmed him at night when he was a young boy, the same soft voice that would reprimand him with love, and tell him funny stories that had kept him awake at night wanting more instead of putting him to sleep as her intentions were.

It was, without a doubt, the voice of his mother.

Chapter 22

Seth turned to look at her, nearly collapsing when he looked into her familiar blue eyes. He choked down a strangled cry as he pulled his mother into his arms.

"I thought you were dead," he sobbed and laughed at the same time. "I'm so glad I didn't lose you, Mom."

"That woman you were about to bury; she's my sister," his mother said. "She's actually your birth mother, but she's also my twin sister, Beth."

"What are you talking about? I didn't know you had a twin," he said. "Why didn't you ever tell me?"

"It's a long story," she said. "Let's sit down and talk for a minute so I can explain."

He followed her to the back pew where Caleb's mother had just sat only moments ago. That was a shock to him, and now, he knew just how Caleb must have been feeling.

She sat down and faced him, her cheeks tear-stained.

"Jack left me after we had a fight when all this came out just a few months ago, and I've been in hiding this whole time," she explained. "I was embarrassed that Jack had left me because he thought I was lying to him. I was angry with him, and we had words. He said he was leaving me, and there was no reasoning with him. I thought he would come back home after taking a drive to cool off, and we could talk and work things out. In the meantime, I figured I would warn Zeb that Jack had threatened to kill him for taking advantage of me—which never happened."

"Tell me first, how did I get to be your son?" he asked.

"My sister had come to stay with me while Jack was out of town on business. She and I gave birth on the same night, and we were alone with a midwife. My own son was stillborn, and my sister, Beth, also gave birth to a son. She asked me to raise him—you—as my own, because she was a single mother, and the child—you—belonged to Zeb Yoder. She didn't want to raise a child with him because he was a brutal man even then, and we knew of his other indiscretions; it was a small community. So, she replaced my stillborn son as her own and told Zeb the child died so he would leave her alone. But somehow, he found out and threatened to expose us all. He threatened to tell Jack I'd betrayed him, and by that time you were about seven years old, and I'd grown very attached to you. Beth made a decision to visit Zeb once a week to appease him and keep him from revealing the truth. We both accepted the burden to keep peace and to keep you safe."

"That doesn't explain why Jack—dad strangled you—her—my birth mother."

"I went to Zeb to warn him Jack had found out, and he should just come clean with everything, but Beth was already there, and Jack was not thinking straight. He was angry and wouldn't listen to Beth. He accused her as if she was me, making accusations that I'd betrayed him, and said he didn't believe a word I'd said. He even accused me of being with Zeb, and claimed he wondered if the twins were his children. The whole thing was a mess. He fought with Zeb and knocked him out, and then fought with Beth some more, still thinking she was me. Then, he began to strangle her. I screamed, and it distracted him toward me, and that's when Zeb shot him. I ran off before Zeb could catch me, and I went to Florida as planned. I wrote the letter before I left and dropped it in the mailbox, claiming we had been in Florida all that time, and that Jack was with me because I had to get away from Zeb. I was terrified he would find me and come after me and kill me for what I saw."

"Is that why you brought the police here now?"

"I read in the newspaper about the funeral— my funeral and Jack's, and knew you'd be here, devastated. So I went to the police and told them everything."

"So Jack—my dad, really did strangle the woman he thought was you?"

He hung his head, feeling shame that he had two fathers—and both of them were murderers.

She laid a hand on his arm. "Don't let this be a reflection on you," she said gently.

"I wish I'd known her. I wish I'd known Beth."

"You did!" she said. "Every opportunity we were away from the house, she would take my place and spend time with you."

"Didn't Jack know you had a sister?"

She shook her head and lowered her gaze. "She kept her Amish heritage, and became part of another community. I was so busy being an *Englisher* to be with Jack, that we didn't intermingle around him. When we made that pact that night for me to raise you, she never came out in the open again—except to see you."

"It almost seems that she was killed just for being my mother," he said with a deep sadness.

She tucked her finger under his stubbly chin, forcing him to look at her. "It was a burden she was willing to bear. She loved you!"

"But she gave me away."

"She gave you up hoping you would have a better life than being raised by a single mother who was a slave to her sin with Zeb Yoder. That's what killed her; it wasn't because of you."

He rested his head on his mother's shoulder, feeling as if the whole world had turned on him. He struggled to grasp the reality of having his mother back—the woman who had not given birth to him, but had raised him as her own. It was tough for him not to feel like an orphan—even with all his new family around him.

Chapter 23

"Do you think you'll ever get baptized into the church?" Seth asked Caleb.

"Nah. I don't have much faith in their ways now, since they turned their backs on me and Amelia when we were just innocent children. They might have been able to give us some support and even protection, but they were more concerned with banning the family because of our father's sins."

"Not all communities are like this one," Selma offered.

"We have our roots here," he said. "And with the baby coming, we're content to stay in our new home on land we own."

"I know one thing is certain," Seth admitted. "I'm finally going to put my bad-boy days behind me and fulfill the promise I made to my mother. I don't want my bad habits to turn me into the same kind of person the old man was."

"I don't think you have to worry about being anything like him," his mother said. "You've inherited the good from my sister. She would be proud to know the man you've turned out to be. Before she died, she made me promise to get you back on the straight path."

"So that was *her* promise I broke," Seth said with shame. "Don't worry, I'll make her proud of me. I've got two brothers now I thought I'd never have, and they've offered me a place in their business so I can stop the gambling and work for a living, instead of thinking I need everything handed to me."

"That's a good attitude to have, partner," Kyle said, slapping him on the back. "I think this *brother thing* is going to work out for all of us."

"I do too," Caleb said, looking at the large family he'd gained overnight.

Amelia sat with her mother knitting booties for her unborn child. She was perfectly content to stay out of the conversation, being too preoccupied with learning all the things her mother had not been able to teach her in her growing years. But now that she was about to be a mother herself, Amelia was grateful to have the woman there to guide her.

She looked up and smiled.

Yes, her new family was going to be good for the child she carried. She hoped, for her husband's sake that the newest brother, Seth would stay and be part of the family the way he had hopes for it.

Then an idea sparked in her. The best way to get a man to settle down was to find him a good woman, and her cousin, Katie, would be perfect for him.

She giggled at the thought of her child's new *Onkel Seth* wearing Amish clothing, but knew if anyone could get him to do it, Katie could.

THE END

Book Four
Pigeon Hollow Mysteries

Samantha Bayarr

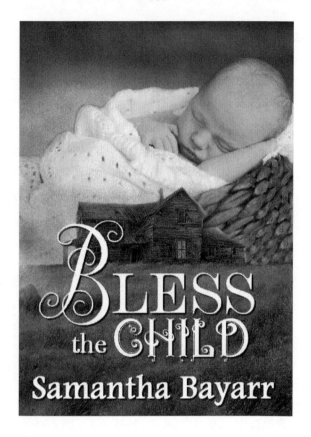

Copyright © 2016 by Samantha Bayarr

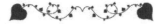

A note from the Author:

While this novel is set against the backdrop of an Amish community, the characters and the names of the community are fictional. There is no intended resemblance between the characters in this book or the setting, and any real members of any Amish or Mennonite community. As with any work of fiction, I've taken license in some areas of research as a means of creating the necessary circumstances for my characters and setting. It is completely impossible to be accurate in details and descriptions, since every community differs, and such a setting would destroy the fictional quality of entertainment this book serves to present. Any inaccuracies in the Amish and Mennonite lifestyles portrayed in this book are completely due to fictional license. Please keep in mind that this book is meant for fictional, entertainment purposes only, and is not written as a text book on the Amish.

Happy Reading

Chapter 1

Amelia plucked the last cloth diaper from the wicker basket and lifted it to the clothesline, pinning it in place and then stepped back to admire the fruit of her labor. She was a proud *mamm* indeed. Before giving birth to little Gabriel, she had no idea that she could have so much love in her heart for such a tiny little human being. Nor did she ever think that he could go through so many diapers in a day. She giggled happily, and she picked up the basket and rested it on her hip. She looked up at the sun for a moment, taking note of what a beautiful summer day it was.

A sudden commotion from inside the house, followed by the high-pitched scream of her infant, sent a chill of terror through Amelia.

Amelia let the basket fall from her hip, as she pushed aside rows of diapers hanging from the clothesline, trying to push her way toward the house. Her feet felt stuck in mud so thick she could barely lift her legs, her muscles straining to push her to reach her infant. Her chest heaved as she ran the length of the yard toward her back door, intermittent cries escaping her lips, as her mind reeled with thoughts of her infant being in danger as he continued to scream.

"God, please let him be okay," she cried out, as she entered through the kitchen door. When she reached the inside of the house, the hair on the back of her neck served as a warning that something was not right. Gabriel suddenly stopped crying, but the commotion from the other room had not stopped. Chills turned her blood cold when she realized that someone was in the house.

Someone was in her baby's room.

Someone could be trying to hurt him.

Her gaze turned to the kitchen window and peered out to the driveway, making note that it was devoid of any vehicles, either horse-drawn or other. Being in such a remote area, Seth had tried hard to persuade them to install a telephone, but Caleb would not hear of it. He'd argued that just because they were not part of the community, that did not change their commitment to their Amish heritage, and a phone would hinder that commitment.

With no way to reach anyone, and her husband and brothers-in-law both working with him, no one was here to help her. Her mother had taken lunch to them at the construction site, and she would not return for at least another half hour—too late to help her.

Before she could think of what to do, a man— an *Englisher,* entered the doorway carrying her infant. Her heart slammed against her ribcage, and her throat constricted at the sight of her infant in the arms of the stranger. The man's expression turned from surprise at seeing her, to instant anger.

"What are you doing with my baby?" Amelia screamed. "Give him to me!"

The man gritted his teeth and narrowed his eyes "I'll give him back when you give me the money!"

She reached for her son, but he pulled back, causing Gabriel to cry.

Tears streamed down her face and she could barely breathe.

"I don't have any money," she sobbed. "I don't have any money; please give me back my son."

"You have money here, and I know it," he said. "I read all about it in the newspapers."

It slowly dawned on Amelia what he was talking about, and her heart sank at the reality that there was no money to give him.

"We don't have any money," she continued to cry. "Please, please," she bawled. "Give me back my baby; you're hurting him!"

"I'm not hurting the little fella," the man said as he jostled her son about carelessly. "We're just getting to know each other, but we're going to know each other real well if you don't get the money, because I'm taking him if you don't hand over the cash right now. You owe me!"

Chapter 2

"For the last time," the man said through gritted teeth. "Are you going to hand over the money in exchanged for the screaming kid, or am I taking him with me?"

"No!" Amelia screamed. "Please don't take him. I don't have any money to give you, but if I did, I'd give you all of it."

The man wandered over to the kitchen window and looked out as if waiting for someone—an accomplice, perhaps.

"I happen to have it on good authority, little Amish girl," he said. "You have a lot of money tied up in this land, so you're lying."

Amelia reached once more for her screaming infant, but the man jerked him away so hard, she worried that he'd hurt him if she didn't back off.

"At least let me calm him down," Amelia pleaded, trying to remain between the man and the kitchen door.

"Sit over there," he said, as he gestured with a tilt of his head to the side. "Sit over there in the corner—away from the door, and I'll bring him to you, but you better quiet him down," he ordered her.

Her heart melted with relief as her son was returned to her arms, even though she feared it was only temporary. She held him close to her and whispered prayers in his ear, hoping to accomplish two things. First and foremost, she needed to calm her infant, and secondly, she intended to plead with God to spare them the danger that she feared was to come.

"I'm going to need some diapers and some bottles," the man said, looking around nervously.

Amelia's breath hitched and she started to sob all over again. "Please, Sir. I don't know how to get you to understand that we don't have any money."

He charged toward her, anger in his eyes. "You're lying! I read about the robbery in the newspapers, and I know that you found the money hidden under the floorboards of your house."

"We turned the money in," she said. "They gave us a small reward, but my husband and his brothers used it to build their business. There's no more money left."

"You better come up with some," he demanded. "Even if you have to rob another bank, or I'm taking that boy with me." he said, pointing to Gabriel.

"No! I won't let you do it," she said, gritting her teeth. "I'll fight you to the death!" she surprised herself by saying.

He took a step toward her, causing her to jump instinctively.

"Oh, now you're threatening to kill me?" He asked. "Is this whole family full of murderers?"

"I'm not a murderer!" she said. "But I'm not going to stand by and let you take my child from me. I'll do whatever I have to!"

"You don't have a choice, Amish girl," he said. "Now tell me where that crying brat's diapers and bottles are so I can be on my way."

"Please, Sir," she pleaded. "He doesn't take a bottle. I nurse him."

"I guess he'll have to get used to taking a bottle until his mother decides she's going to trade him for the money," he said coldly.

"Please, no," she begged, sobbing.

"Does your kid have a car seat?" the man asked. "I can't hold him while I'm driving, and he'll be no good for ransom if he's all banged up."

Amelia gasped as she pointed to the opposite corner of the room where his car seat was. It had only been used to bring him home from the hospital since she had decided against a home birth. She sobbed as she wondered why she was helping him, but the thought of him taking Gabriel without the safety of the car seat filled her with absolute terror.

"I'm begging you not to take him. He'll die if I'm not there to feed him."

"Lots of babies take bottles," the man said, mocking her. "If you won't get me a bottle I'll get one for him. But we can avoid all this if you just hand over the money."

"I already told you," she sobbed further. "I don't have any money."

"Then I suggest you get together some bottles and diapers and clothes, because from the sounds of things, it's gonna be a while before you get me that money."

She jumped up toward him, pulling Gabriel close to her.

"Please, take me with you!"

Chapter 3

"Hey, it's me," the man said to the person on the other line. "Bring the car around, we're taking the kid!"

"No!" Amelia screamed.

She stood between the man and her child, who slept peacefully in his car seat, oblivious to the danger he was in.

The kidnapper reached out a hand and pushed her down into a chair. "Don't make me tie you up before I leave!"

"Please," she pleaded. "Take me with you so I can feed him. You won't get any ransom if my son is dead."

"Now you're talking the way I want you to talk," the man said. "I knew you had money."

"No!" She said. "You're wrong! We don't have any money, but I'm sure they can try to raise some. I don't think it'll be as much as you're asking for, but we can get you a little bit—a couple thousand maybe."

The man threw his head back and laughed heartily. "You think a measly few thousand dollars is going to satisfy me? I want the half a million that was stolen from the bank!"

Amelia collapsed to the floor and hovered over her son in his car seat and began sobbing uncontrollably. "I won't let you take him. I won't let you go without me."

"Fine, Amish girl," he said angrily. "Maybe the old man will pay more for the two of you."

"Are you talking about Zeb Yoder?" Amelia asked.

"Of course I am," he said. "I'm talking about the murderer. The one who murdered Rachel Miller, and the other two people—and who knows how many others."

Amelia felt her blood run cold through her veins at his statement. Who was this man? She looked deeper into his angry face, noting that he looked very similar to the way Seth had when she'd first met him. He had that same anger in his eyes, though he had no resemblance to the old man.

"Is your mother Rachel Miller?" Amelia asked sincerely.

"Rachel Miller is my wife's mother," he said. "Zeb Yoder killed her and put her in another woman's casket."

Amelia was all too familiar with the story of how the woman had gone to see Rose, Caleb's mom, and died from the tea that her father-in-law had laced with poison and sleeping pills. Rose had blamed herself for not thinking that the gift Zeb had given her could be tainted, and it was the cause of her friend's death. It had haunted her ever since that day when she'd unknowingly served her the poisoned tea. She'd blamed herself, and had to live with the guilt of that day, especially since she'd run away like a coward.

"She was the woman who was buried in my husband's mother's grave," Amelia said. "But if you think Zeb Yoder is going to give you a single penny for ransom for me and his grandchild, you're wrong! He doesn't care any more for me than he did for your wife's mother when she died because of him!"

"You sure seem to know a lot about my business! That *woman* was recently dug up," he said angrily. "Because your husband thought it was his mother buried there. But my wife's grandmother had filed a missing person's report when her mother had come up missing several years ago, and the detectives recently put the cases together and asked my wife to submit to a DNA test. Surprise, surprise, it was a perfect match. But why did you think she was *my* mother?"

"I just sort of assumed because of all these bodies showing up seemed to be women, and they seemed to be linked to Zeb Yoder in some way," she said quietly. "What about your wife's father?"

"Her father died before she was born," he said raising his voice.

"Do you know that for sure?" Amelia asked cautiously.

"Of course I know it because my wife told me that, and she's never lied to me. Why are you asking me these questions? Are you questioning my wife's morals?"

No, but I'm questioning yours!

"No, I'm not," she said, holding her hands up defensively. "It's just that my husband recently found out he had two brothers and it was because his father, Zeb Yoder, had fathered two other children with two other women–Amish women. We've suspected there were more siblings, and we especially suspected that the woman in the grave may have had a child with Zebedee Yoder. Your wife could be that child! If she's related to us, we'd be more than happy to help *both* of you."

"My wife is no relation to that murderer!"

Chapter 4

Amelia looked at the pregnant woman who'd entered her home to help the kidnapper, and knew immediately she was related to the old man. She could see a lot of Seth in her. She had the same darkness in her eyes that he'd had when they'd first met him. Despite the terror that ran through her, Amelia felt sorry for the young woman he called *Faith*.

"Get the baby's things!" he ordered the woman he'd claimed was his wife.

The young woman was clearly Amish, and he was an *Englisher,* and they seemed terribly mismatched. She supposed the woman may not have lived in a community since her mother's death.

"Please, Zack, I don't want to do this," she begged him.

He backhanded her, and she immediately raised a hand to her cheek to cover the welt, and began to weep.

Amelia was tempted to comfort the poor woman, but she had to remind herself of the immediate danger she and Gabriel were in.

Faith picked up the diapers and blankets that Zack had thrown at her, as she flashed Amelia a sympathetic look.

"What was that?" Zack questioned her. "You feeling sorry for that rich, Amish girl?"

He took a swing at her and she ducked away. "No! I just don't think this is the way to get the money."

"You let me worry about how to get the money for that kid you insist on having! I say we're taking her kid for ransom so we can pay for that one you're carrying!"

"No!" Amelia screamed. "I'll find a way to get you some money, but please don't take Gabriel."

Her lower lip quivered, and tears ran down her cheeks as she looked at his innocent face. He'd worn himself out crying, and was still sleeping peacefully.

"Please, God," she cried out. "Don't let them hurt my baby."

"God didn't help Faith's mother when Zeb Yoder was killing her. Why should he help *you?*"

"I'm sure God was with her in her final moments on this earth," Amelia said quietly. "Don't take it out on my baby what that man did. I had no control over that."

Zack leaned in close to Amelia and gritted his teeth. "I'm taking your kid for ransom. It's nothing personal. I just want my share of the money."

"I don't want that money, Zack, I've already told you that," Faith said. "Don't take her baby."

He slapped Faith again, her cry startling Gabriel, and he began to wail.

"Please," Amelia begged. "Let me comfort him."

"No!" Zack barked. "He's all strapped in, and we need to get out of here. We've wasted enough time already. Get his things, Faith, and we're going to walk out of here."

"What about me?" Amelia sobbed. "Please let me go with you so I can feed him."

"You better stay here so you can tell your husband we mean business," he said. "And if you try anything, I might have to shoot you!"

Amelia's breath caught in her throat, even though she hadn't seen a gun yet. That didn't mean anything; he could have kept it concealed.

She flashed a pleading look at Faith, and the woman made brief eye-contact with her, but it was enough for Amelia to know that she would help her.

She shook as she watched them leave her home, and she searched for a piece of paper to write a note. When she didn't see one, she tipped over the sugar bowl onto the table and scribbled the word *HELP* in the mess, and then crept out the door while Zack's back was turned to her. With him preoccupied with strapping the car seat into the back of the car, Amelia managed to slip around to the other side of the car unnoticed, praying the entire way that the door on the other side of the car was open.

The familiar sound of the clip-clop of horse's hooves filled her ears, and she knew it would only be her mother, but prayed the woman would intercept them, even though she knew there was nothing her mother could do to stop them.

Amelia crouched down at the back of the car and waited for Zack to walk around to the front so he could get into the driver's seat, and then she made her move. She threw open the back door and slid into the seat and slammed the door before he knew what was happening.

He looked at her from over his shoulder, screaming for her to get out of the car, but Faith interrupted him.

"Close your door, Zack!" she urged him. "Someone's coming and we're gonna get caught!"

Zack took his eyes off Amelia long enough to look toward the end of the long driveway, where the horse and buggy had just pulled in.

"Is that your husband?" he asked.

"I don't know who it is," she said, knowing he could not see who was in the buggy at this distance.

"Let's go before we get caught and you go to jail," Faith urged him.

Amelia didn't know if the woman was on her side or not, but she wished it had been Kyle's truck that had pulled in instead of the horse and buggy.

Zack jumped into the car, grinding the tires in the gravel driveway as he sped down the lane toward the buggy. He veered off the path when he neared the horses, and Amelia pressed her face against the glass, praying that her mother had seen her in the car.

Chapter 5

Abigail steered the horses out of the way of the oncoming car that came barreling down her daughter's driveway.

"Melia," she cried as she watched her daughter fly by in the speeding car. She hadn't missed the look of terror on her little girl's face, and Abigail knew she was in trouble.

Had something happened to the baby? The couple who were in the front seat of the white BMW were not any of the normal drivers for the Amish, and she wondered where they would be taking her daughter and grandson in such a hurry. Amelia would have had no way of contacting them, so it just didn't make any sense. Turning around as they sped away, she noted the vanity plate read: *HSR-DDY.*

Then a thought hit her, and she wondered if the old man was behind this in some way.

She slapped the reins to move the horses toward the house faster. She had no idea what she would do once she got there, but she hoped, perhaps, that her daughter had left a note that would explain.

As she approached the house, she ran up to the open kitchen door. Seeing the message written in sugar on the table, she scrambled back out of the house and hopped into the buggy.

She urged the horses faster down the road to the construction site where her son-in-law and his brothers were putting a roof on a new house.

When she reached the site, she didn't even bother to slow the horses before jumping out of the buggy. She ran fast to reach Caleb, screaming to get his attention. He dropped the tools in his hands and ran to her, placing a hand on each of her arms to calm her.

"What's wrong?" He asked.

"Did Amelia make arrangements to have some *Englishers* take her and the baby somewhere today?" She asked, trying to catch her breath.

"No, why? What happened?" he asked.

"When I drove back to the house after bringing you boys your lunch," she said, still out of breath. "She was speeding away in a white BMW, and the baby was with her. But when I went into the house, I saw that she'd scribbled the word *help* in a pile of sugar on the table."

"What are you talking about?" He asked. "That makes no sense."

"I don't know how she would've gotten word to the people that were driving her, but when I saw them go by, she had her face pressed to the glass, and I could see she'd been crying. I hope nothing has happened to the baby."

"Maybe we should go to the hospital and see if they went there. But why wouldn't she have taken the time to write a proper note explaining where she was going?"

"I don't know, but let's go."

By this time, Seth and Kyle were at his side, and had heard the whole thing. Seth offered to put away all the tools and then meet them at the hospital, while Kyle offered to drive them.

Seth tied up the buggy at the site deciding it was best to leave the horse there for now.

The three of them piled into Kyle's truck and he sped off toward the hospital, which was about eighteen miles down the road.

None of them said another word the entire ride there; tensions were high. When they reached the hospital, Kyle let Abigail and Caleb off at the emergency room entrance, and went to park the truck. When he made his way to the entrance to the hospital, Abigail and Caleb were running back out.

"She's not in there!" Caleb said.

"They said it's been a slow day for them. The nurse told us they've only had two senior citizens come through today, and no one with a baby."

"Where can she be?" Kyle asked.

"I think we need to go to the police," Abigail said. "I told you Amelia looked like she'd been crying, and that car was driving way too fast down the driveway. I don't know why they were in a hurry, but I've got a bad feeling about this."

They all got back in the truck and drove down to the police station another several miles down the road.

"What are we going to say when we go in there?" Kyle asked.

"I guess we need to tell them all we know," Caleb said. "Is there anything you left out, Abigail?"

"I noticed the license plate, and both the driver and the woman in the front had dark hair, but they were going so fast and I was busy trying to get the horses out-of-the-way so they wouldn't hit them, that I didn't get the best look at them like I should have."

"What was the license plate?" Kyle asked.

"It was HSR – DDY," she said.

"Hoosier Daddy--who's your daddy?" Kyle said with a sigh. "Not very original is it?"

"I didn't know that's what that meant," Abigail said. "But I guess it makes sense now that you figured it out."

"One thing's certain," Caleb said, as they entered the police station. "It should make it easier to find them."

"Let's pray that it is so," Abigail said.

Chapter 6

"I'm afraid I have some bad news for you," the officer said as he entered the lobby where the four of them had been sitting waiting to hear the results of the record search for the license plate.

"Let me guess," Kyle said. "The car was stolen!"

"I'm afraid so," the officer said. "The owner reported it missing yesterday afternoon. But the good news is, we have officers in the area, and we'll see if we can find them."

"I'm afraid you can probably search the area all day long and won't find them," Kyle complained. "They've obviously ditched the car and have found another one."

The officer turned around as another officer called him back to a locked door. "Excuse me just a moment," he said to them. "I'll be right back."

Caleb paced back-and-forth in the lobby, while Kyle watched out the window at Seth, who was leaning against his car and smoking a cigarette. He'd been so good about not smoking, and here he was, out there on his second one already. It was obvious he was having trouble handling the stress.

When the officer returned, his face did not look as if he was bearing any good news. "They found the car abandoned in an alley about 12 miles from here," he said. "We can search the area, but my guess is that they've stolen another car in order to get where they need to go. That means that if we get another report of a stolen car, we'll be checking it out to see if they fit the description of your wife's abductors."

Kyle went to shake his hand, and thanked him.

"I'm afraid I have some worse news than that," the officer said sincerely.

Caleb shook, and Kyle could see he was thinking the same thing—that they found evidence like blood or something in the car.

"Maybe you folks should have a seat." He gestured back to the chairs where they were sitting in the lobby, and everyone sat down robotically; the room was so quiet it was almost deafening.

"Please just tell us everything," Kyle pleaded. "No matter how bad it is; we need to know."

"Well, I guess you need to know what you're dealing with," the officer said. "We just got word that your father has escaped again."

"What?" Caleb said, jumping up from his chair. "When did he wake up from his coma?"

"Apparently he just woke up yesterday and they were getting ready to move him back to the prison, and he managed to escape again."

"We don't think he's going to make it far, because he's weak from being in a coma for so long."

"He isn't dumb enough to go back to his house; he knows that's the first place you'll look."

"We doubt he'll go back to his house this time since we found him there the last time," the officer agreed. "I imagine he's going to hide out somewhere until he feels it's safe, or he could even be planning on leaving the state."

"If he's holding my wife hostage, then…" he couldn't finish his sentence, and Abigail pulled him into a hug.

"We'll be patrolling the area just in case. I'm afraid I don't have anything else for you, but we'll keep an eye out for your wife and your son. In the meantime, my suggestion is that you go home and prepare yourself for a possible ransom note. I imagine your father's freedom is going to be the price he'll be asking for."

"What about the couple I saw driving her away from the house?" Abigail asked.

"They might be working together," the officer said. "There's no way to be sure, unless we get word from someone, either in the form of a ransom note, or a phone call."

"Now we need to be on the lookout for the old man on top of everything else," Kyle said soberly.

"You don't think he'd hurt his own grandchild, do you?" Caleb looked at his brothers, tears welling up in his eyes. "After all he's done, I just can't trust him anymore. It seems to me, that our father is the type of man that would hurt even an innocent baby if he got in his way."

"So who do you suppose we should be looking for: your father?" Abigail asked. "Or Amelia?"

"Unfortunately," Kyle said. "I'm afraid we're going to find them in the same place."

"Do you really think he would hold his own grandchild hostage for his freedom?" Caleb asked. "It doesn't make sense."

"It makes perfect sense," Kyle said. "Do you forget that he held my mother hostage to keep his secrets hidden from the community? He did it to keep his standing here, and let's not forget his being arrested interrupted his last hope of getting the Bishop to listen to his confession and welcome him back. I think that's all he's wanted all along."

"You think so?" Caleb asked.

"Let's not kid ourselves," Kyle said angrily. "The Bishop was not going to welcome him back. He only wanted the confession."

"Perhaps if we could somehow get the Bishop involved and get him to promise our father amnesty, perhaps we can put an end to all of this."

"It's possible that might just work," Caleb agreed. "The only problem is; how do we get the Bishop to go along? You remember he had all of us shunned, and he doesn't want us in his community. He certainly doesn't want our father to be a part of the community. I'm not sure at this point that he would even agree to listen to his confession so he can be forgiven."

"Caleb," Seth said, stepping into the conversation. "I thought forgiveness was what the Amish were all about? Kyle and I didn't grow up Amish like you did, but if there is no forgiveness in the community, where do we stand?"

"I'm not sure," Kyle said. "But right now, I think that's our only hope."

Chapter 7

"Why are we switching cars?" Amelia asked her abductors. "Why would you leave your car here in this alley? Aren't you afraid someone will steal it?"

Zack chuckled at her. "You naïve little Amish girl, we stole that car!"

"I didn't know he was gonna steal the car," Faith said trying to defend her innocence. "And I didn't know we were gonna take you or your baby."

Zack raised his hand toward her, and she ducked.

"Shut up Faith! Shut up now!"

"It's not too late to turn back and stop all this, Zack," she pleaded with him. "You told me those people owed you money. I didn't know you were going to resort to stealing cars and kidnapping. I don't want my baby's father to go to jail."

"No one is going to jail. I told you to shut up!"

They all piled into a rusty gold Pontiac that smelled of dirty feet and cigars inside. Amelia coughed at the smell when she got in, pushing aside trash that was on the floor at her feet. She tried locating the buckle to the seatbelt so she could strap Gabriel's seat in, but it was buried deep beneath the sticky, gummy, dirt-stained seat.

She winced as she put her hand down between the seats and felt amongst sticky dirt to locate the other side of the buckle. When she pulled it out, her fingers were black with dirt. She wiped them on the already dirty upholstery, realizing that they weren't going to come clean. It wasn't important in the grand scheme of things, but it certainly made matters worse. She shrugged it away and strapped him in, thanking God that he hadn't yet woken up.

Zack tried several times to start the car, but it stalled each time, and Amelia prayed it wouldn't start and they would get caught. On the fourth try, it started, but then backfired, causing Gabriel to startle in his sleep. It started on the next try, and Zack revved the engine. Gray smoke billowed out from the back of the car and filtered into the windows, causing Amelia to cough.

When the car took off, she was grateful for the breeze that blew out the exhaust smell from the car.

Zack followed the same path leading almost directly back to her home, and she thought for a moment he'd changed his mind. When he turned into the driveway of the old man's farm, she feared that she was in bigger trouble than she originally thought.

"Why are we turning in here?" Amelia dared to ask.

Zack chuckled. "I thought it would be pretty smart to hide you directly under their noses. Besides, I already told you that old man owes us for what he did the Faith's mother!"

"And I already told *you*," Faith complained. "No one owes me anything, and I don't want anything from that old man! My *mamm* has been dead for a lot of years, and I've had a long time to get used to it—for plenty of years before I met you."

He grabbed her arm and shook her, gritting his teeth as he swerved the car, causing Amelia to brace herself against the door.

"And I told you that you had no life before you met me!"

Faith buried her face against the window and began to cry quietly, but Amelia could see from her shaking shoulders that she was crying. It was tough for her not to feel sorry for the woman, knowing how lucky she'd been to find such a gentle and caring husband who would never raise his voice or a hand to her. But no matter how she felt about Faith, she had to keep her head about her and not get emotionally involved. She had to remember to keep her wits about her in order to keep herself and her son safe.

Their very lives depended on it.

Chapter 8

"Have you got any more bright ideas?" Seth asked his brothers when they left the Bishop's porch. "That old man wouldn't even let us in."

"I can hardly blame him," Caleb said. "He doesn't want to get involved, and I understand that even if I don't like it."

"I thought men of God jumped at the chance to minister to sinners—especially murderers!" Seth argued.

"Well, one thing is certain; I can't stand around here waiting for my family to either be returned to me, or get word that they're no longer alive."

"Maybe we need to see if we can figure out where the old man is hiding out," Kyle said.

"He had so many mistresses, it's possible he has places he could stay that we don't even know about," Seth said with disgust.

"Who do you suppose the couple could be that took her?" Kyle asked. "Abigail said they looked like they were about our age. Who do we know that would do such a thing?"

"No one! But the thought had crossed my mind that we could have a fourth brother," Seth said with a half chuckle. "Maybe he has a chip on his shoulder like the old man, and he wants revenge!"

"Well, there was another body that turned up. Why don't we ask Aunt Rose to tell us a little more about the woman who was buried in the grave that was supposed to belong to my mom," Kyle said. "Maybe she had a child, and that child could be the one we're looking for!"

"That's a long-shot," Seth said. "But it's all we have to go by right now."

They went directly back home, knowing that all three of their mothers were at the main house waiting for any word about Amelia and Gabriel.

"Rachel and I weren't the best of friends," Rose said sadly. "We were classmates, but we were never really friends. She and her mother had come from another community, and they just didn't have any family here, and they never really tried to fit in. They were only there for the last year or so of school, and then they moved away. When she began to work at the bakery many years later, we started talking and realized we knew each other when we were young. I do remember a young girl going to visit her a couple of times at the bakery. She had dark hair, and she would be about the same age as you boys. I don't remember her since she was only there for a minute or two to drop something off to Rachel. At the time, I asked her if it was her daughter and she said she was, and that her husband had died before her daughter was born."

Kyle ran out to his truck and grabbed a stack of newspapers and brought them into the house. He flipped through them furiously until he came to the article about Rachel Miller.

"Look here," he said pointing to the newspaper. "It says here she left behind a daughter named Faith. Faith Miller. And she's our age!"

Kyle turned to his aunt. "Why did she come to visit you that day if the two of you weren't close?"

"When she dropped in that day, she said she had something weighing on her mind—a confession of sorts. We never did get around to talking about what it was she wanted to say because the tea caused her to feel dizzy, and when she went to use the bathroom, she stumbled and fell on the table. She died instantly."

Rose began to cry, remembering that day she'd had an upset stomach and didn't think she could drink or eat anything, so she hadn't even taken a sip of her tea yet. When her friend stumbled, she knew then it was because of the tea Zeb had given her as a gift.

Seth jumped up from his chair. "I'd be willing to bet her confession had something to do with her daughter and the old man. He must be her father!"

"You mean we could have a *sister?*" Caleb asked.

"I think it's possible," Seth said. "All we have to do is find this *Faith Miller,* and I'd be willing to bet we'll probably find Amelia and Gabriel."

"I thought you gave up betting," Kyle teased him.

"Not when it's a sure thing!" Seth admitted.

"It might not be that simple," Kyle said. "What if she *is* his daughter, and she's as bad as he is and they're working together? You have to admit the timing of Amelia being taken, and the old man escaping is probably not a coincidence."

Seth pulled out his cell phone and called the police detective listed on the business card they'd gotten earlier. He abruptly hung up the phone, frustrated that he'd had to leave a message because the detective was not available.

'We can't just sit here and do nothing,' Seth said. "How do we find this Faith Miller? Maybe someone at the bakery would know. What was the name of the bakery, Aunt Rose?"

"It's called The Brick Oven, and it's right downtown in Hartford."

Seth pulled out his keys. "Who's with me?"

"I'll go," Kyle offered. "You stay here, Caleb, in case we get word. I'll leave my cell phone with you just in case."

"That won't do me any good," Caleb complained. "I don't know how to use it."

"I do," Selma spoke up. "You boys be on your way. We'll stay here, and I'll call you if there's any word, and you do the same."

They each kissed their mothers goodbye, and Seth flashed his brother a sympathetic look. He hadn't been part of the family for very long, but he was already emotionally attached to every one of them, and Amelia's and his nephew's disappearance hurt him more than he could ever let on.

Chapter 9

Amelia felt awkward feeding Gabriel with Zack so close nearby, but he wouldn't allow her to go into the other room to feed him in private. Faith had found her a throw-blanket that was tossed over the sofa so she could at least keep herself hidden from the evil man.

He'd joked with her several times, stating how funny it was that he should hide her right under the noses of her own family, but knowing the history of her family, they were more likely to start their search on the old man's property.

She would never tell him that.

Amelia was hoping to get a moment away from Zack so she could talk to Faith about her hunch that they were related. She felt certain Faith was her sister-in-law, and she hoped the information would get the woman to be completely on her side. It was obvious to Amelia that Faith wanted no part in her husband's crimes, but in her condition, she probably felt there was no other way but to go along with the unreasonable man.

Zack had found jars of fruits and vegetables tucked away in the pantry that the old man had canned, and he was preoccupied at the moment with eating, though he hadn't offered any to the two women, least of all his pregnant wife.

Faith sat near her. "You know, he wasn't always like this," she said quietly. "When we first met, he was very gentle and very kind. He was so romantic, I married him only one week after meeting him. But now I wonder if I should've thought that through."

Amelia reached a hand out and touched her cheek that still boasted a deep welt from where Zack had slapped her.

"I'm afraid you're going to have a bit of a black eye," Amelia said gently.

Her lips formed a thin line, and tears welled up in her eyes. "It wouldn't be the first one. I told myself after that first one I wouldn't stick around for another," she said, as she patted her belly. "But this little one here has changed all that."

"Well, if anything," Amelia said as kindly as possible. "That little one should bring the two of you closer together."

Faith lifted a hand and waved it at her. "Oh, don't mind him," she said, defending him. "He's just nervous about all the money the baby's gonna cost us. It's been worse since he lost his job."

"There's a lot of things that he can do. I'm sure my husband and his brothers would've been more than willing to let him work with them.

But now, well, after what he's done, I just don't know. I couldn't speak for them."

"People like you don't help people like us," Faith said, lowering her head in shame.

"You know better than that!" Amelia said to her. "We're both Amish. Weren't you raised Amish?"

"Only slightly; my *mamm* was too ashamed to be a part of the community since I was born out of wedlock."

"I thought Zack said that your father died before you were born."

"That's what she used to tell me, so I tell everyone else that to keep from shaming her— especially now that she's gone. But we got in a big fight one day before she disappeared, and she admitted the whole thing to me. She said she'd needed to get it off her chest for a very long time, and she felt relief after telling me the truth. But there's no forgiveness from the community for her since we couldn't be part of the community because of it. I know the Amish ways are about forgiveness, but sometimes those ways come with flaws—flaws that don't fully forgive a person's mistakes."

"I know what you mean," Amelia said. My husband and I were both shunned because of the mistakes that our parents had made, and we were just innocent children. We fell under the ban because of them, and at that time, we really could've used the community's help. But they turned their backs on us, mostly out of fear, but my husband feels that was no excuse."

"I agree with your husband."

"We know now that had more to do with the Bishop than the people in the community, because we have a lot of friends within the community."

"That's good that you have that," Faith said. "But that won't help us."

"Let me help you," Amelia pleaded with her.

"After what we've done to you, why would you want to help me?" Faith asked, tears in her eyes.

"Because I think you're my sister-in-law!"

Chapter 10

Zack charged toward Amelia, and she started to wince, but caught herself. She was tougher than this. She knew if she showed fear, it would be all over for her.

He raised a hand to her. "I told you my wife ain't related to that murderer!"

Amelia stood her ground. "She looks so much like my brother-in-law they could be twins! That would make her my sister-in-law, and you can't change that if it's a true fact."

He raised his hand higher, but she kept herself from cowering.

"You think I'm afraid of you slapping me in the face the way you smack your wife around? I shot a man when I was ten years old, and then I spent the rest of my childhood in an orphanage, so I know how to fight!"

Zack backed away. "You're not worth it. I won't get much ransom for you if I send you out with a black eye."

Amelia slowly let out the breath she'd been holding in so he wouldn't hear, as she watched him go back over to gobbling a Mason jar of peaches. She sat back down next to Faith and kept quiet, not wanting another confrontation with him.

When he finished, he picked up a pad of paper and a pen from the kitchen table and tossed it at her.

"Let's get to writing that first ransom note!"

"Why me?" she asked.

"I figure if it's in your handwriting, your family will know you're not hurt or anything," he said.

When he turned his back, Faith whispered in her ear. "He didn't finish school, so he doesn't read or write so good."

That was good news to Amelia, her mind immediately reeling to the possibilities of codes she could encrypt into the message. She'd have to be careful, figuring he'd probably have Faith read it before it went out, and she wasn't entirely sure if the woman would let a blatant cry for help pass by her without telling her husband. Even if she wouldn't say anything, her expression might give it away, and Amelia wasn't about to take that chance.

As Zack relayed to her what to put in the note, she was busy trying to figure out how to word it to send her husband a message within the message. When they were kids, they'd used homing pigeons to communicate, and they'd developed a way to send an extra message that only they knew by making certain words less obvious by using upper-case letters to spell out another word. It had been fun when they were kids, but she'd had no idea then that such childhood play could one day save her life.

caleb,
Please go to sister Felicia At fenwIck hall (THe oRph - Anage) and have her release my inheritanCe tHat was LEft for me. ransom is to be haLf a million dollars. more instructions later
~Amelia

Zack snatched the note from her and handed it to Faith so she could read it to him.

"Who's Sister Felicia, and why does she have your money? I thought you said you had no money!"

It wasn't a lie, but she knew she would have to skate around the truth to convince him the money was there.

"I had money that the state is supposed to grant to me on my twenty-first birthday from my parents' estate, but I'm sure they'll release it early if it's an emergency. When I left, I'd asked them to hold it until then, since I didn't want the money. I thought it was from the robbery. I didn't figure I would ever go back for it."

"How much is it?" he asked, his eyes lighting up with greed.

"Two hundred fifty thousand!" she answered.

His eyes lit up even brighter, and the corners of his mouth turned up into a sickening smile.

She'd meant *pennies,* but he didn't have to know that. The gleam in his eyes let her know he was falling for it, and she would not have to lie to convince him, rather than confessing it only amounted to twenty-five hundred dollars.

His expression quickly changed to anger. "That's a start, but it's not nearly enough!"

Faith tucked her arm in his and smiled weakly.

"That's more than enough, Zack. Let's not be greedy!"

"I'm not being greedy! I want what's coming to us!"

I have a feeling you're going to get exactly what's coming to you!

"After dark, you can walk around and put the note on the door of her house."

Faith looked nervously between her husband and Amelia, fearing the woman would not be alive by the time she returned.

"That's a long walk, Zack," she complained. "Will you go?"

"If I go," he growled. "I'm tying the two of you up!"

"Why me? I'm your wife!"

His gaze traveled between the two women.

"I don't trust her not to convince you to let her go," he growled. "Ever since you got pregnant, you've become weak, and she's already put ideas in your head that she wants to help you, and you're falling for it. So what's it going to be? You delivering the ransom note, or am I tying the two of you to a chair?"

"Tie us to a chair!" Amelia said with a bit of an edge in her voice. "She doesn't need to be walking all that way in the dark in her condition!"

He chuckled angrily. "Have it your way, Amish girl."

Chapter 11

Seth walked out of the *dawdi haus* that he'd agreed to share with his brother, Kyle, until Amelia and the baby were returned home safely.

He needed a cigarette, and he'd had to wait until Kyle was asleep to avoid reprimand from him. He'd made promises to quit, and he had been truly trying, but his tension was so high right now that he needed one, and he needed it in the worst way.

He crept out the door and walked far enough up into the driveway, hoping to avoid Kyle seeing him.

Reaching into the pocket of his pants, he pulled out his Zippo and flicked it open, lighting it with one quick motion. It was something that he'd practiced for a long time until he'd gotten it right. Now, it seemed like such a trivial thing. He shrugged and lit the cigarette anyway, knowing how badly he needed it.

He walked further up toward Caleb's house, noticing there was a light on in the kitchen even though it was well past midnight. He knew his brother was probably not sleeping any more than he was.

He took one last drag of is cigarette and snuffed it out with the toe of his boot, and then walked up to the kitchen door. He knocked lightly, and while he waited for his brother to answer, he grabbed the slip of paper that was stuffed in the doorjamb.

Without waiting for Caleb to come to the door he tried the handle and it was unlocked. Caleb sat at the kitchen table, his head in his hands, and he appeared to be crying. Seth put a hand on his brother's shoulder to comfort him while trying not to get emotional himself. He sat down next to him and opened up the sheet of paper to show him.

"It looks like we got a ransom note after all," he said. "Someone put this in the doorjamb."

Caleb's head popped up, his eyes puffy and red, but he took the note and read it.

"She's put a message in it for me," he said, his eyes growing a little brighter.

He grabbed a notepad and a pen, and picked out the capitalized letters within her message, hoping to spell out her whereabouts. He scribbled the letters and showed it to Seth.

"Faith and Rachel."

"So she's with Faith?" Seth asked.

"There's more to it than that," Caleb said. "Felicia is the administrator of the orphanage. She isn't one of the nuns. The word, *sister*, stands out. What do you suppose she mean by that? Do you think she's figured out that Faith could be our sister?"

"It's sort of looks that way!" Seth said, feeling a bit of hope. "So now all we have to do is find Faith, and we'll probably find Amelia and the baby."

"The last line says more instructions will follow. That must mean she has more to tell us. But why would she be asking for half a million dollars? She probably couldn't put too much in one message, but that's probably a good thing. At least we know she's safe."

"She's safe as long as her kidnappers— whoever they are, don't catch on that we don't have that kind of money to give her."

"I don't think it's going to come to that," Caleb said. "If I know my wife, she's going to lead us right to her. In the meantime, let's call that detective and get him looking for her."

Chapter 12

"What time did the note get here?" The detective asked as he sipped the coffee Caleb got for him.

"I went out to smoke–uh, get some fresh air," Seth corrected himself. "It was around midnight. I saw the kitchen light on in the main house, so I came up to the door to see if Caleb was awake. That's when I noticed the note was stuffed in the doorjamb. We all parted ways around eight o'clock, so that's a four-hour window that he could've shown up."

The detective sighed as he took notes. "That doesn't give us much to go by. Your wife is smart for encrypting her message, but I hope it didn't put her at risk with her kidnappers. I know she wrote it by hand, and it's not as easily detected, but that doesn't mean she isn't risking her safety. Let's hope that finding this Faith woman is going to be the key, and we can put an end to all of this."

Seth could barely open his eyes when his cell phone started ringing beside him. The bright sun coming in through the window would have normally been enough to wake him, except that he and Kyle were up half the night plotting with Caleb to get his family back

"I'm going through the drive-thru to get a large coffee, can I come over and talk to you boys when I leave here?" the detective asked from the other end of the line.

"We'll be here," Seth said.

He pushed his feet to the floor and rubbed the sleep from his eyes, stretching his weary muscles. He felt as if he'd run a marathon, the tension in his shoulders painful enough to make him reach for a bottle of ibuprofen at his bedside table. He popped a few in his mouth, and smoothed out the wrinkles in the shirt and pants he'd fallen asleep in, and shuffled his way toward the main house, where he hoped his brother would have a fresh pot of coffee ready.

No sooner had he sat down at the kitchen table with his brothers than the detective pulled up to the house.

Caleb greeted him at the door, and asked him to sit. He could tell by the look on his face that he didn't have good news for him.

"I wanted to talk to you boys together so there wouldn't be any misunderstanding," he said.

They all looked at each other, worry lining their faces.

"I'm afraid we haven't found Faith Miller," he began. "We checked her paperwork that she signed to identify her mother's body, and it gave an address for her and her husband, Zack

Farmer. The apartment looked like it was recently abandoned, and after talking to a few of their neighbors, it seems Zack lost his job recently, and they started hearing a lot of constant fighting. They also said Faith is pregnant, and that she'd be close to six months along by now."

"That's a lot of good information, but the only thing it helps is for us to understand that Mr. Farmer must have gone off the deep end when he lost his job, and thought kidnapping my sister-in-law and nephew and holding them for ransom was a good alternative for making money the honest way," Seth complained. "I know I have no room to talk because I used to have a gambling problem, but I didn't put a pregnant wife in the middle of a dangerous situation because of my selfishness."

"Where does our father, Zeb Yoder, fit into all of this?" Kyle asked.

"We haven't established a connection yet, since we've been unable to find him, so we don't know for sure if the two incidents are related."

He pulled out a couple of pictures from an envelope. "We were able to pull the video feed from the surveillance camera at the morgue when she went to submit to the DNA test to make an identification of the body that we excavated. We took a few stills from that video so at least we know what they look like."

Seth took the pictures of Faith. "She's Amish, and he's English!"

Kyle moved the picture up in front of Seth. "Do you see the resemblance?" he asked Caleb.

"The two of you could be twins!" he said.

He held the pictures out and studied them, realizing he couldn't deny the strong resemblance.

"Do you think she knows the old man is her father?" Kyle asked.

"You don't think they're working together, do you?" Caleb asked the detective.

"If I had to guess, I'd have to say her husband is the *brains and brawn* of this operation," he said. "According to the neighbors, she's always been very quiet and reserved, and he's become pretty aggressive with a temper. They suspected he started abusing her physically after he lost his job about three months ago. Faith doesn't fit the description of working with a seasoned criminal like your father."

"Sounds like he could be pretty dangerous if he decided to join forces with the old man!" Seth said. "And if she is our sister, he isn't going to get away with abusing her with us around!"

The detective put the pictures back into the manila envelope, and rose from his chair. "We put out an Amber alert with the description of his car and his license plate, so hopefully, he'll lead us to his new hideout. If you get a new ransom note, let us know, and we'll get right on it. In the meantime, I'm going to keep an officer out here on duty hoping we'll catch him when he tries to deliver the next note."

"That sounds like a good idea," Caleb said. "Thank you for all of your help."

He bid them a good morning, and was on his way. Caleb felt discouraged that they'd come up with nothing so far that would bring his beloved wife and son back home to him. He missed them dearly, and said a prayer that if Faith was his sister, and she was aware of it, that she would help Amelia escape unharmed.

Chapter 13

Zack looked at the final ransom note written by Amelia, pretending he could read it.

caleb,
On thursday, at 4pm,
Leave the money Down
inside the tunnel at the
new pavilion at Mans -
Field pARk on elM st.
~Amelia

"It looks good," he said. "I'm going into town to get a cheeseburger. I can't eat this *farm food* anymore. I can either take the two of you with me, or I can tie you to a chair. What'll it be?"

"I'd rather we went with you," Amelia offered.

Faith nodded, feeling a little uneasy about parading around in public with their *hostages.*

Once again, they piled into the dirty, rusted out Pontiac, and Amelia prayed it would backfire and draw attention from her own farm. Unfortunately, the strong breeze blowing in the afternoon storm would muffle the sound of the car from this distance with the rustling of the trees. If not for it being summer, she knew they would have been able to see the lights on last night from her kitchen window, but the thick cover of leaves on the trees camouflaged their presence from her family's view. The few acres between the two farms suddenly felt like a non-crossable border of a new country, making it seem further away than it really was.

When they pulled onto Main Street in town, Zack pulled up in front of the liquor store.

"Why are you stopping here, Zack?" Faith asked. "You promised you wouldn't drink anymore."

"Get off my back, Woman!" he said. "I'm not gonna drink. I'm looking for someone to deliver the ransom note."

It didn't take long for the owner of the store to kick out a few underage kids and yell at them for trying to buy beer.

"Bingo!" he said.

Zack opened the driver-side door, but turned to Faith before he exited the car. "Don't try anything funny. I'll be right there, and I'll be watching you!"

He pulled the keys from the ignition and walked toward the young boys, who were loitering near the entrance to the store.

"Hey boys," he said. "I just saw what happened. Why did he kick you out of the store? You're not causing trouble, are you?"

"No!" they all said together.

"He said my license was a fake, and refused to sell me some beer!" another one said.

"Let me see your license? He's got to be mistaken. Sounds to me like he's discriminating against you just for looking so young!"

The kid pulled out his wallet and handed Zack his license.

"That doesn't look like a fake, Mr. *Jones!*" he said. "But that doesn't help you since he isn't going to let you go back in there and get what you came here for. I'll tell you what. How about if I go in there and get you the beer?"

"Okay," they said together.

"I just need you to do me a favor first," Zack said, holding up the envelope containing the ransom note. "I need you to deliver this letter to a farm about ten miles down the road, and then I'll get you the beer."

"How do we know you'll still be here when we get back?" one of them asked.

"I'll give you twenty dollars, and then when you get back, I'll take my twenty dollars back, and you can give me the money to buy the beer. Then we can both be on our way!"

They took the money from him, and Zack waited until they were out of site to get back in his car.

"Did I hear you tell those boys you'd buy them beer for delivering that note?" Amelia asked.

"Yeah, so what?" he said casually, as he started his car and revved the engine to keep it from stalling.

"Those boys aren't old enough to drink!" she said angrily. "Why would you promise them you'd get them beer?"

Zack turned around in the seat and leered at her.

"Get off my back! I'm not going to justify myself to you!" he said, gritting his teeth at her. "I don't have any intention of getting those kids any beer. They ain't old enough to drink, and they're trying to use a fake license to buy beer."

"Then why did you promise them you would?"

"So they would deliver the note!" he said, putting the car in reverse and backing out of the parking spot. "I have a feeling they're gonna get caught delivering that note, and they might get arrested, and hopefully that'll scare 'em straight! I wished I'd had a chance to learn that lesson when I was their age, b'cause then maybe I wouldn't have turned out the way I did."

"So you're sending them into the lion's den?" Amelia asked.

"If you mean, I'm letting them take the fall for this, then yes!" he answered. "By the time the cops catch up to those kids, we'll be long gone from here," he said, as he squealed his tires and sped toward the old man's farm, forgetting all about the cheeseburger he'd claimed he couldn't live without, but Amelia had a hunch he'd just given those boys his last dollar, and he was in for a rude awakening when he discovered there wouldn't be any ransom money.

Chapter 14

Zeb cringed at the mess that someone—squatters perhaps, had left in his house since he'd been gone.

Was it too much to expect that his son would take care of the place in his absence and run off any low-life moochers trying to take his land from him?

He moved about slowly, still weak from being in a coma for so many months. His muscles had all but completely atrophied, and he wasn't certain how much further he would have made it if not for the kindness of the young boys who'd offered him a ride.

Within minutes, he could hear sirens, and for some reason, he just wasn't afraid this time. He'd had enough of running; his only goal was to see the Bishop for his confession—his last confession.

Uncertain if he'd even make it much longer in this life, he needed redemption more than ever.

But now, with the police closing in on him, he didn't hold out much hope of getting to see the Bishop before he was caught.

"I suppose it's your will, Lord," he mumbled. "But you know I need forgiveness in this life if I want to go on to the next life, and you know my days here are few. I can feel the end is near for me. Please give me a sign that I can receive the redemption I desperately need."

It had been so long since he'd breathed such a sincere prayer; he'd forgotten how liberating it could be.

He peered out the side window, noting that the young boys who'd given him a ride had been stopped by the police, and he knew it would only be a matter of time before they would be at his home to arrest him and take him back to jail.

He didn't think he'd make it even one day in jail. His energy was spent and he'd become so frail while he'd been sick, he was surprised he'd even survived the fall into his cellar, let alone the drowning.

He'd never forget the deep sadness he'd experienced when he'd felt his life slipping away. It had filled him with a lot of regrets—mostly over not raising his children right. He'd finally realized what a gift they were, and now they would never know how much he regretted not bringing them up with a good example. He'd spent his entire life only thinking of himself, and mourning the loss of the community and his standing in the eyes of the Bishop—a mere man, that he'd missed out on the most important thing in this life—to know his Savior.

When he'd been in a coma, someone—a minister, perhaps, had visited his bedside regularly and had read to him from the Bible, and he'd heard the word of God, and understood what it meant for the first time in his life. He knew then that he had to get well and make amends to everyone he'd wronged—somehow, he had to.

Chapter 15

"I already told you, officer," the boy said. "This guy gave us twenty dollars to drop off a note for him. He told us to put it in the mailbox. That's all, I swear!"

"What did he look like?" the officer demanded.

"He was kind of tall and had dark hair," the boy said. "I saw him get into a gold colored car with two other girls—oh, and there was a baby crying!"

The officer held up the pictures of Faith and asked if that was one of the women.

"I think so," the boy said. "I can't be sure."

When he showed him the surveillance pictures of Zack, he was able to make a positive identification.

"I'm going to need you to go down to the station and give a full statement.

"I'm not going to the juvey, am I?"

"At seventeen, you won't go to the juvenile center; you'll go to jail if you're involved. That man kidnapped a woman and her child!"

All the boys in the car began to fight with the driver, blaming him for agreeing to take the note.

"We didn't help anyone kidnap anyone," one of them said. "We just wanted some beer, and he was going to buy it for us. He just wanted us to deliver the note first. Honest."

"Beer?" the officer said. "Now you're all under arrest for attempting to buy alcoholic beverages, and for being an accessory to kidnapping!"

The officers made all four boys get out of the car, and then they read them their rights and handcuffed them, putting them in the back of two patrol cars.

Zeb watched the boys being taken away, feeling relief that it wasn't him, and that whatever they had done wrong, that they had spared his life.

"I promise you, Lord," he declared. "Since you've given me this second chance, I'll do whatever it is that you need me to. I want forgiveness that much!"

Chapter 16

Zeb peered out the window of the living room when he heard a car coming up the long gravel drive that led to his house. It was an older, gold car—not one he recognized.

Instinctively, he went to the closet in the hallway and stomped on the floorboard in the corner with his heel. The plank flipped up, and he reached in to retrieve his shotgun and a box of shells. He quickly loaded the gun and stuffed a few extra shells in the pocket of his trousers, and then closed himself inside the closet.

He found himself praying again that God would guard him from further sin, and that he would not have to use the gun to defend himself. In his weakened state, it was his only defense against intruders, but for the first time in too many years, he felt God had heard his prayer.

A loud, male voice caused his heart to jump.

"It won't be long now, Amish girl," Zack said. "And I'll have the money, and as long as you cooperate, I'll set you free."

"What is that supposed to mean?" Faith cried. "You promised you wouldn't hurt Amelia and her baby!"

Zeb sucked in his breath. Were they talking about Caleb's Amelia? The mention of a baby was a surprise to him. He'd never thought of the possibility of being a grandfather. From the sound of things, they were in danger, but he decided to listen a little more to see if he could figure out what their plan was, and how many he was up against.

"Shut up, Faith!" Zack said.

Faith?

"I told you not to get emotional over this. The old man wasn't emotional when he poisoned your mother with that tea. Now his son's wife and kid are gonna have to pay if we don't get the money from that robbery he committed!"

Zeb had no idea who that man was that he heard, but he now knew it was his own daughter that was in danger, as well as his son's wife, and his own grandchild.

He had to save his family!

He breathed a prayer for courage as he burst out of the closet, shotgun ready for whatever he needed to do.

Both women screamed, and Zack held up his arms in defense.

"Zeb," Amelia said. "What are you doing here?"

He aimed the gun at Zack and raised it as if to threaten him. "I could ask this one the same thing! From the sound of things, you're up to no good, and you seem to have yourself a hostage situation here. I can't let you do that, Son. I'm not going to let you hurt my girls, or my grandchild."

Amelia's breath hitched. "Girls?" she asked.

"Faith is my daughter!"

Zack took a step forward. "She's not your daughter! She wouldn't be kin to no murderer!"

Zeb looked at Faith's swelling belly and then back at Zack. "Well, from what I can see, she's going to be *married* to a murderer if you aim to do any of them harm. I'm afraid I just can't allow that!"

"What are you going to do, old man? Shoot me?"

"If you force me to, yes!" he said. "Girls, I have some good strong rope in the kitchen on a hook by the door. Tie him up!"

Faith wiped the tears from her eyes, wondering why she was getting so emotional. Was it that she finally knew who her real father was? Perhaps disappointment at what kind of a man he was? Or maybe, just maybe, it was relief that he was sparing her and her unborn child from going to jail for her husband's foolishness.

Her emotions were overwhelming, but she did as she was told. He was, after all, her father.

Chapter 17

Caleb read the note one more time and confirmed to the officers that Amelia was being held at his father's home. Though the old man had not been mentioned, he still worried he was involved somehow.

"You stay put," the detective warned Caleb and his brothers. "You'll only be in the way, and as tough as this is to trust us, this is what we do. Be patient, and say a few prayers that we'll be back here in no time with your son and your wife."

"We will," he answered, looking at his brothers in a challenging way.

He watched the officers leave, and then stepped over to the kitchen window straining to see through the thick of the trees. The officers snaked their way over to the house, and Caleb prayed their presence wouldn't spook the kidnappers.

His brothers stood next to him and prayed quietly, but all he could concentrate on was the scene unfolding in his backyard.

Resisting the urge to run over there when he saw that the officers were encroaching on his father's property, Caleb felt his throat constricting, his face covered in perspiration as if he'd plowed his entire cornfield in one afternoon.

"Go on now," Zeb told the girls. "Go get help and I'll hold him here until you get back here with Caleb and his brothers."

"I don't want to leave my husband here with you," Faith said. "I don't want you to hurt him!"

"I won't hurt him," he promised. "I give you my word. But before you go, I want you both to know how sorry I am for everything I've done to hurt you, and my sons—and your mothers."

Amelia looked at him, tears welling up in her eyes. "I believe you," she said softly. "I forgive you, and I know Caleb does too."

Faith began to cry. "If she can forgive you, then so can I. What about you, Zack?"

"I don't know if I'm ready to forgive," he said. "But I'm ready to surrender. No amount of money is worth dying for, and I don't trust this old man! Get me out of here!"

Faith went to him, sobbing and giggling slightly. She looked up at Zeb with a pleading gleam in her eyes.

"Is it okay to untie him?"

He nodded. "On one condition."

"You name it," Zack said.

"I may not be around much longer, and I want you to take good care of my daughter, and my grandchild she's carrying."

Zack hung his head. "But I lost my job! I can't even pay for our rent, let alone for the birth!"

"I'm willing to take the blame for this kidnapping because I'm going to spend the rest of my life in jail for other crimes I'm not proud of, which means my house will just sit here."

He turned to Faith. "With Amelia as a witness, I'm willing to give you my house, but only if your husband promises to work hard and take care of you and the baby. There isn't any money for you to gain from this, only *familye,* and that can be worth far more than money. I regret that I didn't learn that until now!"

Zack's eyes lit up. "I'd appreciate that, Sir," he said. "But I gave the ransom note to those boys to deliver. They can identify me!"

"What did the notes say?" Zeb asked.

Amelia told him, and he chuckled.

"Were they full of code messages, the way you and Caleb used to write when you were children? The messages you sent with the pigeons?"

She smiled. "How did you know?"

"I found them on the floor of his room. He never picked it up when he was young. And I soon learned to break your code!"

"So then you know that, by now, Caleb knows where we are, and the police are probably on their way here," she said.

Zeb nodded. "That means we don't have much time. I'll tell the police I was holding you against your will and that I made you write the notes. I'm willing to take all the blame, if you agree to start fresh and be a good husband and father—not like me!"

Zack nodded. "I give you my word. Thank you for taking the blame for my mistake. I don't know what I was thinking. I lost my head because of the stress I was under when I lost my job and our apartment. We've been living in the car for two weeks."

"You have a house now. Don't mess this up!" Zeb warned. "I can see in my daughter's eyes that she believes in you. I don't think you're a bad man like me; I just think that you're a mixed up young man who's lost his way, and I pray that giving you a way out of the mess you created will set you on the right path again."

Still tied up, Zack turned his attention to Amelia. "I'm truly sorry for what I did. I'll do my best to do right by you and your family."

"We're *your* family now. I'm sure my husband and his brothers will want you to work with them now that they have a sister to look after."

The two women hugged. "I've always wanted a sister," Amelia said.

"Me too!" Faith agreed.

Faith untied her husband, and he kissed her and apologized for letting stress turn him abusive against her, promising not to let it happen again.

The three of them walked out of the house, Amelia holding Gabriel close to her heart.

No sooner did they get out the door, than the police closed in on them.

"Stop where you are!" one of them said.

Zack threw his hands up and dropped to his knees. "Don't shoot!"

Chapter 18

Caleb ran from the house when he saw Amelia exiting his father's home. He'd been so afraid and so overwhelmed, that tears now streamed down his face as he ran the length of the field. In the time that his father had been in a coma, Caleb and his brothers had torn down all the barbed wire and electric fence that had separated the two farms.

Now, he ran freely through the corn field full of thick, healthy stalks he'd planted with his brothers.

Amelia heard Caleb calling for her from the cornfield, and for the first time, she did not fear the maze of rows she could not see through. She trusted, as she followed the calls of her future that echoed over the silk tassels swaying in the warm summer breeze that felt refreshing against her cheeks.

The barriers were down, and perhaps now they would truly be free to live their lives without the fear of the past. There were no more ghosts that called to her from within the rows that confined her; she heard only the sweet sound of her husband's voice calling her.

When she reached his waiting arms, a shield of safety surrounded her in the warmth of his embrace.

"I was so frightened," he said, as his lips ran across the top of his wife's head until they found her lips.

"We're fine," she reassured him. "Our troubles are over—finally!"

"How can you be sure?" he asked, pulling his son into his arms and searching his wife's eyes.

"Your *daed* has asked for forgiveness, and he's willing to change his life around. He's found *Gott* again!"

Caleb's eyes teared up all over again, and his lower lip quivered, slowly turning into a smile.

"That's wonderful news," he said, realizing his father had been behind the abduction.

It no longer mattered. If his father was looking for forgiveness, Caleb would give it to him freely.

Chapter 19

Amelia found Caleb's hand and pulled him back through the cornfield toward the other side.

"Come with me," she said. "There's someone I want you to meet!"

They walked hand-in-hand through the length of the field toward his father's home.

When they reached the perimeter, Caleb stopped to watch police officers putting his father into the back of a patrol car. It was a scene he wasn't sure he would ever get used to, but it was a reality he'd have to learn to accept.

He dropped his hand from Amelia's and went to the car, still holding his son in his arms.

"May I talk to my father before you go?"

The officer nodded and opened the back door to his patrol car.

Caleb peered in at his father, who was pale and thin. It saddened him to see the man in such a state, but he'd brought it all on himself.

"I'd like you to meet my son, Gabriel," Caleb said to his father.

"I saw him, Son," he said, with a shaky voice. "I want you to know how proud I am of the man you've turned out to be, and I thank *Gott* that you did not follow in my footsteps. You're a *gut mann,* Caleb, and so are your brothers. I'm sorry for everything I've done to you and everyone else. I know it doesn't change what happened, or take back any of the consequences of my selfish behavior, but I pray that you learn from it, and promise to always listen to *Gott.*"

"I will," Caleb said, swallowing back tears. "I want you to know, *daed,* that I love you, no matter what. And I forgive you."

"That means a lot to me, Caleb—probably more than you could ever know."

By this time, Seth and Kyle had reached the farm, and each wanted to talk to their father.

Each of them accepted his apology, and blessed him with the gift of the forgiveness he so desperately needed. He'd confessed to the police officers before they'd taken him from his house, and the truth had finally set him free. There were no more shackles of guilt that weighed on his heart. No more ghosts of the past taunting him back to his sinful ways.

His sins had been confessed and forgiven.

It was all he needed, before taking his last breath.

Chapter 20

Zack took a deep breath in and blew it out slowly. It was good to get all that off his chest. He knew that by the old man's example, he had to accept responsibility for his actions, and to be willing to accept the consequences, whatever that may be.

Caleb lifted his head from the deep prayer he'd been engrossed in while he'd listened to Zack's confession.

"I think I can speak for each of my brothers, that we will leave this alone. Our father has accepted the blame for all of this, and he blessed you with a gift; the gift of a clean slate. He'd accepted the responsibility and took your mistake on himself in order that his daughter, our sister, would have a better life, and you both could have a fresh start. We, as a family, will take care of you, and help you in any way. You're more than welcome to work with my brothers and me, and you're free to live on the old man's farm the way he gifted it to you. There's been enough death and destruction in this family, and it's up to us— the blessed ones, to make a new path for our children, and to leave them with a better heritage than was left to us."

"I couldn't agree more," Kyle said.

Zack teared up, and thanked each of them, realizing how truly blessed he was.

They were all blessed to be the children of a repentant and forgiven man.

Seth leaned in close to Zack. "There's one last thing I want to make clear. If we ever see another mark on our sister, or even so much as a look in her eyes that makes us *think* you're not treating her right, my brothers and I will take you out to the woodshed and have a nice long *talk* with you," he whispered. "Do we understand each other?"

Zack nodded his head, and Seth slapped him on the back and pulled him into a man-hug.

"Well, then welcome to the family!"

THE END

Thank you for reading this suspense series. Please leave a review on Amazon and let me know how much you enjoyed it. I always love hearing from my readers.

God Bless!

ATTENTION:

ALL my future books will be offered for 99 cents for the FIRST few days!

If you would like to be informed of new books published so you can take advantage of this special price, PLEASE sign up on my <u>FACEBOOK fan page</u> for my email list, to take advantage of this

SPECIAL OFFER.

Thank you!

598

You might also like:

99 cents on Kindle

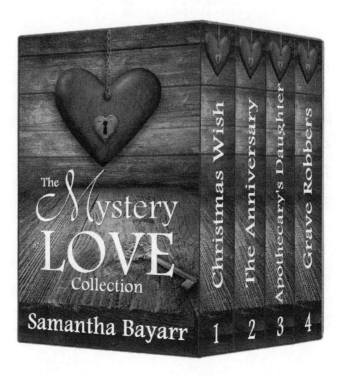

99 cents on Kindle

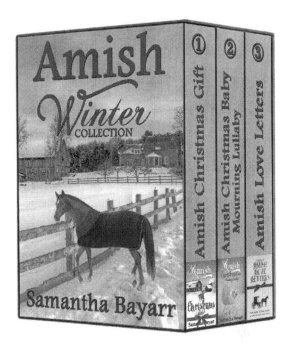

99 cents on KIndle

99 cents on Kindle

99 on Kindle